Lying
in bed

M. J. Rose

Lying in bed

Spice

Spice

LYING IN BED

ISBN 0-373-60508-0

Copyright © 2006 by Melisse Shapiro.

www.Spice-Books.com

Printed in U.S.A.

For Suzanne Beecher who asked for this book, and
for Susie Bright who opened the doors
that have made this book possible.

Part One

"Well, so many words, because I can't touch you. If I could sleep with my arms round you, the ink could stay in the bottle."

—D. H. Lawrence, *Lady Chatterley's Lover*

Chapter 1

August 28, 2004

"Tell me the story…" he said.

We were lying in bed, making love. I pretended that I hadn't heard him and instead breathed in the sweet smell of his hair mixed with the rougher smell of his skin slicked with sweat. I licked the part of his salty neck that was pressed closest to my mouth. The tendons were hard ropes against my tongue.

I hoped this would distract him but it didn't and he asked again: "Tell me. Who is he?"

The words came from his mouth, but I heard them first between my legs, where they halted the faint and faraway sensations that I had been hoping would, like a tight bud, open and flower.

Until five words ago, it had been only sensations that had my attention. (You know how it feels, not like a pain that you can pinpoint but a breeze of stinging electric-blue pleasure surging through you.) Now it was his question that I felt. So intrusive it repeated itself. If not actually, then in my mind. Drawing my thoughts where I did not want them to go.

I needed to focus, to keep my mind in the present, to stay and not slip backward. *Focus,* I told myself. *On being here. Now.*

I took in the half-life of the room smothered in the dark. Listened to his short breaths. Panting. Like a dog overheated. To the silence of the 2:00 a.m. street below. Felt the smooth sheets, pillows crushed beneath me, warm skin sticking to mine, my own insides, holding him in, clenching around him as if this would keep me tethered and prevent me from sliding into the past.

This was what I craved: sensation to overwhelm me and keep me in the moment which made the present all that mattered—and by doing so, made *us* all that mattered. But it never came.

Until then, Kenneth had never questioned me about my past.

What had changed?

Five minutes before the call, we'd been sitting on the bed, not yet making love but, given the wine and the conversation and how many days it had been since we'd seen each other, it was clearly where we were headed. When I heard the phone ring, I'd glanced over and seen the old and familiar number on the Caller ID. Leaving, I picked up in the living room.

At that time of night, with Kenneth there, I normally would have let the machine answer, but I didn't want to guess at what the message might be. And I didn't want Kenneth to overhear it, no matter what it was.

We'd only talked for a minute or two at the most. On my end it was hushed, on his, it was loud. But surely Kenneth couldn't have heard that. He must have thought it was odd, though, that I'd gotten up just then—which it was—and so he must have tried to listen and probably had heard snatches of what I'd said.

I pushed my body closer to Kenneth to entice him to resume our mutual seduction. So the past wouldn't matter. So the present would be all that did.

He didn't respond with his body. The interruption had done damage.

Don't you wish men didn't worry about who you were before you met them?

But they do.

Not at first.

Sometimes not for a long time. Sometimes not for so long that you get fooled into thinking that this new man will not care, will not ask. That he has the strength somewhere inside him to accept what came before him and leave it be.

But eventually every one of them does ask.

Except for the first one. Ah. Lucky him. He knew you were pristine and empty. No other sperm stains. No flesh touched by other hands or hips that ground too hard into hips. No bruised heart.

But there can be only one who comes first and then there are all the others who come after and lust to wipe you clean. If you are lucky they want to do it with love. Unlucky, then with force.

The worst thing is if you care about it, too. If you also wish you could be cleansed.

Beware the wish. It makes you long. And longing makes you weak. It's an emotion I have managed to avoid for the past eight years.

"Guess what?" I said, my voice more sarcastic than was smart. "I can't get rid of what happened. Can't change it. No matter how much I wish I could. Or you wish I could. So why don't we just forget about it."

"I won't judge you. I promise. Just tell me."

That, I knew was a lie, even if Kenneth didn't.

The room was redolent with a sandalwood candle and the burnt bitter wick that sputtered out some time ago. I pushed my face closer to his chest, I didn't want to smell incense, I wanted to smell my lover's scent.

"Tell me."

How many times could he ask?

"Not now."

"Yes, now." He stroked my back, as if his touch could coax out the words. "Trust me, Marlowe. Tell me."

Kenneth wanted more from me than I could give. He always had. But until now he had been patient. Why couldn't he be satisfied with the way my legs had opened to clear a path for him? Why wasn't it enough that we were together? Even if he didn't get as much intimacy as he wanted yet. I was getting there.

Now I was supposed to believe that he would be accepting. That what I would tell him would not affect him. But he was lying in my bed. How could I take the chance? What if I did tell him and it was more than he wanted to know? What if it damaged us?

It had, after all, already damaged me.

We were both motionless. A frozen snapshot of our tame but real passion interrupted. I was lying in my bed, on my side. He faced me, arms around me. His rust-colored hair was silky on my cheek. I pushed my lips into his, still trying to make everything about us.

"Tell me," he said after what turned out to be a lackluster kiss. I had been trying too hard and he had been preoccupied.

"Or?" I tried to make my voice light and teasing.

He frowned. "Don't do that. It doesn't work. You making something serious into something frivolous never does. And you do it too often. You are afraid of conflict, Marlowe. You know that? It's not good for you."

"Whoa. Where did all that come from? When did this get so serious?"

He didn't answer, just looked at me, disappointed and hurt by what I'd said.

"When wasn't this serious?" he asked, a little-boy pout playing on his lips.

I always forget that women are tougher this way. If our positions were reversed, I would not have been upset by my comment, but men can be more sentimental—they just often hide it better. This wasn't one of those times, though, and I knew I'd made a mistake. Not the last of the evening.

"There is no glory in honesty if it is destructive. And no shame in dishonesty if its goal is to offer grace," I said, still trying to convince him that my answering would not be in our best interest.

"Tell me," he urged, this last time a whisper against my

cheek. Intimated in his tone was the promise of what would come after my confession, and what would be withdrawn if I chose to withhold it.

We had been lying in bed for long enough that I had almost been ready. He knew that. Knew how long it could take me and that when it finally started to build, I would do anything not to lose it. Even though I almost always did.

My orgasms are extremely infrequent and hard fought. Like battles I have to win. My present against the intrusion of my past. In the last six months I'd only won once or twice.

Additionally, our lovemaking was not as frequent as was probably typical of two people our age. For one thing, Kenneth traveled so often. For another, we were simply not as connected that way as we were in other ways. And sadly, it was because the erotic was the last holdout of the lands I didn't want to travel to. Too rife with memories and embarrassments I hadn't been able to erase from a memory bank overflowing with episodes I wished I could erase.

When I thought about our lusterless sex life, I went back and forth thinking it was his make-up, or mine. Obsessing about the fact that we, at twenty-seven and twenty-nine, could go months without making love. And then convincing myself it wasn't a problem. We were not experimental. We were kind to each other. That mattered more.

Didn't it?

The thing was, I loved him. Because he listened so well. Because he cared about my work as much as his own. Because he was smart and gentle and patient and seemed so satisfied with us, and that made me grateful. And because he never dug into my psyche. He did not wonder if there were other selves I hid from him. I was safe with him.

Or at least that was the way it had been until that night.

Focus. Focus. Stay on the sensation of his hands on my back, his breath on my neck, on the feel of his arms under my fingers. The muscles beneath the flesh, solid and defined.

It had been bothering me less and less that our passion was so pale. And lately I had been able to get pleasure from touching alone, accept that pleasure didn't always have to bring release, and see that one day I might find the path to more satisfying trysts.

Outside in the street a woman laughed. Like crystal shattering. High. Thin. Clear.

I was losing—everything was distracting me now.

He felt my efforts and knew my semiconscious dream state had been broken. He needed to work harder if he was going to get either of the two things he wanted.

His hand moved between my legs and stroked my thighs, lightly, tantalizing, retreating and advancing, going just a little higher each time his hand returned.

The humming started up again in my head.

"Tell me," he said again, and it all broke apart.

"Damn it, Kenneth."

He'd had me and he knew it. I'd wanted what he had and I was close. This time I knew it had been within my reach.

And because of that ephemeral goal, in short staccato sentences I told him, expecting that as soon as I finished explaining, Kenneth would begin the lovemaking again, that I would let go, that we would disappear into sensation for a time.

But that didn't happen.

The problem was that as he listened he guessed I was lying. He told me that as he pulled back. Our skin, glued by sweat, made a sucking sound as we separated. My legs struggled to hold him to me, but he was stronger and I lost.

No part of his body any longer touched any part of mine. He moved away, stood up, turned his back on me and walked out of the bedroom.

I felt the prick of depression, of being let down too fast.

I had always known that one day a man would ask. But still it had come as a surprise and I was not prepared. Not for Kenneth's question. Not for his reaction to my response.

And not for what came next.

Chapter 2

August 30, 2004

Dear Marlowe,

Venice is a city for lovers and you are not here. But you are with me in your way. No matter where I go, I see through my eyes but thrill to it through yours. Everywhere I go, I find gifts for you.

This journal is something I found today in a small shop off St. Mark's Square. You walk down three worn stone steps and into a single overcrowded room that smells of leather and oil paint, turpentine and candle wax. Smells together that take you back to some other time.

Paulo's father owned the store before him and his father before him, back to the mid 1600s. And in an even more crowded workroom, this family of Venetians have been making leather journals like this one and dipping marbleized papers the same way for almost half a century.

I'm sending this journal to you, along with the glass fountain pen I'm writing this entry with. It was blown in Murano. Like everything else in Venice, it is old and to use it you have to dip it in ink. This process changes how you write…you will see when you try…the procedure gives you time to think between the words—something the computers we love so much do not allow.

I found the pen in an antique shop down an alley I am sure I could never find again, even with a map. Serendipities like this are nothing out of the ordinary in Venice but that doesn't make them any less magical. The city is, like the collages you make, full of unknowns: juxtaposed centuries, cultures, images that surprise, startle, please.

Which is just one of the reasons you and I have to come here together.

I want to take your arm and walk with you down quiet narrow streets at twilight when the sunset shines on the canals like flecks of glass. It will shine off your golden hair and warm your skin. We'll walk till the night falls heavy and thick the way it does. It will wrap around your shoulders like a velvet cloak. And I'll kiss you. Oh, Marlowe, how I will kiss you.

Time is out of time here. There is no present, no future. There is just beauty. Just like you.

I know I could call you now. But the phone seems a science fiction artifact here where I am ensconced in this high-ceilinged room in this villa—this fine old palace built more than 400 years ago. And in my room, I am back in that time. Or no time. Or any time.

I wonder who we would have been if we had lived in fifteenth-century Venice? How would we have met? Would we have been in masks? Making love in dark corners, behind thick silk curtains, waiting to hear footsteps coming down the corridor? Your father? Husband? Other lover?

I'm sorry we fought.

Will you forgive me?

In this serene city of deep intrigue and sensual preoccupation, I go over and over what I asked you and the answer you gave…the lie gleaming in your eyes…a lie that I now understand you told for both our sakes.

That I was jealous of your past is not something I can take back. I was narrow-minded. Closed off. Like these serpentine streets of Venice. I could tell from the argument you were having on the phone that you were talking to an ex-lover. I wanted to know who he was. Why he was still calling. What he wanted. How you felt. Why you talked to him so long. What he meant to you. What he still means to you. If he is at the heart of the problems we have in bed.

But now, forcing my emotions to calm, I know that we become who we are because of who we were and who we have known and what we have done. And so. To love you I have to love all the men you have been with. I have to be grateful for every kiss that has been pressed on your lips, every tongue that has slid up your thigh. Every finger touched to your cheek. Every hand that has cupped your breast. Every pair of eyes that have seen you naked. Every minute of love that you have made. All of these things—damn…all of these men—have made you the woman I want.

One day, when we are old and weary, I want us to look at each other and smile, alive and young again with all that we did and all that we have been and given to each other. To get there, I have to learn to love what I despise.

It's late. The night is starting to lighten and the sun is starting to rise. And so I'm putting down this pen, closing this book, wrapping it all up and sending it off to you so that you can write to me here in this book and tell me that you forgive me. So that your answer will be waiting for me when I come home next week.

Kenneth

The letter had been written on the first three pages of the leather-bound journal, which he had sent me, via priority mail from Venice, Italy. It arrived five days after he had left, around 11 a.m. on a Tuesday morning. Two days before he was expected back.

I was reading it for the second time when the phone rang.

It was Grace, Kenneth's sister. Her voice was controlled but tight and I knew something was wrong from just hearing her say hello.

She was calling to tell me that he had been in an accident—a train wreck—on his way from Venice to Florence and that he had been killed.

When I got off the phone, I sat motionless for a long time in the chair in my living room. I did not move. Did not even weep. Not yet. What I did was reread the letter. Over and over. With my forefinger touching the paper, running over the sentences as if something of him would rub off on me. As if he was there in those words, still.

I got to the end.

What he had asked of me came as a shock. The shock I needed to finally make me realize that he was gone. That my idea of my future was gone.

Once again I read the end of the letter.

He had asked me to forgive him. He had asked me to write him back.

But I no longer would be able to do either.

Chapter 3

Eighteen months later
February 1, 2006

"I don't want to be in the picture," I said as I stood up from behind my desk, hoping to prevent the photographer from getting a clear shot of me.

Vivienne Chancey continued to search me out with her sleek silver box. "You'd give the article a more interesting slant. The face of the woman who writes the letters."

Click. Click. Click.

I was talking to a camera but it wasn't even slightly disconcerting. My mother is a photographer. So are my stepfather and my stepbrother. I am the only one in our family who doesn't look through a lens to see the world.

Click. Click. Click.

"The letters and stories don't need my face. They speak for themselves," I laughed. Hoping she would, too. That my levity would deter her.

It didn't. She was still aiming her machine in my direction.

It was a blessing, I thought, for the sake of the shoot, that I had my father's last name and that my mother had kept her maiden name. And that my stepfather and stepbrother had different names altogether. If Vivienne knew who my family was, she'd barrage me with questions that would make this session even more uncomfortable. Isabel Scofeld was too well known. Cole and Tyler Ballinger were, too.

Vivienne is lovely: small and slight with pale blond hair, cut short and smartly to show off her perfectly oval face. Her hands are the most expressive part of her. Long, strong fingers, unadorned by either jewelry or nail polish. Her fingers danced—they didn't just move. I knew those hands. My mother's have the same economy of motion. So do Cole's, my stepbrother, and his father's.

"Why don't you want the people who read the article to see you?"

"Because," I told Vivienne, "I write letters and stories for other people. Me, my personality, my likes and dislikes, have nothing to do with what's in them."

She was snapping shots, one after another without a break, and the sound punctuated what I was saying. Each click was like a period at the end of my thoughts.

I hadn't let anyone take my picture in ten years.

In that last photo I was lying in bed. Naked. Nineteen years old. I didn't mind when the picture was taken. I didn't know how exposed I was going to appear. How naked I was going to look. You think there is only one kind of undressed? There are layers. Innocent nudity.

Then suggestive nudity. Then bare and brazen sexual nakedness. And since that day, I have never been that undressed again.

And since then, I have not had my photograph taken by anyone except the New York City driver's license bureau and the man in the small store in the bottom of Rockefeller Center when I needed a passport shot. And in both cases I was wearing my glasses. Big, round glasses with thin black frames. They are the barrier between me and everyone who looks at me. I could wear contacts but I like the curtain of glass—slightly, ever so slightly tinted blue—that I wear to separate me a little bit from everyone's eyes.

I didn't want a stranger to take my photograph, even if it would have been good for business. That hadn't been the plan. The magazine's art director hadn't told me she wanted me in the shots when she'd set up the shoot. She'd said the photographer would photograph some of the collage letters/short stories for a pre-Valentine's Day issue of New York's weekly glossy magazine. My work was to be part of a section on perfect gifts for the man or woman who has everything.

"How do you do that? Get out of your own way and keep yourself out of the letters that you write?" Vivienne asked.

"It's my job," I told her.

The job we were talking about was writing love letters and erotic stories for other people. Sexy sweet letters. Suggestive stories from one lover to another, using their names as the characters. Poignant ones. Seductive ones. Dirty ones. I also decorate them, turning them into exotic collages.

For the few months before the shoot, men had been hiring me to write Valentine tales for their girlfriends and mistresses. Women had been hiring me to create fictions out of their fantasies to give to their boyfriends. I worked with people who couldn't express themselves but wanted to offer words as promises or to immortalize their most passionate wishes and dreams. Sometimes I simply personalized and altered one of the three dozen letters or the two dozen short stories that came with the job—written by my predecessor's predecessor.

But I also wrote originals for a slightly higher price.

And while I don't know if I did it better than anyone else—or even if there was someone else out there doing it—I do know that I did it well enough to have a steady clientele who had found me via word of mouth. And that gave me the time to work on my own collages that I hoped would someday hang in an art gallery.

Vivienne moved to a corner of my office, looked through the viewfinder, shook her head and then moved to the opposite corner. That angle must have been better because she stayed put and the clicking sound started again.

"I'm serious," I said. "I really don't want to be in the shots." I moved out of her line of sight.

I was annoyed but also amused because I knew firsthand how incredibly obstinate photographers can be.

My mother would respect our wishes when my sister, Samantha, and I stamped our little feet and told her we were done, that we wanted to play or watch television or get away from that single, never tiring glass eye, but not until she got off one more shot. And I never minded when I got a little older and Cole, my stepbrother, began to photograph me.

Until I minded too much.

Once Vivienne couldn't find me in the frame, the sound stopped. She lowered her Canon and looked for me with her eyes. Spotting me standing almost behind her in front of a large flat file case where I keep supplies and samples, she grinned at my game of hide-and-seek.

"Do you care that my editor is going to be unhappy?"

"Yes. I'm sorry about that. And I'd be happy to make it up to you. If you ever want me to write a letter for you, you have an IOU for one at no cost."

Her eyebrows raised. "Really?"

I nodded.

"You *really* don't want your picture in the article."

"You guessed!"

We both laughed. I liked her and wouldn't mind writing a letter for her for nothing if she ever claimed it.

"Okay. Let's look through some of the letters," she said. "You will let me shoot the letters, right?"

I smiled and pulled out one of the drawers.

Vivienne came over but she didn't glance down. "Here, look at this shot. Are you sure you won't change your mind?" I thought she'd given up.

She shoved the digital camera in front of my face so that I had little choice but to see the photo she was showing me.

The woman had straight hair, parted in the middle, skimming her shoulders. Brown streaked with gold. She was tall—almost slim but not quite, wearing a plain white tailored shirt with a starched stand-up collar. Her shirt-tails were untucked and hung loose over khaki pants. A black sweater was tied around her waist.

Through my oversize, round glasses, I looked at myself in my oversize, round glasses.

"I look like a tall, colorless owl."

"No. A smart owl. Beautiful, too, in a nontraditional way." It wasn't a compliment but rather a statement made by a professional assessing what she saw in the camera.

"Thanks," I said quickly. "Now, can I tempt you with some love letters?"

Finally she looked down at my profferings.

There were more than a dozen letters and stories in the file. Each was a collage combining words, pictures, fabrics, papers and various other ephemera. They glittered and shone, bits of metallic paper or gold picking up the overhead lights. The inks were greens, purples, turquoise; ribbons and bits of lace, velvet, satin or silk decorated the sheets of prose.

Vivienne picked one up: deep fuchsia-colored ink covered a rich vellum paper that had petals of roses imbedded in its weave. She read it silently to herself and, over her shoulder, silently to myself, I did too.

Your skin is what I think of when I close my eyes. How it warms me when I slip into bed beside you, cold from the outside. You take away the freezing air. Heat me up. With what?

How do you manage to start the process as soon as I walk into the room?

In the darkness I feel your eyes on me. Can just make them out, orbs of luminescence, stroking me from eight feet away. My hands reach out before I have reached you—my hands have a memory of you that they trick me with when I am out in the world.

I touch a silk tie and feel your skin. Pick up a glass and think it is your wrist. Run my fingers down a line of figures on a sheet of paper and they are running down your thigh as you lie on the sheets under me. And the sensation, for one second, takes my breath away.

When she put down the letter there was a faint blush on her cheeks. The same color as the rose petals.

Chapter 4

Three months later
May 16, 2006

"Are you hurt?"

I looked up at the man who belonged to the voice. A quick impression of dark hair, strong features and a beard. Then he reached down to help me up.

I'd fallen. Cut myself. My reactions were slower than usual. Instead of getting up, I stared at his hands for a moment. They were heavily scarred. The older cuts showed as pale lines, almost impressions of wounds, whereas the recent ones were deep red and raised.

The pain throbbed in my own hand, and I grimaced. A few seconds before I hadn't even known I'd cut myself. I bent my head and sucked on the heel of my palm, the fount of the nuisance. It tasted sweet.

Then I inspected the source of the stinging injury.

Carved into my flesh was a clean, curved gash which, as I watched, refilled and then overflowed with blood.

"You've cut yourself. C'mon, let me help you up," he said in a voice that sounded like wind through a canyon. Strong, evocative, determined. And concerned. His hands were opened to me. Still slightly dazed, all I could do was stare at them, not realizing that was what I was doing.

On the heel of his left palm was a crescent moon of thickened flesh. Almost the exact same shape as the cut I'd given myself.

How could that be? It suggested something portentous but I didn't believe in fate. We were not in a fantasy but in New York City, in SoHo, on Broadway between Prince and Spring streets, inside the store where I work, called Ephemera, which sells papers and ribbons, stickers, pens, boxes, journals, glitter, glues, scrapbooks and stationery predesigned or to order.

Grace—the owner, my employer and my friend—and I debated the issue of fate when business was slow. Over cups of take-out cappuccino from Dean & Deluca, the gourmet emporium across the street, she always tried to convince me to pay attention to the signs that the universe presented. An eternally optimistic woman, she loves with an exuberance that I find enviable and am thankful to be the recipient of. Grace believes in magic, several religions, as well as parapsychology, the healing power of chocolate and good red wine.

Her belief in predestination was as strong as my opposition to it. And we argued about it, both of us enjoying the fight. She used to be distraught that I didn't want the comfort her belief system offered, but I remained unwilling to accept that I could be locked into a fate that was not of my own making.

But, here was a stranger who *was* marked in an almost identical way to me. Both alike in how we were damaged—at least on the surface, in the flesh.

He would have once felt the very same pain that was flashing through my hand.

I had been spending too much time listening to Grace, I thought. Our having the same shape cut in the same place on our palms didn't mean anything. Even if the gash were similar, it was impossible that his psyche was ripped in the same places as mine or that the glue that mended me would be the same as had mended him.

Still, I was mesmerized by his injury. Hypnotized and angered by its familiarity. I wanted to rub it off him and erase the coincidence of it, annulling what I couldn't understand.

No.

I didn't want to erase it.

In what seemed like an obscenely short amount of time—mere seconds—I knew that I didn't want his scar to disappear. I was fascinated by it and I wanted to touch it.

Maybe I had been momentarily stunned from getting hurt. Or I was simply curious because of the odd parallelism of the way we were both marked. The why didn't matter—I was fixated on the scar.

Or maybe Grace, with all her talk about predestination and symbolism and how there were no coincidences, had primed me for that moment.

Grace made prophecies. She brought in amulets and crystals and left them on my desk the way someone else would leave flowers. I adored her. She was the older sister I never had. And so I took her offerings and respected her. But I had never believed any of what she told me when she went all "New Age" on me.

Or so I thought.

Because the truth was, in that moment, looking down at the scar on his hand, a mirror image of my own fresh one, all I could think about was what Grace would say it meant and how she would interpret my reaction to it.

Maybe the pain in my hand *had* made me hypersensitive to other feelings, or perhaps it was the sound of the man's voice or the way he looked so familiar in the instant when I'd seen his face, I didn't know. But my reaction was both completely unexpected and foreign to me. I disliked it. And so I mistrusted the man who had aroused it in me.

I wanted to dissect his scar. Explore it with my fingertip and read it like Braille. Examine its contours and ridges just as I had done to my own cut. I needed to prove how distinct it was from mine, how dry, how healed compared to my open, sharp-edged and wet wound.

"There's blood everywhere," he said. The wind in his voice now a worry. "How bad is that cut? You might need stitches." He gripped me by my elbow and lifted me up.

As I stood, shards of broken glass fell from my skirt and hit the tile floor with a high-pitched sound that rang out like bells.

In one swift motion he pulled my hand toward him, bending over it so quickly that I didn't get a chance to see any more of his face, and instead found myself studying his hair which was burnt umber—a deep brown color I used when I painted—and fell forward in thick curls.

"Are you a doctor?"

"No. But I know about cuts."

I was quiet while he studied my hand. A customer in the store who had come to my aid. A stranger who I had no reason to notice. He was much taller than me, wore blue jeans and a black turtleneck. He was lean and gangly and almost disheveled but not quite.

I was aware of his strong fingers on my skin. Where we made contact, my nerve endings pulsed. Similar to the throb of pain, sensation spiked and retreated, and then repeated itself.

It made me uncomfortable and uneasy. I was too aware of his touch. The accident had made me nervous.

"This cut isn't deep enough for all this blood. You must be hurt somewhere else." He picked up his head and looked at me. "Are you?"

Once he wasn't bending over my hand anymore, I examined his face while I explained that what he thought was blood on my clothes and the floor was only ink and how I'd been kneeling, searching on a low shelf for a box of gold leaf paper, heard the phone ring, rushed to get it, pulled myself up using a shelf above me, but somehow yanked out and spilled a box of six bottles of vermilion ink in the process. How all of them had broken around me, sending glass and splashes of red liquid everywhere.

"Something else is wrong, though. What is it?" he asked when I'd finished.

"What?"

"Something other than the pain is bothering you."

"How did you know that?"

He shrugged. "I can see it in your eyes."

"But you don't know me."

"That's true. But I do know what concern looks like. And you're concerned."

I couldn't tell him about all of the reactions I was having to him. So I chose the most innocent. "It's only that you look like someone and it was driving me crazy who it was." I've studied art and painted for years and still look at people as if I was going to draw them. I forget that it's rude, intrusive and confusing. I forget people on the other end of it find it disconcerting.

"So who is it? Have you figured it out?"

I nodded. "You look like a man in a painting. A fresco in the Metropolitan Museum of Art. Roman. Third century BC."

And he did. The same dark wavy hair, wide, almond, intelligent eyes—deep set and harboring a haunted expression. The same arrogant, high cheekbones, aquiline nose and long neck.

I pictured the portrait that I'd stopped in front of a dozen times on my way in or out of the Egyptian wing because the man's gaze—even though it was only pigment on stone—demanded it.

"Only your toga and crown are missing."

He tilted his head and looked at me as if he was figuring something out. Then he smiled. "I'll have to go see him, then. I'd like to see how I look in a toga. And the idea of a crown is very appealing. I haven't been to the Met in too long anyway."

"It's a wreath really."

"Build up my ego and then dash it to bits in mere seconds. You're heartless," he joked.

I don't know what it was that gave me the feeling he was

so secure, but listening to him, I didn't think anyone could dash his ego. Except it wasn't egotistical or obnoxious. It was a good thing that this man was sure of himself. It was as if he wore an invisible cloak that kept him slightly removed from the dangers and weaknesses that could attack the rest of us mere mortals.

Or was I projecting what I felt about the man in the painting on to his twenty-first-century double?

Some people's faces are open. Their expressions easy to read, all their features following in a certain logic. Their lips and eyes and their facial lines declare the same emotion at the same time.

This man's face did not fall into one easy-to-read communication. Yes, he was smiling—his lips moved, the left side lifting a little higher than the right, and the grin showed irony and humor. But his eyes retained something more serious and deeply curious. At the same time they were rebellious. As if he didn't only accept what he saw but challenged it.

As he continued cradling my hand in both of his, I was aware of where we made contact but I didn't know why.

It was unexplained.

And the unexplained troubled me.

It occurred to me, standing there, in the store, with a man I didn't know but felt as if I did, that it would be better if I disengaged my hand, stepped back, excused myself and asked Grace to help him.

But I didn't. Didn't pull away. Didn't run away.

Instead I let him continue to hold my hand as a shiver of—what? recognition? pleasure? fear?—shot up my arms and down my neck and pushed my pulse into overdrive.

How long did it last? Probably thirty seconds? Maybe ten minutes. A day? Two nights? I didn't seem to be thinking straight.

"Do you have a first-aid kit here?"

I said there was and that I'd clean up the cut.

"You won't be able to do it with only one good hand. Show me where the kit is." He wasn't asking, he was mandating.

"No. I'm fine."

I had assumed he'd drop my hand and walk off. But he didn't. He just stood there, his continued presence as clear a communication as if he'd spoken.

"Okay, it's this way."

I led him to the restroom, where I pulled out the first-aid kit from under the sink and handed it to him. After gently rinsing out the cut and looking at it closely for a long time to check there was no glass in it, he poured peroxide over it. It stung and I winced, involuntarily jerking my hand away, but he'd anticipated that and held on.

"I know. Hurts like hell doesn't it? It'll stop in a minute."

He was right. By the time he'd finished dressing the wound, the sting was gone.

Done, he gently ran his finger around the edge of the Band-Aid to make sure it had adhered.

"Cut still throbbing?"

"A little."

"But it's not stinging anymore, is it?"

"No."

We were still standing in the small white-tiled room, by the sink. I put the first-aid kit away and he followed me out into the hall.

"You were right," I said.

"I never mind being right." He grinned—and the corner of his mouth tilted upwards again. "But right about what?"

"It would have been hard for me to do that with my left hand. Now, how can I help you? Can I find something for you? Obviously, you didn't come into the store to play doctor." I cringed at the double entendre, surprised that I even noticed it. Hoping he hadn't. "But thank you."

He nodded.

"So…what can I help you with?" I asked.

"Marlowe Wyatt, is she here?"

He wasn't joking.

"I'm Marlowe."

A frown creased his forehead, and I felt as if I'd been dropped from a high distance and was in a free fall.

It occurred to me to ask him why he was disappointed that I was the person he'd come to see. But I didn't. Partly because his face had relaxed so quickly that I was no longer sure I'd read his expression correctly.

"Marlowe," he repeated my name as if he was getting used to it. "I called earlier. Someone named Grace told me that you'd be here and I didn't need an appointment."

"No, you don't. Except for the eight weeks before Valentine's Day."

"Yeah, I read about you and Valentine's Day gifts a few months ago. That's why I'm here."

Since the article had run I'd been incredibly busy. Sending lovers, husbands or wives sexy letters or stories had become a popular gift. I'd gotten more than thirty clients. Including the woman who'd shot the photos for the article, Vivienne Chancey. First she'd taken me up on my free offer and then hired me to write three more letters for her. She was on the road, working on a travel book and was trying to keep a new relationship going while she was gone. The long distance, she said, wasn't working in her favor.

I'd been surprised she'd had to try so hard. She was a talented, successful woman, not someone who I imagined needed the help of erotic letters to attract anyone.

When I told Grace what I thought, she said Vivienne's soul swam in shallow water and it would stop her from succeeding at the kind of relationship she craved.

How did she know? I asked.

Grace had winked—code for the spirits, the stars and magic.

"Grace told me someone had called. Mr. Brown, I think she said. Is that you?"

"Gideon," he said as he extended his hand and then withdrew it. "Forgot about your cut."

"Thanks again. For helping me. For walking in when you did."

I opened the door to my studio and he followed me inside.

"So," I said. "How can I help you?"

Chapter 5

"How many of these have you written?" he asked me after I'd given him the heavy scrapbook of my work. On the front, in hand-tooled gold letters read: Lady Chatterley's Letters.

"I don't know. Maybe a few dozen originals…a hundred personalized from pre-existing stories."

Examining the cover, Gideon ran his long fingers over the letters, tracing their outlines. I responded as if he were drawing them on my bare skin. The *L* slid down my spine, turned and then swaggered halfway across my waist. The *C* curved in a smooth semicircle under my breast.

When he stroked the leather cover, I felt his hand glide between my thighs.

"You aren't sure?"

"I never counted."

I had an insane desire to tell him that the number was immaterial, that the only thing that mattered was the one letter I could never write because there was no address to send it to. Of course, I didn't. I had never discussed that last letter from Kenneth asking me to write him back and forgive him. Not with Grace or any of my other friends. I certainly was not going to disclose it to a stranger. That I'd even had the thought astounded me.

He opened the book.

The fluttering inside my stomach could not have been more intense if he had literally pushed my legs apart with his knees.

Forcing my concentration back to the desk, the scrapbook, my work and the store, I tried to ignore my body's intense reaction.

Where was it coming from? Why was it happening? This wasn't like me—to be attracted to someone I didn't know.

Men who are attached to other women, yet manage to move you, are dangerous the same way a mercury spill is. The mineral glitters and teases, attracting with its pretty, slick smoothness. Looking at it you can almost forget that it is, in fact, poison. But you mustn't.

"Here," I said, pulling the first letter out from the clear plastic sleeve. "You should look at it the way the person does who receives it. The letters are as much about touch and feel and smell as they are about words."

I leaned over my desk, awkwardly using my left hand, since my right was hurt. His eyes took in my movements, and my skin burned where his eyes traveled.

If he looks up at me now, I thought, *I'll ask him about this combustion. If he feels it, too. If he knows why it is happening.* But he was already looking down at the letter I had removed and handed to him.

The words were written in a vibrant green ink on parchment paper that I had decorated with pressed flowers, a scattering of pine needles and a border of moss-colored ribbon. An original Victorian vignette of a brilliant red cardinal perched on the crossbar of the large capital *H* that began the first word.

"You're an artist," he said, sounding surprised and—what was it? Disappointed? Annoyed? Something I couldn't figure out.

I shrugged. "This is only how I earn my living. What I really do is create collages." I nodded toward my wall where some of my personal work hung. "But it's not easy to make a living in fine art, and garrets don't appeal to me. Besides there are no garrets in New York anymore."

"No, I imagine not." He laughed, and looked around my little office now, his eyes taking in the sketches on the wall and the three hanging boxed collages. If people even noticed them, they usually merely glanced at them, but Gideon put the letter down on the desk, got up and walked over to inspect my work more closely. He stood silently in front of the first, looking at it for a long time, and then gave the second an equal viewing.

"You have an amazing imagination and great eye," he finally said. He sat down, picking up the letter again. "So, do you design every letter?"

"Yes. Unless someone hires me just to be the author. Then they write it out in their own handwriting on their stationery or cards that they can pick out here."

He ran a finger over the smooth nap of the translucent paper and down the satin border. He touched everything, I realized. My hand, the Band-Aid, the cover of the book.

As if he knew it better by touching it. Then, lifting it to his face, he inhaled.

I'd used real pine needles, rubbing and crushing them into the back of the paper, infusing it with the green, minty scent. And he was taking it in.

I expected him to read it, of course, but what I hadn't anticipated, what had never happened in the months since I had started writing Lady Chatterley's Letters, was that he would read what I had written out loud.

But he did. Unlike his own staccato way of talking, the story had an abundance of words, and he read them smoothly and much to my surprise, lushly. His voice was dark and his head was down, so I couldn't see the expression on his face, and he couldn't see the one on mine. For which I was thankful.

"Hearing the music, I thought it was the sound of a brook running through the forest. Smelling the perfume, I thought there were flowers growing deep in the woods. The taste of the air had to be the taste of the trees.

"I didn't expect you to be the source of both the sounds and the scents and tastes.

"The tree trunk was as thick as two men and hid me well so I stood there holding on to the bark, letting it bite into my fingers while I watched.

"I should be sorry I stole time that we could have been holding each other but I had to watch you there by yourself, I had to see you like that, unaware of me, but waiting for me.

"The bed you had found for us had a canopy of

leaves, interwoven, criss-crossed, filtering out all but slim rays of light that fell on your breasts. The headboard was made of rocks covered in soft moss, two inches thick."

I had never heard anyone read aloud what I had written. Even though I had consultations with my clients so I could tailor the content to personal taste, I composed the letters and stories alone, in my apartment, after I came home from work, dinner with friends or one of the many disappointing first or second dates that rarely inspired me to accept any more.

And so hearing Gideon read my story disoriented me. Listening to the phrases that until that afternoon had existed only as thoughts inside my head or in calligraphy on paper, filtered through his voice, was a violation of my privacy. Invading without invitation.

Who was this man to walk into Grace's store to buy one thing and instead steal something else?

I wanted to reach across the desk, grab the letter and the book and tell him to go away the way I might tell a man I didn't know well to leave the room if he had accidentally walked in on me while I was getting undressed.

Instead I crossed my legs, moved my arms into an X on my chest, shifted in my seat enough so that I was facing away from him, bit the inside of my cheek and waited for him to finish. I didn't ask him to stop reading even though it was what I wanted to do. Instead I convinced myself I was overreacting, and waited him out.

Grace had taught me how to treat clients, to be polite and respectful, even when I didn't feel they deserved it.

So I sucked in my outrage and tried to think of something else—anything—so I wouldn't hear his articulation of my secrets.

But I couldn't.

"You were naked, your skin dappled with the yellow light that sneaked through the trees. A single beam flashed off the flute you held up to your lips as you pressed a kiss to the opening.

"It was like watching you take another man in your hands and into your mouth. And I was jealous that you would treat an inanimate object so intimately: coaxing melody from its shaft the way you coax pleasure from mine.

"There were leaves woven into your hair, caught up in the curls, and flecks of earth on your bare back and legs. Wide bracelets made of soft willow branches braided together decorated your wrists and ankles.

"It was difficult, in that low, green-tinged light to know where you began and where the forest ended.

"I tried to stay quiet and still but the moan escaped of its own volition. And when you heard it over the music and turned, when I saw how happy you were to see me, I wasn't sorry anymore that I had stolen those five minutes to watch you when I could have been with you, on you, or inside you. I would have missed the expression on your face if I had. And *that* would have been a shame."

Chapter 6

Finally he stopped reading, slipped the letter back into its plastic sleeve and turned to the next page. But I couldn't just sit there and watch him read another. I got up.

"I feel sick…" I mumbled, and I walked out of my office.

I used to know what it was like to be stripped bare in front of a man but I had no interest in experiencing anything like it again.

It was only when I stepped out onto the floor that I knew I was looking for Grace. To ask her to take over for me with Gideon Brown. To hope she would read something in my mood or my inflection or my eyes that would encourage her to take me in her arms and hug me and tell me that everything would be all right. To be, for a few minutes, the recipient of the motherly grace that was the best she offered.

I'd never walked out on a client before. But she and I had talked about the possibility of needing to when I first went to work for her. She warned me that it was conceivable for a man or, for that matter, a woman to come in ostensibly to hire me to write a letter, but to take advantage of our being in a room alone together. The fact that I wrote erotic letters and stories for hire might not be that far a leap for someone to make and assume I would perform for them in some erotic way also. So we had a protocol set up: an alarm button under my desk that I could press without anyone noticing, which would alert her and most of the rest of the sales staff.

I'd never had to use it. I'd never been in danger with a customer. And the kind of danger I felt from Gideon was not like that. It was inside my head.

I'd forgotten to use the button. My need to get away from him quickly had been that urgent.

In front of me was the central, wide-open aisle that branches off into all the different areas of the store. Grace might be working in any one of them.

First I walked through the ribbon department where Debra, a saleswoman, was working with a customer in front of the kaleidoscopic wall of ribbons, arranged row after row by color.

Debra was taking out spools of different blues, holding them against a sheet of foil wrapping paper, waiting for the customer's yea or nay, and then putting them back. Ephemera stocks more than 500 different ribbons that sell by the foot or the yard. The most expensive, at fifty dollars a yard, is made of hand-sewn lavender florets surrounded by leaves.

Some ribbons are edged with gold, others are wired so that once the bows were formed they would hold their shape. There are heavy satins and silks in every hue, in several different thicknesses, from a quarter of an inch to three inches. Grosgrain, chiffon, tapestry, patterns and solids. We even stock a ribbon made of real silver so thin you could use it to sew with.

Grace wasn't in the decorative paper department either, where there is a selection of more than 100 different designs from all over the world. Large sheets, twenty-four inches by thirty-six inches, hanging over wooden dowels the way newspapers are sometimes displayed in libraries.

We have more than two dozen different marbleized papers all made in Florence, Italy. Flames of gold, oranges, reds, or swirls of turquoise, azure and purple. Other papers came from China and Japan, some made from rice with petals of real flowers woven into their fibers, or printed with vibrant colors, repeating patterns of fans, butterflies or wisteria blossoms.

You can also find paper in several sizes in every solid color from rustic browns to shimmering sea-green. Most have envelopes to match.

Continuing on, I glanced at the wooden glass-fronted cabinets that display a wide assortment of writing instruments—from expensive lacquer Mont Blancs to unusual, old-fashioned fountain pens that need to be dipped in ink wells. But she wasn't working there. Nor was she at the showcase of antique seals or two shelves of sealing wax in brilliant shades.

Crisscrossing through side aisles of arts and crafts items, greeting cards, the premade stationery, journals—some covered in alligator, others in suede; date books and photo albums—I kept looking for her. Usually walking through this Ali Baba's cave of delight stimulates my senses. Normally I stopped to look at the ribbons, the papers, the imagery on the stickers, to hunt around the hundreds of rubber stamps and get inspiration on how to decorate the letter I was working on.

But that afternoon I could only see the afterimage of Gideon Brown sitting at my desk reading my work and feeling as if he was rifling through my underwear drawer.

No one had ever requested a letter that I hadn't been able to write. But I was sure that no matter what he wanted, it would be beyond my ability, so I wanted Grace to intercept. To go to him and tell him I'd gotten a phone call, or gone out into the street for a cigarette and been struck down by a car, or arrested, or taken away in an ambulance. Anything.

I found my boss, working in the personalized stationery area near the front with an elderly woman dressed in an expensive gray linen suit.

From the number of sample books on the table in front of them, it looked as if the appointment had been going on for a long time. An effort that would exhaust me, energized Grace. She is an artist with type and color and paper, and so good with people she never cares how long it takes to match the design to the occasion.

She looked up when I approached and read my face in an instant.

Grace Greene is thirty-eight years old, with a rounded physique that Renaissance painters would have loved. Her reddish blond hair, thick and wild, sets off her heart-shaped face like a baroque frame around a fine oil. Her clothes are vintage from the forties or fifties and she wears them with antique paste jewelry that blazes with rubies, emeralds or sapphires. She's a work of art in progress, someone you notice, who makes you smile, because she so clearly enjoys herself and her life. The eternal optimist, the most supportive friend I've ever had and someone who has never failed to offer me the best advice. As long as she doesn't tell me she divines it, I try to pay attention.

Her parents had first opened Ephemera as an art supply store named Greene's Arts in the early seventies at the same time that SoHo was being claimed by artists who were attracted to the old, rundown warehouses that offered huge spaces with cheap rents, great light and a law that granted them the right to live as well as work in these previously commercial buildings.

In the early nineties, along with the help of their two children, Grace and Kenneth, the Greenes had morphed the store into what it is now. They'd also opened two other branches, both farther uptown.

Grace has been managing the SoHo store as well as the amazingly successful Ephemera Web site since she graduated from Wharton Business School and, until he died, Kenneth had been the buyer, traveling all over the world, searching and selecting the papers, ribbons, journals and albums, pens and other unique items on the shelves.

"Are you okay?" Grace smiled as she looked up at me and pushed her hair out of her eyes.

"I didn't know you were busy."

Turning to her client, she asked her if she would mind if she took a moment and then pulled me into a small office next door to the showroom.

"What's wrong? You are emitting so much negative energy I can feel it."

I shook my head. Once I was standing there with her, I wasn't sure what to say or how to say it without sounding like a fool.

There's a man in my office who I'm scared of because I'm attracted to him in a way I haven't been attracted to anyone in a long time. Ever. Maybe. I want you...no, I need you to get rid of him for me.

"It's silly... There's a man..." I shook my head. "It's nothing."

"It's not nothing. Marlowe, tell me."

Then she noticed the bandage on my right hand and pointed to it. "Did he hurt you?"

"No. This is a cut. I broke some ink bottles. I'm fine. My hand is fine. Go back to your client. I'll—"

She put her arms around me and hugged me close. I shut my eyes and just felt the embrace and the comfort it offered.

A phone started ringing. Not the desk phone but her cell.

"Take your call. I'll catch up with you when things are less hectic."

She held up her hand for me to wait. A glass ruby, elegantly set in rhinestones, flashed on her pinky. "No. I'll take a message, I want you to tell me what's wrong."

But I didn't wait. I was being childish. I needed to deal with this myself.

"Helen, I was hoping you'd call..." she said, greeting the caller.

As I walked away, I heard the smile in Grace's voice as she greeted one of her large circle of friends.

Chapter 7

As I trudged back to my office, I gazed at the pens, the journals, the papers, the ribbons, letting the rainbow of colors fill my eyes, and I convinced myself that Gideon Brown would be gone. He would have read a few more letters, realized that he didn't like my style and walked out of the store.

When I got there, I was relieved to find that I was right. He was gone. My sample book was back on top of my desk. The chair he'd been sitting in was empty. There was nothing in the room to indicate he'd ever been there.

I sighed in relief. And then I realized I was wrong. He had left proof of having been here.

When he'd helped me up and bent over my hand to inspect it, and then when he'd cleaned the cut, I'd smelled him: woodsy, dark and leathery all mixed up with something else, too, some spice. Was it cinnamon?

Now I smelled it again, in my own office. Uninvited and unwanted.

I lit the vanilla candle I kept in the corner of my desk. Let it burn. Then breathed in the newly refreshed air.

Yes, that was better.

He was completely gone. His eyes weren't looking at me. His smell wasn't lingering.

The office was mine again.

The letters and stories—my words—were mine again.

Chapter 8

Nothing was working. I'd already gone through a yard of fabric without getting the right effect. Trying once more, I used the scissors to notch the cobalt-blue silk fabric, then pulled and ripped it down the middle.

The tear still didn't have the kind of frayed edge I wanted. I threw it down and walked away from my drafting table. The collage was due the next day, and I didn't see how I was going to make the deadline. I'd been working on the cover design for three weeks but I couldn't get it right. I was almost there, but something was missing.

Every few months I got a book cover illustration assignment from Jeff Harding, who was the art director at a New York publishing house. This time he'd said his deadline was tight—that he only had three weeks. But that should have been long enough for me.

I hated the thought of blowing it. The jobs Jeff gave me were both creatively satisfying and good for my portfolio, and I wanted to get more of them. I also was good friends with Jeff and didn't want to disappoint him.

I'd met him years ago when he and my stepbrother roomed together in college. He'd come to our house for many holidays back then, and all of us thought of him as another member of our family. And it was through Jeff, years later, at a New Year's Eve party, that I met Kenneth and started to date him.

I threw out the piece of blue silk and cut another square out of the bolt I'd bought at a flea market months before and saved, knowing one day I'd want to use it in a collage.

This cover was for a novel called *Soft Water* about an American woman who moves to Venice, lured there by her lover, to help restore a famous painting he owns, only to find that it's a fake.

Part love story, part mystery, the book had kept me turning the pages and at the same time had been so well written I'd seen the sun glinting off the spires of St. Mark's, heard the city's music and tasted its wine.

It was past 2:00 a.m. and I needed sleep. And I would rest, I told myself, as soon as I figured out what was wrong with my design. I got up and stretched, bending over to reach the floor with my fingertips. The cuffs on my over-size, man-tailored shirt fell down and I pushed them back up. It was an old shirt of Kenneth's that I'd appropriated from him shortly after we'd started staying over at each other's apartments. There were glue stains and glitter on the sleeves, splotches of paint on the tails and a rip where the fourth button should have been.

I walked around the loft and tried to figure out what was wrong with the design.

First I switched on the lights in the bedroom area and shut off the lights in the kitchen area to give myself something to do. Then I kicked a pile of magazines under the old leather couch and moved a box of paints off the seat so that I could sit down if I wanted.

I lived in a fifteen-hundred-square-foot space that had been, a hundred years before, a section of the fifth floor of a warehouse that manufactured glass beads. Sometimes still, I'd find a sliver of one in the cracks of the oak floor. The space was divided into areas that included a kitchen and a bedroom with a wall of bookshelves.

When I'd first rented it, I'd imagined it would be a real home. Shortly before he was killed, Kenneth and I had decided he was going to move in and we'd begun making it less like a workplace. We hadn't gotten very far, though. It still appeared to be a large artist's studio that accommodated my occasional need for eating and sleeping. Three drafting tables dominated what could be a living room. A table Kenneth and I had bought, imagining lovely dinners being eaten there, was now where I laid out vignettes and illustrations I cut out of magazines. Currently, the table was covered with cutouts of young women, all with their backs to the camera. Almost a hundred different angles and sizes and shapes. One of whom would go on the book cover.

There were empty boxes piled in corners, some made of wood, others plastic. Ready to be filled with collages. File cabinets lined the walls, overflowing with illustrations and artifacts that I'd collected for my work.

The space under the window in my bedroom area was stacked with finished projects, research books and volumes of poetry I used to find quotes in. Unread novels lay piled on the half of the bed where I never slept.

There was clutter everywhere.

The only place to find relief was out the large windows that ran the whole length and up one side of the loft. They faced east and north, and during the day afforded me not only a view of the streets five stories below but miles of sky above.

That night I could see a sliver of moon hiding behind a pearl-gray cloud. But stars were hard to come by. They always were in Manhattan; there was too much ambient light.

With my forehead against the window, I looked down on Spring Street. A taxi cruised by.

What was wrong with the cover concept?

I closed my eyes, and when I opened them I saw a couple, holding hands, walking close together, meandering up the block toward Broadway.

As they reached the corner the stoplight changed and they stopped. Bathed in a red glow, the woman tilted her face up toward the man's. In sync, he bent toward her. They kissed, and from my perch it seemed as if the music playing on my stereo, bluesy jazz from the thirties, was underscoring their movements.

There was no reason for me to stand there and watch. No reason for me to walk away, either.

The man's hands moved languidly over the woman's back, across her shoulder blades and down her spine. Then, with a sudden fierceness, he grabbed her ass, pulling her to him in a move that was less loving and more desperate than how he'd been touching before.

I held my breath—wondering how she would react—whether this was what she wanted or not.

She melted deeper into him.

The light changed and shone green on them. I could see they didn't care. Nothing sounded or intruded. An invisible envelope had surrounded them and obliterated everything outside of them. There were no smells except what was on the other's skin, no air except what the other expelled after each kiss, no sound except each other's blood beating and their half-intelligible urgent whispers. Words that would have sounded thin and hollow, if not for the context of the tangle of arms and legs and lips.

More.

Please.

Your lips.

You're crazy.

Feel me.

Oh.

No, that was my imagination. I was already superimposing my story on their actions. I didn't know what they were saying or hearing. What they were feeling. Except for their own kind of passion.

Locked in their embrace, they remained on that corner for a few more seconds until the woman started backing them away from the street, toward the side of the building where they disappeared into a small alcove.

To anyone walking by, they would be veiled in shadows, but they were still visible to me.

And as if to prove it, a car drove past, its light illuminating the rest of the sidewalk, but not catching them in its beam. I was glad for them, for finding a place to be hidden, yet in plain view.

His back was up against the bricks, she was leaning into him, her arms were around his neck, his around her back, his hands were burrowing into the waistband of her short jean skirt.

Oblivious to any possible danger or intrusion, urgently now, the woman hiked up her skirt, exposing more of her thighs. She thrust forward. The man maneuvered. I couldn't be sure but from the way his shoulders moved, I thought he might be unzipping his fly and entering her.

Their slow thrusts were the movements of a sexual dance. With heads bowed and hands gripping arms, their hips gyrated in circles, moving faster and faster until they slowed down for one long, aching sequence of kisses and lunges.

I held my breath, squeezed my arms with my own fingers, pressed my pelvis hard up against the window ledge while I kept watching them, staring, living out their whole pleasure in my head.

I'd had sex with a few men since Kenneth had died. I'd even enjoyed it in my own way with two of them, but I hadn't come close to longing for anyone, hadn't been pulled toward anyone with such a force that I would have made love to him on a street corner in the middle of the night. Even with Kenneth I'd never been sexually adventurous like that.

Passion—hungry, yearning, overwhelming—found its place in the stories I wrote for clients. But those were fantasies. I couldn't imagine living that kind of desire.

To feel it required living it. It required exhibitionism

of the body and of the mind, a baring of more than your flesh. You have to open up to someone and show him what is inside you to feel passion. And that was something I'd learned to be afraid of a long time before I'd met Kenneth.

Except for my first real relationship with a man, I'd never managed to merge my fantasy life with my reality. Back then, with my first lover, I'd lived out my eroticism easily. Given and taken freely. But since I'd broken that off at nineteen, for the past ten years, there had been a deep gulf between what I imagined and what I lived. My daydreams and nighttime dreams were thick with lust and wet with pleasure. But when I was with a flesh-and-blood man, I became tight and dry. Withholding. Selfish. Preoccupied.

The letters and stories I wrote, the artwork I did, fulfilled me. And I was all right with that. Not everyone could manage to merge their wishes with their deeds, their imaginings with their actions.

I stepped away from the window, leaving the couple to zip up and pat their clothes back into place. And as I turned back to the living room, I realized exactly what my problem was with the cover of the novel I'd been working on. It needed the hint of lovers. Two shadows embracing in the night.

I didn't think of Kenneth—or miss him—too often anymore. Weeks could go by without me consciously focusing on him. I didn't cry anymore or wonder what might have become of us. But the cover design for the novel that took place in Venice had brought him and his awful, surprising death back to me. And there, in the nighttime, alone and powerless to fight the memories off the way I could during the day, I had become melancholy.

The cover had made me think of what I'd lost with Kenneth.

At least, that was what I thought.

Chapter 9

Mornings were mine. I never went to the store until noon. And then only four days a week—Wednesdays through Saturdays. So, that Tuesday I should have been able to sleep in. But as tired as I was from having worked all night, I needed to get up early and get to Jeff's office for our 10:30 a.m. meeting.

He smiled and kissed me and gave me one of his great big hugs after his assistant had taken me back to his office. Jeff always wore elegant, old-fashioned clothes. Tweeds and bow ties. Three-piece suits. He was slightly foppish—but in a charming way—with his round wire-rimmed glasses, pocket hanky and little Dutch-boy haircut.

He offered me water, which I accepted, and he moved over to a refrigerator in the corner by the window and we talked about his wife and two-year-old baby while he pulled out a green bottle, opened it, and poured the sparkling water equally between two glasses.

The cold bubbles were welcome and I took a few gulps.

And then I pulled the artwork for his cover from my portfolio and put it down on his desk, facing him.

His eyes took it in quickly. "Wonderful," he said right away.

"Thanks."

He was still inspecting it. "It works perfectly. The title will go right here." And he pointed to the sky. "Great job, Marlowe."

"This one was tough."

"Really?" He looked up at me, puzzled.

"Yeah. I was surprised, too. Couldn't figure it out. It was the Venice connection. It threw me."

He knew about Kenneth and understood what I meant right away. "Aw, Marlowe, I'm sorry, baby, I didn't realize. I shouldn't—"

I interrupted him. "No. I didn't realize it, either. It's okay now."

"I feel awful."

"You can make it up to me by getting me some more water." And I held out my glass. When I did, I accidentally jostled some papers on Jeff's desk, revealing a photograph. I recognized it immediately.

The photograph was black-and-white in a thousand subtle shades of gray. Provocative, it pulled you in, demanded that you look at the woman's open mouth. The lips moist and swollen. The unmistakable expression of passion. And a single mark on her cheek. Which could have been anything. The blemish of a man's fingerprint. Inky and dark. Smudged. A moody brand, suggestive and disturbing. Yet, as a work of art, the photograph was beautiful. I could see that, regardless of all the other feelings the photograph brought out in me.

I didn't have to ask; I knew who had taken this photograph as well as I knew my own body in the mirror. I just wasn't quite sure why it was on Jeff's desk. His back was to me as he put the green bottle back in his minirefrigerator, so, not really caring if it was any of my business or not, I pushed away the other papers to reveal that the photograph was part of an invitation.

On the bottom, in tastefully small type it said:

"Nude Muses: The Photography of Cole Ballinger"

I picked it up and turned it over.

You are invited to Cole Ballinger's first one-man show.
June 2 / 6:00 p.m.
Kulick Gallery
34 West 26th Street, NYC
RSVP: 212-222-3333

Cole Ballinger. A name I stared at as if I had never seen it before, because in that context it was foreign. No, worse than that. It was unsettling. A low-level worry started to hum deep in my stomach. My hand started to shake.

I wanted to take the invitation and rip it into a hundred pieces. At the same time I felt an overwhelming wave of weariness and lethargy. The sense that I'd never be able to move out of the chair, never be able to drink the water Jeff had put in front of me, never be able to put down the photograph but be doomed forever to sit in that chair and stare at the blight in my hand.

No matter how I'd found out about Cole's show, it would have bothered me, but like this? By accident?

Looking up, I was not surprised to see Jeff watching me closely.

"I didn't know Cole was having a show."

"A one-man show," he said, clearly imparting the importance of it.

"Do you know anything about this photograph?" I asked, holding my breath after I'd released the words, watching Jeff's face carefully.

"Nothing except how much attention he told me it's getting."

He meant it. I could tell there was nothing Jeff wasn't saying. No duplicity in his eyes. No looking away, no embarrassment, which there would have been if he had known.

"I would have thought your mom would have told you," Jeff said.

"I think she tried. A couple of months ago she started to tell me that something terrific had happened for Cole, but I didn't ask and she didn't pursue it."

Jeff shook his head. "Neither of you has ever asked me to get involved. But I think it stinks. After how close we all were. After how much the two of you mattered to each other. That you can't work out your differences doesn't make sense."

"Cole's never asked because he knows what a shit he is and doesn't care. And I care too much to want to have anything to do with him anymore or to put you in the middle of it."

"It eats him up inside," Jeff said.

"Really?" My voice was as arched as my eyebrows.

"Really. Does that surprise you?"

"Most of what *Cole* does surprises me."

"Isn't there any way for you two to work out whatever is keeping you apart?"

"Maybe a long time ago but…" I had to force myself not to look down at the invitation again but instead keep my eyes on Jeff. "Not anymore. So—" I took a long drink of the fizzy water "—let's not do this, okay?"

"When *was* the last time you talked to him?"

I shrugged. "Before Kenneth died. He's called since. I've erased his messages without listening to them."

"Why won't you hear him out?"

"Because the only thing that would matter to me is the one thing he won't do. If he did, it would interfere with his plans."

"I don't understand that." Jeff was clearly confused.

"I know. But I can't explain. Don't want to, really. It's the past. Or at least it was the past…" I couldn't help it. I looked at the invitation again. Quickly. Then I forced my eyes away. I didn't want to go backward. Didn't want to deal with my stepbrother. Our relationship was too complicated. Too embarrassing. It had meant too much. To me. But clearly not to him. Never to him.

Cole was on a one-way track to success, and nothing was going to get in his way. For as long as I'd known him, he had been devoted to his career to the exclusion of anything else. And I couldn't imagine anything that would change the single-mindedness of his determination. I knew about wanting success but I didn't understand how it could be more important than the people you cared about. He'd tried to explain his drive, his philosophy, to me a long time ago, in different ways. None of them had been sufficient to clarify how he could be so insensitive. Bullshit. He knew what he'd done was wrong, and he knew how to right it—but to do so would have derailed his plans. And there had always been plans.

Cole was now thirty-one, and one of the bad boys of photography. Sexy, clever, talented, and pushing every edge. His heroes were Robert Mapplethorpe and Helmut Newton. His shots were sexual and progressive. Angry and beautiful. They made viewers uncomfortable, which made them think his work was important. Was it? I was too close to know. But Cole was getting attention and press at a time when most people felt everything had been done already. He specialized in photographing private moments in a way that made viewers feel as if they were intruding in someone's life—stepping into a room where they were not invited and witnessing an act that was not for public consumption. And that was exactly what Cole did. He took your emotions, your longings, your wants, your passions, and exposed them with a click of a camera. He recorded fragments of your soul. And while he was doing it, you didn't even realize what you were giving away.

In several cultures, taking someone's photograph is forbidden. The fear is that the camera steals your personal essence, robbing you of part of your self.

Cole and his work were proof to me that the superstition was true to some extent. That the camera can capture a piece of you. And danger can follow when that part of you is lost, even worse when it is given up to the public, allowing them to gape at an emotion you have never even seen on your own face.

In other times, in other cultures, Cole might be considered the devil.

"Marlowe, can't you give him another chance? He's not happy that the two of you are estranged."

"I don't believe you. He knows—he knew exactly what he could have done to work things out with me. He chose to do the opposite. I'm sorry. I'm being cryptic. I don't want to be, but I don't want to talk about this anymore. And please, don't tell him I saw this. If you do, I'll never talk to you again, either."

"That's a little melodramatic, isn't it?"

"No. Considering the breach of trust involved, that's the last thing it is."

Chapter 10

I couldn't go home. Not yet. If I did, I'd focus on Cole and his photographs and our estrangement and the upcoming show. So I went to Ephemera. Even though it wasn't a day when I was expected, Grace was glad to see me.

"To what do we owe the pleasure?" she asked.

I shrugged.

"Tell me."

For a second I heard Kenneth saying the same thing, and that made me sadder than I'd have thought it would. "It's nothing... No...it's not. It's about Cole."

"Why don't you tell me—"

"Grace, I love you. But no matter how many times you ask me, I'm not going to talk about our relationship. It's between me and Cole. I've just gone through this conversation with Jeff and I'm sick of it. I love you, but I don't want to hear about forgiveness and families right now."

She looked at me with that sweet, concerned expression she gets when she senses that I'm upset, put her arm around me and let me into her office. Her touch started to work its magic and I felt the edge of my anxiety start to dissolve.

As soon as we were sitting on her couch, she pushed a dish of chocolate back in my direction. Grace is a chocolate connoisseur. At least once a week, she rescues me from my office and we take a long walk to the City Bakery on Eighteenth to imbibe their heady hot chocolate, made the French way—not with cocoa powder but with melted bittersweet chocolate mixed with milk, a secret recipe they won't reveal. The bark she was offering, deep, dark and shining, studded with fat almonds, came from an even more exclusive shop, La Maison du Chocolate, which was on West Forty-Ninth Street, where everything cost so much it was a true extravagance. Impossible to resist, I broke off a piece, put it in my mouth and let the chocolate start to melt. And then I chewed. And then it was gone and I was sorry. I eyed the dish, almost took more, but managed to control myself. The stuff was addictive.

"Better?" she asked.

"Yes. If only it was a real cure not a temporary distraction."

"What happened?"

"Can I tell you the details later and leave it at the fact that I got yet more proof that I have a stepbrother who is a brilliant photographer and a very selfish prick?"

She reluctantly agreed, and we spent a half hour talking and trying not to finish off the whole dish of chocolate, but we failed.

When her client showed up, I returned to my office and sat down to work, buzzing from the caffeinated confection, trying not to let my anger bubble to the surface now that I was out of Grace's calming presence.

The project I wanted to work on that day required a special rice paper, which I'd ordered, so I went into the back room where deliveries were unpacked to look for it.

Ripping open boxes and unwrapping the packages was therapy. I pulled at cardboard with my fingers, not caring if I broke nails or shredded skin. I picked out staples with my fingertips and tugged at tape that seemed cemented on. I went to work on box after box as if the thing I was searching for might actually be found there.

One box was full of velvet ribbons. About three dozen rolls in pastel colors. Interrupting my search for the rice paper, I took each roll of ribbon out and put it on the unpacking table in the middle of the room, creating a tower of hues and tones. Baby blues the color of robins' eggs, pinks the color of little girls' ballerina skirts. Greens and yellows that looked like the fancy mints made with white chocolate that my mother bought every Easter and put in a bowl for guests after dinner.

The colors were like lullabies, finishing off the job Grace had begun, calming me.

I cut strips off eight of them and laid them aside on the table as I continued to search through the boxes for the rice paper, which I finally found.

The paper and streamers of ribbon in hand, I went back to my office, more tranquil than I'd been after leaving Grace's office. Much more so than after leaving Jeff's.

I opened the door to my office. The windowless room was waiting for me. Small. Cramped. Overflowing with half-finished projects and supplies. It didn't matter. It was a space that was utterly without emotional connections to anyone or anything in my personal life, and I was free to work there without being bombarded by any of my ghosts. The dead ones, or the ones who were still living.

Chapter 11

At 4:00 p.m. I realized I hadn't eaten anything all day except for Grace's chocolate, so I grabbed some money from my bag and went across the street to Dean & Deluca to get some coffee and an apple.

The store is a food museum with every item displayed as if it were a treasure. The fruit and vegetables rest in towering, glittering piles, everything bigger and better and more intensely colored than what you see at an ordinary supermarket. There are strawberries the size of your fist. Carrots, thick and robust with deep green leafy stems—beautiful enough to be a bouquet. Giant artichokes from Israel that seem sculpted from jade, Meyer lemons all year long. Raspberries and blueberries that beg to be eaten straight out of their wooden crates. Fresh herbs and more choices of lettuce than you could try in a week, all sparkling with diamond droplets of water from the tiny automatic sprinklers that spray the produce every few hours.

Glass cases show off an extravagant array of cheeses,

chocolates and pastas as if they were expensive jewelry. The bakery offers more than fifty types of scones, muffins, croissants and breads, and when you stand in front of its counters, the scent is so overwhelming you have to hold yourself back from reaching out and breaking off a heel of a three-foot baguette or ripping into a sourdough loaf.

There is something to lure even the most worn-out foodie, from the glistening caviar and sushi to the opulence of thirty different kinds of honey, three dozen types of salts, four dozen jams and jellies, and almost a hundred varieties of olive oil and vinegar.

Usually, I wandered up and down the aisles, allowing myself to give in to the temptation of one treat: a portion of lobster saffron ravioli for dinner, a bottle of extra virgin olive oil infused with garlic, along with one perfect head of butter lettuce, or a small sack of *fleur de sel* tied with a black ribbon.

But not today.

I grabbed one green apple and went straight to the counter at the front and got in line for coffee.

"Next!" the barrista called and I stepped up to the register. Ignoring pastry, panini, soups, slabs of carrot and zucchini cake, wedges of pie and cheesecake, I ordered black coffee. Plain. I wasn't in the mood for a creamy cappuccino or a sweet mocha. All I wanted was a cup of coffee, hot and bitter.

After paying, I walked over to the window and sat down at the six-foot-long marble-topped bar surrounded by high wooden stools.

Dean & Deluca is almost always crowded, but this afternoon there was only one other person there: a young woman wearing a paint-stained shirt who was sipping a tall iced tea and eating a brownie in tiny, tiny bites as if she was trying to make it last forever.

Removing the top from my paper cup of coffee, the steam escaped, and I took the first sip, inhaling the dark, aromatic scent.

The woman smiled at me. There were rings of paint around her cuticles and more splattered on her hands. I liked seeing her there. SoHo had become so gentrified that artists were now greatly outnumbered by business people and tourists.

Cole—my anger with him, my disappointment with him, my embarrassment that I had been fooled by him—was like a splinter. I felt him there.

For years, too many times, I'd taken the needle and tried to fish out the remaining sliver of him that seemed lodged forever under my skin, but I hadn't been able to extract him. I had to figure out a way to clean him out of my system. Finally.

"You were pretty damn rude the other day to walk out on me, after I did everything but kiss your hand to make it better."

Once again, I didn't see his face first, but his hands as he put a plate of chocolate chip cookies and a cup of espresso on the table beside me.

Then, pulling out the stool, he sat down.

I didn't want to be interrupted. Didn't want anyone to intrude on my self-pitying anger at my stepbrother. Didn't want to be polite to a potential client and didn't know how to extricate myself from a stranger who had made me feel undressed in my own office.

"Why did you do that?" he asked. "Is that how you treat all your potential clients?"

I fumbled for a reason, something that wouldn't be personal but that would satisfy him and prevent him from asking me any more questions.

"I didn't walk out on you."

"What would you call it?" He'd swung from sarcastic, kindly banter to a moment of sincere anger. Looking at it from his point of view, it was not undeserved. I had left him sitting there.

He took a gulp of his coffee and then waited for me to say something. I didn't. Not right away.

Gideon was wearing blue jeans again. And a sweater with thin stripes of blue, indigo, green and white. His hair had the same tousled look as before, and when he reached up and brushed his hand through it I knew why. His habit of running his fingers through the dark curls and pushing the lock off his forehead gave him a perpetually breezy look. That, with the slightly insolent slant of his cheekbones and the sparkling but hard-to-read eyes— unusual eyes that were like fine Italian marble, green with threads of black swirling through them—engaged my curiosity. Despite myself.

"I didn't mean to be rude," I said sincerely.

"What happened, then?"

I knew I probably owed him an explanation, but what could I say that would make sense?

Always try for some version of the truth, my stepfather had taught me. *You are simply a lousy liar,* he would say. *Your face always gives you away.*

"I'd never heard anyone read one of my letters out loud before," I explained. "It was like standing there and being undressed by a total stranger."

He didn't respond to that except to push his plate of cookies closer toward me. "Have one," he said, implying how good they were. How did he do that? I didn't think I'd ever met anyone who conveyed so much in so few words. Or so much behind his words.

They smelled delicious, and eating was something to do instead of just sitting there feeling even more foolish than I had before I'd blurted out the thing about being undressed, so I broke off a piece and took a bite. It was soft and sugary and started to dissolve as soon as I put it in my mouth. First Grace's chocolate and now the cookies, I was going to be on a sugar high for the rest of the day.

It was as strange to be sitting beside him doing something as ordinary as sipping coffee and eating cookies. Just as strange as it had been to have him read my own words to me in my own office. I was too aware of all the tastes and smells and how he moved and what I said and how I sounded. I didn't feel like myself in Gideon's presence, and I didn't know why. No, that wasn't right. I felt like a version of myself I hadn't been for years. Open. Vulnerable. Wired. Receptive. Angry. Aware of every fleeting feeling.

"So...I'd like to talk to you about an assignment," Gideon said as he brushed crumbs off his hands and shifted so that he was facing me instead of the window. "How long have you been writing these stories?"

"About six months."

"How did you start?"

I took a sip of coffee, then spoke. "The woman who had the job before me had quit, and while Grace looked for a replacement she asked me to fill in. It was easy enough. There were a few dozen letters and stories already written, I only had to insert names and places and little facts to make them personal, and then decorate them. I never intended to stay on. And I never thought I'd start writing original letters or stories. I'd never written seriously but—" I stopped. Why was I telling him my life story? I shrugged. "The letters provide good money, and selling collages doesn't."

"Not the whole story, is it?"

Typically clients spent most of their time looking through my samples. Generally they are either giddy or giggly or slightly embarrassed. Usually happy and excited. They almost never ask me about myself.

I played with some of the crumbs on the marble, rolling them around under my fingertips, buying time, trying to figure out if I had to answer him, and finally deciding I didn't.

When he realized I wasn't going to respond, he changed the subject.

"Who owns the letters and stories that are originals?"

"The client does."

"They can't show up in your sample book?"

"Not if a client doesn't want them to. But most clients don't mind and agree to let me show them with the names changed."

"And your boyfriend—or husband—what does he think about you writing love letters to strangers?"

"That's not what I'm doing—the letters aren't *from* me. I help clients figure out what they want to write. What kind of fantasies they want me to create. There's a long questionnaire they fill out that gives me a lot of information and insight."

"But the ideas are yours."

"No. I'm just the translator for people's emotions."

"They're your thoughts written down in your voice."

"They aren't my thoughts. That isn't my voice."

"I read them. It's your voice. Has to be. Unless you ask each client to describe what it feels like to touch someone, kiss them, make love to them. You don't, do you?" He didn't wait for my answer; he knew this, too. "When you write, aren't you feeling your own heat? Isn't that what you're transferring to the page?"

Something was buzzing under the top layer of my skin again. I reached up and touched my glasses. Almost as if I was making sure the screen that kept people at a distance was still in place.

"You're the seductress, even if you are hiding behind some stranger's signature."

I couldn't tell if he'd insulted me or complimented me. And I was even less certain why it mattered. All I knew was that listening to him was like being buffeted by a storm, not sure how far you've been thrown off your course until the wind finally dies down. Then realizing you're lost.

"The letters aren't personal to me. They are anything but. I don't give them half as much thought as you're giving them. I'm not describing what it feels like for me to kiss someone, or touch someone or make love to them. You're making a lot of incorrect assumptions."

"You're angry?"

"Of course I am."

"Capturing an emotion. Violent or passionate. Isn't that the goal of an artist?"

I took another sip of what was left of my coffee. He had me all mixed up. So it had been a compliment. "I'm not making art. The stories are just a job."

"Right," he said, making it completely clear that having upset me pleased him in some way. "While I waited for you the other day, after you walked out of your office, I read a few more of the letters."

I felt my cheeks get hot, wondering which ones. Using my forefinger, I pressed down on one chocolate chip that was left on the plate and brought it to my mouth, letting it liquefy and savoring its intense flavor.

Before I figured out how to respond, he said, "Since what's in the letters isn't what you feel, but what your clients feel, your clients are all, amazingly, very sensitive and sensual and able to communicate awfully well." His voice was complicated, the way the chocolate was both sweet and a little bitter at the same time. But mixed in with the sarcasm, I heard the shadow of his disbelief and concern for me.

I'd never wondered before if the people who read the sample letters thought that the fantasies, emotions and feelings I described belonged to me. I had assumed everyone knew they were fictitious dreams created to satisfy my clients' needs, to express their emotions and desires. Why didn't Gideon understand that? Why was he judging me against the words and trying to make us fit together?

"Okay," he said, his word ending the exchange. "You're

a modern-day Cyrano. Only without the nose. Have I got it right now?"

Finally I laughed.

"What do you charge?" His seemed resigned, as if he hadn't been sure before and then once he'd made the connection between what I did and Voltaire's sixteenth-century novella something had been settled for him.

"Fifty dollars to customize an existing letter or story to—"

"Originals," he interrupted.

"Four hundred and fifty dollars. A hundred less if the customer only wants the words and not the collage."

"Any discount for more than one?"

"No, sorry."

"Accommodating, aren't you?"

"It takes me the same amount of time no matter how many letters someone wants. Each is original."

I wasn't doing my best selling job. Clearly I was ambivalent about him giving me work. He was too present. Too intense. Besides, I was having a hard time believing that he wanted to. He seemed too self-possessed to ask anyone to write a word for him.

He stood. "Thanks for answering all my questions. It's all very interesting."

"No problem."

"I've got an appointment that I'm going to be late for. So I'm sorry, but I'm going to run."

"Thanks for the cookie."

He smiled and shook his head, making it clear the thanks weren't necessary. "I might want to hire you," he added.

I nodded, but something about him made me doubt he would.

As if he could read my thoughts he said, "I know my own talents. What you do isn't one of them."

As I watched Gideon walk out of the store, noticing how his shoulders sloped and how lazy his walk was despite his having somewhere to go, I wondered about him.

How had he wound up there at the exact time I'd been there? Did he work in this neighborhood and had come for coffee himself and seen me there? Or had he gone to Ephemera, asked for me, and someone told him where I was? And who would have done that? I hadn't told anyone where I was going.

It could be another coincidence. Like our mirror-image scars. Grace would never accept it as sheer chance. But that's all it was and was just as meaningless.

Hundreds of people stopped by Dean & Deluca because they were hungry, thirsty or curious. Why couldn't his motives have been as innocent?

Later that day Grace told me I was denying all the obvious signs because what was happening to me was beyond my rational interpretation of how things worked. "If you can't touch it, you don't think it's real," she said. "But kismet *is* real."

"You don't expect me to believe that," I countered.

"Expect you to? No. But I want you to. There are reasons for things that we don't understand, for the unexpected and the unexplained. They have their own logic, Marlowe. Just because you don't know what it is doesn't mean it doesn't exist."

Chapter 12

At ten o'clock that night I got undressed, putting on the dark ruby silk robe that Grace had found for me in an antique store on West Broadway. I hadn't even noticed it; Grace had spotted the robe hanging on a hook by a painting that had me mesmerized. Ordinarily I didn't like vintage clothing. While I could appreciate the design, the idea of wearing what someone else had once worn didn't appeal to me. My curiosity over who had owned it and when she'd worn it and how it had wound up for sale fifty years later was too vexing. I didn't want my clothes to come with another woman's history.

But the robe still had its original tag attached. How had it escaped being sold for all those years? That in itself was enough of a mystery. Had it been a gift that had stayed in its box under the bed? Had it been purchased by a woman to wear on a trip that had never been taken?

I'd owned it for as long as I'd been working for Grace, and it had become my writing robe. I'm not superstitious.

I don't have talismans. But when I'm going to write someone else's story, I slip into it, feel its smooth silk against my skin, shiver and then settle down at my desk, ready to take the hours when I used to sleep or watch television or read while Kenneth sat beside me, and give them over to strangers.

I had two rituals: I always wrote the letters and stories in my ruby robe, and I always wrote them by the light of a candle I used to keep on the bedside table. The same sandalwood candle that had lit my derailed lovemaking with Kenneth.

I wasn't sentimental. It was all part of a process. The low light made it easier to glide into the words.

None of it felt like work. I was lucky for that. Other artists I was friendly with worked at tedious jobs in offices, or tiring stints in stores or waiting tables in restaurants. I got to fantasize other people's lives. But it still required effort and energy that I had spent on Kenneth—first loving him, then mourning him. It was a relief to finally offer all that up to the letters and stories. I donated the hours that had been ours to the words. And even though they were written for strangers who paid me to turn their half-realized erotic imaginings and outpourings of passion or love into prose, they were still, in a way, intensely private.

Until that night, I'd never thought about it quite that way, but Gideon had made me see differently. And I wasn't sure I was happy he had. If I became self-conscious about what I was writing, I would fail. And more than not wanting to fail, I didn't want to lose what had become a welcome escape, and had come to represent something much more complicated to me.

The process began with choosing the pen. Each was different, and picking one was like the first step a woman takes when deciding what to wear to seduce someone. A black lace bra? A short rose silk teddy? A lemon-yellow camisole with nothing else?

Whatever one selected would set the tone for the rest of the ceremony. And so it was for me with the pen.

That night I equivocated between a sleek maroon lacquer Mont Blanc, an exotic Waterman Serrisima that was curved like a man's penis, or an antique gold pen that had no barrel and had to be dipped after every few sentences. I picked the dipping pen. The deliberation it required fit the mood of what I was going to write.

The next decision was what color ink to use, like the decision to leave your hair down or pin it up and show more of the naked skin of your neck. For that evening's story, I picked a dark velvet blue-purple, the color of a bearded iris or blueberry juice.

What paper to use was like picking sheets with which to make the bed. It wasn't only that you wanted fresh sheets when you were expecting an assignation, you knew the color and pattern would be a communication in itself. Clean pristine whites that invited a contrast to raunchy lust? Or a dense flowery pattern that inspired soft, sweet romance?

The paper I put on top of my desk was a thick stock in the palest blue.

The options became even more complicated after that. Choosing the first words was like giving someone a small look across a room. Determining an evocative phrase was like giving an openmouthed kiss. Shaping a sentence that

would elicit a thrill was like opening for the first pene-
tration. Or taking a lover into your mouth.

The pen point disappeared into the ink like a swimmer
dipping into a lake of dark blue water and emerged dripping. Once the last of the ink had splashed back into the
bottle, I started to write.

The car was waiting for her when she came downstairs.

She had obeyed all of his instructions, dressing in
a long, black velvet dress that he had picked out for
her. It was high-necked and sleeveless. But it was also
backless and had a slit going up the side that reached
the top of her thigh.

He had been specific. She was to wear stockings
with a garter belt. The one he had bought for her. No
brassiere. No other underwear.

It was a silly game, she thought as she went from
the building to the car and felt the breeze blow the
dress apart and caress her skin. She shivered. It was
late fall and she should have had a coat on. But he'd
been explicit that she not wear a coat.

The chauffeur got out of his side of the car, came
around and opened her door. He wore a pearl-gray
uniform and hat, white gloves and murmured "good
evening" as he held the door for her. She barely
glanced at him as she anxiously climbed into the
limousine, where she expected to find her lover.

He wasn't there, and that disappointed her. She'd
thought he'd been watching her come out of the
building and get into the car. That had pleased her.

No, he hadn't watched. He wasn't there.

But a woman was.

She stared at the seated woman.

Right away, she noticed that the other woman's arms were as bare as her own. That her neck was just as covered. But the similarities went further. Their black velvet dresses were identical. Their hair color was identical. So was the way their hair was cut. The stranger's eyes were lined with the same smudges of eyeliner that Gaia wore. The lipstick that filled in the woman's mouth was the same rose color Gaia used: the color of Gaia's nipples.

Was it also the color of this stranger's nipples?

Even the perfume the woman wore—which was a fairly unusual scent that Gaia's lover purchased for her from an obscure shop in Paris that made its own fragrances—was identical.

A sharp click alerted Gaia that the driver had returned to his seat, shut his door. A second later, the car pulled away from the curb.

"Do you know where we are going?" Gaia asked the woman sitting beside her.

She wanted to ask her other questions. Wanted to know why she was there, who she was, why she didn't seem as surprised as Gaia was at the similarities in their appearances.

The woman didn't answer, but poured Gaia a flute of champagne from the bottle of Cristal that sat in a bucket of ice. After Gaia took it, the second woman drank from her own glass with the same particular mannerisms that Gaia used.

It was mesmerizing. This was her twin. Almost

identical. She wondered how far the resemblance went, and her eyes inadvertently grazed the woman's breasts. Even covered by the extravagant velvet, Gaia could see that they were almost the same size.

The woman watched Gaia watching, and smiled.

"Do you know what is going on?" Gaia asked, apprehensive. Nervous. Excited. She could feel the satin that lined the dress against her skin. Feel the goose bumps on her arms that had not gone away even though it had been several minutes since she'd walked from the cold night air into the warm interior of the car.

In answer, the woman leaned forward so that she was only a few inches from Gaia's face, so close that she could smell the musty scent that was body heat, not perfume.

It was fascinating to look into this face that was so much like her own. Like looking into a mirror. And then the other leaned even closer and kissed Gaia on the mouth. The pressure was exquisite and the texture was luscious, like the flesh of a ripe peach. It was the softest kiss that Gaia had ever felt. Plush lips pressed against hers. A tiny delicate tongue that flicked out and very gently licked the outline of Gaia's mouth. Burning the nerve endings as she went along. Stinging and smoothing. Light and penetrating.

Gaia didn't fight the kiss even though it was unexpected. It was too interesting. So this is what it would be like to kiss myself, she thought. But it was more than that and she knew it. This was something she'd wanted for so long. Dreamt about for even longer. She knew why there was another woman there.

Her lover was giving her this gift. This fulfillment of her fantasy.

One late afternoon, sipping heavy and sweet rum punches on the beach in South Miami, she and her lover lay on chaises and told each other one sexual secret. She told him that before him she had preferred to make herself come because so few men really understood her timing.

And when you played with yourself, he'd asked, what did you think about? Who did you fantasize about?

Honestly? she'd asked, because she'd never told anyone.

He'd laughed and nodded. And she'd told him that she didn't think about anyone; instead she watched herself in the mirror. That she liked how her own face thickened the closer she got to coming. That she liked to pull up her hand and look at it in the mirror, slicked with her own wetness. That seeing it made the throbbing inside her increase.

She had told him, when he talked to her about how she made herself come, that she played a game fantasizing that she made love to herself, and here she was. Facing herself in the car.

Now, what would it be like to reach out and touch her own breasts and feel between her own legs? she wondered.

And wondered, too, if she would have the courage

to do it? To take the offering he had made, and take it as far as she could.

But she didn't have to decide. Because the woman facing her picked up Gaia's hands and pressed them to her breasts and then moved them into the slit in her dress and then she left Gaia's hands there and moved her own hands between Gaia's legs and began to stroke her, softly, gently raking her fingernails over Gaia's skin, raising tiny goose bumps in excitement.

Meanwhile the woman kissed her again. Moving from her mouth down along her jawbone to her neck. Gaia was feeling the wet lips and the hands fluttering between her legs and feeling the fur and moist heat on her own fingertips as she explored her twin.

The woman's tongue flicked down the side of Gaia's neck in a teasing motion like a butterfly alighting and then taking off and then coming back for more nectar.

Then the sound of a zipper.

The feel of cold air.

The woman had pulled Gaia's dress down and was rubbing her hair against Gaia's breasts, not touching them yet with fingers or lips, when suddenly Gaia thought of the driver.

It was difficult to raise her head, to force herself to pay attention to anything other than the sensations of the silken hair against bare skin and pulsing flesh against her fingers. But it bothered her. She was willing to do anything with the female stranger, but she couldn't do it in the presence of the driver. She didn't want a man seeing this. And so she looked into the rearview mirror to see if he was watching.

His eyes were there waiting for her, with a little smile playing in them. Because what she hadn't seen before was that he was not a driver that Philip had hired for this excursion.

He was Philip.

And so when the woman's lips moved lower, Gaia opened her legs and looked down at the top of the woman's head, seeing herself, feeling another, and when the first wave of pleasure hit, instead of keeping it inside and swallowing the moan, she let it out. She knew it would circle and circle the way the orgasm was circling inside of her, and that the circle would include the man driving the car into the night.

Chapter 13

Gideon came back to see me at Ephemera at the beginning of the following week. I hadn't thought about him since we'd accidentally shared coffee and his chocolate chip cookies. I'd been working hard during the intervening days, finishing up an original short story for Vivienne Chancey, a letter for Robert Rosenthal and several easy jobs—personalizing stories that already existed. In between, I'd done some decent work on one of my own collages, gotten up early to run every morning and gone out to dinner with friends until late every night. I was overcrowding my days the way you stuff too many unimportant details into a conversation when you want to avoid the one thing you need to discuss. And I was tired. Not only from the hours and the constant activity, but because it was an effort to clear my stepbrother from my mind. It took constant work to fill up my days with enough activity to drive Cole back into the deep background where I didn't need to think about him or his gallery opening or his photographs. Where I'd managed to keep him for al-most two years, until I'd seen the invitation on Jeff's desk.

"You look busy," Gideon said from the doorway.

He was wearing black jeans and a black sweater and car-rying a portfolio.

"Hi." I must have sounded startled because he apolo-gized for surprising me. "No. That's okay. I didn't even know you were there. I didn't hear you. You seem to have just appeared."

"I was watching you. I couldn't help it. You were clearly lost in what you were doing. Artists can do that, can't they? Disappear into their own imaginations. It's a bless-ing. You looked so absorbed."

I felt a rush of recognition as if we were deeply con-nected and understood each other on a visceral level.

Except how could that be? I didn't know anything about him. And what he knew about me was only superficial. But nothing about the way his eyes moved hungrily over my body or the way his voice sounded, as if he were revealing the most intimate secrets, seemed perfunctory or trivial.

I didn't know what to say. "Come in" wound up be-ing my profound response. I was chagrined and caught off guard.

And disturbed.

He walked over to my desk and sat down, bringing with him the sound of the wind, the mixed smell of his cologne, the spring air outside and the very realistic and compelling idea that he was back because he wanted to hire me, which made me glad. I needed the work, having finished up everything in house. I lived on the money I made at Grace's. My rent for the loft—along with every-

one else's in New York City—was too high. The supplies
I used in my own artwork were expensive. It all added up.

But more than that, I needed something new to distract
me from my stepbrother.

"I was finishing up a job. Do you want some water? Or
tea? I'm afraid we don't make good coffee here. We can't
compete with Dean & Deluca."

"No, thanks. I'm fine," he said, and he smiled as he
leaned forward in the chair, moving out of the light cast
by the overhead lamps.

"I'd like to see what you're working on, though."

"I'm sorry, no." I moved the collage to a shelf behind
me. "It's confidential until my client gives me permission
to show it."

"Oh. I thought it was one of your own collages. That's
what I want to see."

"I don't work on them here."

There was a beat. He continued looking at me. As if he
were trying to figure something out. And then he said,
"What's wrong?"

"I didn't say anything was wrong."

"No." He looked confused for a moment. Trying to figure out for himself why he'd asked me that. "You didn't.
It occurred to me as you were speaking that you were unhappy somehow about your own work."

I was. The collage I was working on at home was going
well, but it was deeply personal and painful. I wasn't going
to tell that to Gideon Brown.

Ignoring his invitation to comment I said, "It's nice of
you to ask about my work, but I'm sure that's not why
you're here. How can I help you?"

His eyebrows arched knowingly, as if he understood exactly why I'd changed the subject and was willing to humor me for a while but was also warning me that he might not always be so obliging. To have such a strong sense of what his thoughts were when he was a stranger, bewildered me. To have such a strong sense of anyone's thoughts was unusual to me.

"Have you read a lot of erotica?" he asked with his voice at a slightly deeper register.

I hadn't expected this. "No," I said after thinking about it for a few moments.

"No Anaïs Nin? Henry Miller? Not even Pauline Reage?"

I shook my head again.

"How about D. H. Lawrence?"

"Yes, but I consider that literature."

"Nabokov's *Lolita?*"

"Yes. But again—"

He interrupted. "Some people called what they wrote porn. Banned them for years. I would have thought you'd have read Nin, at least. Didn't you need to study some of the greats?"

"Because of the stories I write?" That was stupid. Why else? "Mr. Brown, I'm not a student of erotica. So I can't defend erotica or even tell you if that's what I'm creating. I don't even think of myself as a real writer. I'm an artist. I'm only doing this until I can get a gallery for my collages. Or until Grace finds someone better and faster at this than me. All I do is talk to my clients and write what they would if they could."

"Gideon," he said.

I didn't understand at first, and it must have showed on my face.

"Call me Gideon. Mr. Brown sounds much too formal for what I'm here to talk to you about." He was still looking right into my eyes. The entire time he'd been sitting there he'd never glanced away. I tried to meet his gaze even though it was disconcerting. People usually looked right at each other, didn't they? It wasn't something I'd ever thought about before. Obviously, there was something different about the way he kept his eyes on me.

"How closely will you work with a client?" His eyes narrowed a little with the question, the way men's eyes do when they move in to kiss you. He was leaning in close enough that I could smell him again: that woodsy, forest-dark scent. His voice was even lower than it had been before, as if he were asking me how I wanted him to touch me and where. But that wasn't what he was talking about. The undercurrent had to be my imagination. I was manufacturing it. Looking for it. And I didn't know why.

There was nothing about him that explained my interest. I didn't know what he did for a living and so it wasn't his job that had me curious. His looks were familiar to me because of the painting in the Metropolitan but that was a meaningless coincidence. He hadn't revealed anything about himself that should have connected us and made me feel as if we were moving together, doing a secret dance.

But that was exactly how I felt.

"A client can be as involved as he or she wants to be," I said, wondering how many subtexts there were to the conversation.

"Orchestrate what each letter is about?"

"You mean, give me ideas and direction?"

He nodded.

"Yes, of course you can do that. In fact, it's easier for me if someone has ideas."

He ran his fingers through the hair that had fallen forward on his forehead, and the movement made me aware that I was playing with a pen. I put it down and the metal clinked on the desktop. The noise filled the silence of the last few seconds.

"I'd like to send a few short stories to the woman I'm seeing. She's traveling. She won't expect this from me, but it should please her."

Of course he would be with someone. Why else would he have been interested in Lady Chatterley's Letters in the first place? Why had I been certain that he was, like I was, alone at his core?

So much for my intuition.

This wasn't the first time I'd read someone wrong. Usually it didn't have serious consequences. Once it had. I should be better at not trying to guess.

I don't have the gift that Grace has of intuiting things about people. I'm subtle and I miss other people's subtleties. Who you are informs what you understand about the people you know or meet. I'd be better off using my perception like a reverse barometer—if I sense something I should automatically assume the opposite.

His hands were on my desk, fingers splayed on the polished surface.

This simple thing, his flesh on the same slab of wood

that I worked on every day, felt like an invasion. I wanted to move his hands away. Regain what was mine.

I could still hear his damn voice reading my words. It had been like him shooting an X-ray of my psyche.

Why did he provoke such a strong reaction in me?

Movies did that. Paintings hanging in the museum did that. So did music. Terrible news on television. Stupidity aroused me. The extremes of great beauty and creativity and the horrible, irrational or cruel.

But men who I met—without knowing them—never did that to me.

Except, he had.

Part Two

"A letter does not blush."
—Marcus Tullius Cicero 106–43 BC

Chapter 14

The ocean roared. The sky was gray and there were rain clouds gathering.

"Why did you want to start with sound?" I asked Gideon as we walked side by side on the beach.

"Because it seemed like the most difficult sense to create an erotic story about," he laughed.

"You have a perverse thing for challenges?"

"You have a perverse thing for questions?"

"Questions lead to answers. The most complicated part of writing a letter or a story for a client is getting inside his head so that I can make it personal."

"Then I haven't been very helpful, have I?"

"Not very."

"That makes us equally difficult."

Gideon and I had taken off our shoes at the top of the wooden staircase that led down to the beach and had been strolling for about ten minutes.

My friend Tina and her husband, Jim, lived in Manhattan and only used their beach house on the weekends. She'd told me that I could park in their driveway and access the beach at any time. She'd even reminded me of where the key to the front door was in case we needed to use the bathroom or the kitchen.

There were other beaches closer to New York City but I'd wanted to go someplace I felt comfortable, someplace private. The assignment had me nervous enough. I didn't know what it was going to be like to come up with a scenario for a story in tandem with a client.

The beach hadn't been my first idea.

Gideon had officially offered me the job over the phone two days after he'd come back to see me at Ephemera and we'd worked out the details of what he wanted: five stories that he would rewrite in his own hand, without any collage work from me. One a week until his lover came home. Each was to focus on one of the senses, beginning with sound, and he'd like to start as soon as possible. Then he'd asked if I could give him some ideas in a day or two, suggesting possible story lines and locations where we might place the first.

That had made me realize he wasn't from New York, or else he would have known the city well enough to propose the locale himself.

I'd come up with the idea that we go to a symphony and suggested a story about two lovers who sit, listening to the music, watching each other and how the notes and chords lead them to a crescendo of feeling so strong they bring each other to climax only with their eyes.

I'd tried not to blush when I'd told him my idea, even though he had been on the phone and couldn't see me.

And I tried not to focus on how much the idea had come out of the way I felt when Gideon looked at me—even though I knew my reaction was inappropriate and a figment of my own imagination, an imagination that was not normally focused on my own sexuality.

He hadn't been sure about that idea, he'd said, asked me to put it on the "maybe list" and requested another. My second choice was about two lovers in bed. She's sleeping. He's listening to a CD and slowly, following the rhythms of the music, he begins to make love to her, arousing her awake.

Gideon responded more positively but still wasn't sold.

Finally I'd come up with a story set at the beach. I didn't have any idea of where it would lead or what kind of fantasy might take place. Just the concept of the ocean being the sound that seduces the lover.

So of course that was the proposal Gideon said he liked the most.

The one that I had the least inspiration for.

As we walked, the sand warm on the soles of my feet, I thought about how different this was from work I'd done for other clients. At least half of my assignments had been reworking the dozens of existing stories and letters that Grace kept from the five years she'd been offering Lady Chatterley's Letters. Of those who wanted originals, I'd never met with one of them outside of my office. None had wanted to be involved to this extent—where he or she would see and feel and explore the idea with me. This made my work for Gideon a challenge.

We walked by a piece of driftwood twisted into a crescent. I stopped and picked it up. It was the sort of object

I could incorporate into my next collage. I'd had the idea that while I was creating these stories for Gideon, I'd do a collage of each for myself. Five pieces—one for each sense. Without knowing it, Gideon would be partially paying me to take an artistic journey of my own.

The idea of concentrating this way on each of the senses, from an erotic point of view, was compelling. Maybe enough so that it would not only engage me creatively but, I hoped, distract me from Cole's forthcoming show.

It hadn't occurred to me until we were walking on the beach, but Gideon Brown's job had come when I needed a diversion. As the date of my stepbrother's show approached, I became more and more preoccupied with it.

I almost laughed. Even when I wasn't thinking about Cole's exploits, I was thinking about what I could do to not think about them.

I spotted a piece of green sea glass, soft and smooth and frosted. A sand jewel, I'd called them growing up. Stopping, I picked it up, pocketed it and then gazed out.

The water was a gray-green with three-foot, white foam-capped waves. Far out on the horizon was a ship, blowing its horn. The low note traveled to shore under the sound of the crashing surf.

If I asked Cole once more, would he reconsider? No. Of course not. What would be different about this time? I had nothing to offer him in exchange, and that was the only way to get anything from Cole.

Damn.

I had to stop thinking about Cole and start focusing on getting an idea. But *wasn't* it odd how Gideon had appeared and presented me with a very real and lucrative distraction from an equally real and disturbing fact of my life?

No. It wasn't odd. It was how shit happened. It was a coincidence.

To think anything else was to deny logic and reason. Leave it to Grace to see ordinary circumstances as manifestations of my own needs and desires. The fates, she would have said, were working hard to help me out.

It suddenly became all right if this job proved more difficult than most. That would make it even more distracting. For the next few weeks I was going to be Gideon's sensory tour guide. And he—even if he didn't know it—was going to protect my sanity.

Chapter 15

The ship blew its horn again and Gideon and I both looked out in the same direction. The fog was rolling in. It muffled the sound and misted my skin. I sucked in a deep breath, smelling the brine. Under my feet the sand felt damper than it had a few minutes before.

"A storm's coming. Pretty fast, too," he said.

"Should we go back?"

"Not yet. You haven't been inspired yet. We are walking toward an idea. As soon as you trip over it, we'll go back."

The surf had turned rougher; the whitecaps rolled up higher and crashed onto the beach with more force, disturbing the shells and sand, depositing more sea debris.

A few yards ahead I spotted a creamy, pink-colored shell.

About four inches in diameter, it was round and swirled to a point like a nipple. When I turned it over, I could see a complicated, pearly, deeper pink nautilus chamber within.

I picked it up and was inspecting it when Gideon said

he saw another up ahead. I followed his glance and noticed several more dotting the beach.

The waves kept coming closer and closer as the tide rose, and with each one that jumped the beach and deposited flotsam, more of the shining wet shells were left on the shore.

By then my hair was curling around my face and both of us were wet from the damp air. It was a warm moisture that smelled of the ocean and enveloped us in its humidity. The atmosphere thickened, smoothing out the edges of the horizon and the houses on the other side of the beach, blurring everything, as if we were looking through a nearly opaque piece of sea glass.

There were occasional raindrops but we didn't pay any attention to them. We were too preoccupied collecting the shells that the waves were bringing us like gifts.

We gathered two dozen of them. Perfectly formed, each slightly different, all creamy pink and golden with their erect nipples on top.

Gideon held one up to my ear. "Listen."

I heard the unmistakable roar of the ocean inside the chamber. The same sound inside that was coming at me from the sea. I smiled.

I kept listening.

And then I heard something else murmured underneath the roar of the ocean. I wasn't sure it was actually there. More than likely I was imagining it. And that I was imagining it made me even more upset than if I had been hearing it. A shell cannot whisper a man's name. But my imagination could. And the name it was whispering wasn't fair.

"What is it?"

I lowered the shell quickly. "It's disconcerting that you seem to know so much about how I'm feeling. What's the deal? How do you do it?"

"Would you prefer if I noticed but didn't say anything?"

"That's not the point. It's the fact that you do notice. I want to know how you do."

"I'm not a mind reader. You just have a very expressive face. When something bothers you, your eyes go from that crazy topaz color to a duller brown. Your mouth purses slightly. A line appears in your forehead. Your face gives you away."

My fingers made circles on the smooth surface of the shell I was still holding on to. The one that could speak. Ridiculous, I thought. I hadn't heard a thing. I picked it up to my ear again and listened. The sea's bellow echoed in my ear and if I paid attention, there was Gideon's name again, like an undercurrent.

I worked at keeping my face emotionless and still while I listened, and then I put the shell away in my jacket pocket.

"Did you listen to them when you were a kid? I thought they were magic," Gideon said.

"I thought my father had put the sound in them."

"My father and I would take them home and look each one up in a huge shell book he had, and he'd help me learn their Latin names."

"What are these called?" I asked.

"You keep doing that. You did it in the car. Whenever the conversation might become more personal about either of us, you redirect it."

"Do I?"

"You don't want to even get close to talking about me. Do you?" he asked.

"No. That has nothing to do with it."

"Of course it does. It's a clever ruse. If we talk about me, then we might wind up talking about you. And that's what you are trying to avoid."

"But you don't need to know anything about me. I'm supposed to write stories for you."

"But we're not talking about the story now. You know, we were in the car for an hour and a half—two people driving with nothing else to do and you never managed to answer a single question I had."

He'd started walking again and I kept pace. It was good to concentrate on how my feet sank into the wet sand and how the water washed over my toes. Even though the ocean was cold, the temperature was tolerable; you could tell summer was coming.

"Why is that?" he asked when I'd thought he'd abandoned this line of questioning.

"Why do you need to know anything about me?"

"Because I'm curious."

"You'd be very disappointed."

"You can't keep deflecting interest with sarcasm," he said with a definite sarcastic tone of his own.

"I can if I want to." Even to my own ears, this sounded childish.

"But why do you want to?"

"Why do you want to know that?"

"Damn you're good at this," he said, laughing.

It was the sound of his laugh, combined with the sound

of the waves crashing and what I'd heard in the shell, that gave me my first idea of what the beach scenario might be. But now that I had a concept, I was going to have to explain it to him.

It was one thing to write a story down, another to suggest it in a brief sentence over the phone; but to actually talk it out in person in situ, as it were, was daunting.

"What if…" I began. Beside me, I felt a shift in Gideon's attention. He focused, turning slightly so that he could see more of me as we walked.

"What if…." I started again. "What if in the story, a woman is walking on the beach and she hears a man laughing. A man she's met before but hasn't seen in a long time and doesn't know well. She's even slightly surprised that she remembers the sound of his laughing. She looks around, but doesn't see him anywhere."

He nodded. We walked a few more feet while I tried to look ahead in my mind—as if a movie were fast-forwarding—to see the next scene. "She's alone. Lying on a towel. Half awake, half asleep. The sun had been out, but the clouds have rolled in and it's dark. When she hears the laugh, she's not sure if it is a real sound. It could have been the sudden disappearance of the sun that woke her up. She might have been dreaming the laugh."

I stopped talking for a moment, seeing more of the mirage of the woman up ahead, lying on her towel. A light blue towel. The color the sky would have been if the storm hadn't rolled in.

"What happens next?" he asked.

His words broke the membrane of the daydream. I lost the sense of where the story had been headed. "I don't know. This isn't how I work. I didn't think you would… What I normally do is work by myself at home writing it."

"I don't expect you to actually write here," Gideon said. "That would be too much pressure on you. I don't imagine many artists can create while being watched. But I want you to talk it out with me. So I can comment. So I can push you in the direction that I think she'd like. I'm sure if you relax, we'll do fine."

"I'm relaxed," I said, an angry edge to my voice that was like the foam on the ridge of the waves.

But that's not what I wanted to say. I wanted to scream at him over the roar of the water and tell him that we couldn't do this. *I* couldn't do this. That this was too uncomfortable for me. That I didn't want such a big challenge. I didn't want to ride ocean swells. I just wanted to glide, to move slowly ahead on a smooth mirror lake. I practiced telling him all that in my head, testing out exactly what words I'd use to beg off.

Meanwhile we walked.

Meanwhile he was quiet.

Gideon was often quiet. Long, slow silences that matched the languid pace of his walk. He must have studied that walk, I thought. To be provocative. To flaunt the length of his legs. To show off his thoroughbred body.

I took a big gulp of the ocean-soaked air and expelled it. I was ready to tell him this wasn't going to work. I knew what words I was going to use. And then I had an image of going back to my loft. Of the drafting table with my collage—the one that was about Cole whether I wanted to admit it or not—staring at me. Knowing if I gave up Gideon's job, what was going on with Cole would consume me. The nights would last longer than the days, which would last forever. And then conversely, perversely, the show would also come too soon.

Waiting would be worse with nothing to do.

And then there was the money. Gideon would be paying me a total of seven hundred dollars for the first two stories— that was guaranteed—and if those went well there would be three more. More than two thousand dollars.

I couldn't freak out now. That was a lot of money to turn down over some feelings I couldn't work out. I only needed to remind myself that I had done more complicated things in my life and had been far more embarrassed than Gideon could possibly make me.

Looking back at the ocean, I started the story again, from where I'd left off.

"She looks for the man. But doesn't see him. There are no other people anywhere on the beach, either up ahead or behind her. Just the ocean and the sand and a dozen shells scattered around. And then, mixed in with the laughter, she hears her name being called. It's coming from far away, her name almost being overpowered by the sound of the waves."

Damn. It was painful. Like stepping on stones. Knowing that, as bad as it is, you have to take that path if you want to get where you have to go.

I turned to Gideon. "So, if that's a good start, then I'll work on it tonight."

"I'm not clear where it leads."

"I'll figure that out and send it to you tomorrow or the next day. We should go. It looks like it's going to rain."

"The storm's still a while away."

"I need some time to plan what else happens."

"Improvise. Pretend it's a collage. Pick another object, throw it into the story." He was playing with the sand, shaping it into a rounded mound. The action of his fingers smoothing the grains was mesmerizing. "If you don't share this part of the process with me, this won't work. I have to be involved. Otherwise it's a complete cheat."

"Except it's not working. It's too difficult."

He shook his head, and his hair, damp now from the fog, fell in his eyes. He pushed it back. "No. It's not hard for you at all. You're doing it."

"How do you know that?"

"I've been watching you, listening to you. Your voice was calm, so were the muscles in your face. Your eyes were shining. Your imagination was totally engaged. You were building the story. Easily. Then something in your brain interrupted and told you that you should be self-conscious. That you can't talk this out. All the musculature on your face changed. Your eyes went dull. I watched it happen. But you're wrong to let that thing in your head interrupt you. You can do it, Marlowe."

He drew lines on the mound. His fingers were so facile, so certain of how to move. He didn't wait for me to answer. "You aren't exactly what you seem. Like the way you look at me, up from under your eyelashes. When I first saw you do that, I thought you were flirting. But that's not it. You're hiding. Or at least part of you is. Then there's this other part of you that's fighting back. That's out there fearlessly mixing up all those outrageous images you put together in those boxes."

The only thing I wanted to do less than make up a

story in front of him was hear him talk about me, and get involved answering his questions. I stood up. He followed suit. Looking down I saw what he'd been making—a sand sculpture of one of the shells we'd found. I had an urge to walk though it, and at the same time, I wanted to preserve it.

"What happens next?" he asked as we continued walking.

"She picks up all of the shells. Gathers them in her sweater. Brings them back to her towel. Washes them off in the water and is amazed at their opalescent color. Like Tiffany glass. Or something painted by Monet. Pinks, yellows, fading into each other."

Even though I wasn't looking at him, in my periphery I could see him nod.

"She holds one up to her ear."

I wasn't sure what was coming next. Turning to face the ocean, I felt the salty wind blow on my face. I shut my eyes and let my mind go blank. Forgetting about Gideon and the job, I absorbed the sounds of the ocean. I took the shell from my pocket and held it up to my ear.

What I heard was too clear. It was impossible. Not a name this time but whole words. Strung together. With meaning.

"First she hears the waves," I said, my eyes still closed. "And then something else. A man's voice. In her ear, coming from the shell. It's the voice that was laughing. The voice that was whispering her name. It's inside the shell."

Wind blew ocean spray up into my face. It was cold and so salty it stung a little. I took a deeper breath, hungry for the ionized air. Needing to swallow some of the spray. Even to swallow the sound. To take it inside me and translate it into the story. To feel overpowered by the sound. To be in its thrall. If I could have gone into the water I would have. I wanted to feel the power of those waves tug at me, pull me out into the ocean, which was like a man insistent on getting closer, determined to get what he wants.

Gideon didn't have to encourage me this time, I started again on my own. "She hears the man's voice say her name and thinks about how it sounds, as if he is talking to her though the waves. As if he were out in the water, submerged, but somehow able to speak to her."

I almost turned to look at Gideon but suddenly realized I could only do this if I focused my attention on the ocean and the feel of the wind. If I could forget he was there I could find the story.

"He's telling her that he wants her to lie down. Here on the sand. Close to the shore. He wants her to lie on her back. Near enough to the water so that she's in contact with the spill of the waves. He tells her to shut her eyes.

"But she doesn't understand where these commands are coming from. She looks around, thinking it's crazy. The voice must be someone she knows playing some kind of trick on her. But the beach is still deserted. The man repeats the instructions, kindly but with determination. He uses her name and cajoles her to do it, entreats her to try, promises that he won't hurt her, that he'll be gentle, that it will be lovely. Seductively he pulls at her the way an undertow does when you're swimming. You think you can go a little farther, that the current won't overwhelm you. So you swim out that small distance more and suddenly you're overtaken. Helpless. Have no power against the swirls of green-blue. And she knows that the smartest thing is not to fight or try to swim against him, but to do as he asks."

I could see the rest of the story, then. I knew where it was leading. But that was as far as I could go using words and phrases. I'd reached the limit of what I could say out loud.

"Don't stop."

"I can't figure out the rest," I lied. He didn't say anything. Why did I assume that meant he didn't believe me? "Gideon, this is too difficult."

"Why?"

"It's too erotic." I could barely hear my own voice, I was talking so softly.

He started to laugh, not like the seductive sound I'd heard inside my head but an insult that felt like the saltwater stinging my face.

"No, Marlowe. I'm not making fun of you," he said, again knowing what I was thinking. "What you said was funny. I hired you to write sexy stories for me and now you're telling me that you're too uncomfortable to tell me what you're making up for me because it's exactly what I asked for."

I got it and smiled. "Okay. Let me tell you what will happen. The voice that she hears in the shell is going to seduce her. She's going to listen to it and—"

"No. Not that like. Please. Keep going. *Tell* the story."

He spoke softly without ever taking his green-and-black eyes off me, but I didn't know what his concentrated glance was trying to say. I didn't speak his language yet.

In another situation I might think that he was interested

in me. But that wasn't possible here. He was with someone. Had hired me to help him with that relationship.

I sat down on a weathered log and looked away from
him, out to the water. He sat down beside me.

"It will get easier. You'll get used to it."

Shutting my eyes, I tried to see the woman on the beach
whose tale I'd been telling, but I could only see Gideon,
the way he looked when he'd been encouraging me to
continue.

I wished that he projected nervousness or anger or
weakness. I wished he was unattractive and looked less
like that nobleman in the Metropolitan Museum of Art.
Or that his eyes were not so eloquent. Or that his voice
didn't blow through me.

"I like listening to you," he said. "The story is very seductive. But it's more than that… I've never seen anyone
create this way. The sentences just spill out of you. I
won't be embarrassed. You won't be, either. I promise."

I'd learned about believing men the hard way. Cole
telling me he'd never make me ashamed. That nothing we
were doing would ever humiliate me. Kenneth telling me
that he could accept my past if I only told him the truth.
And then telling me he'd be home soon.

I knew better.

Except I believed Gideon's promise.

How was that possible?

Maybe going on wouldn't be so bad. What was so terrible about what I was doing? I wasn't showing him any
of myself. It wasn't me on the beach listening to the shells.
It wasn't my passion I was describing. I took another deep
breath.

"The man's voice is cajoling, soothing, and so she listens to it and does what he asks. Once she is lying down on the beach with her feet in the water up to her ankles, he whispers to her to take off her bathing suit. She's not sure what he's saying, so mixed up are the sounds of the surf and the timbre of his voice. But she does it. Quickly, in one smooth movement. The cool air makes goose bumps on her skin but only for a second because she's suddenly warm. As if the air around her has heated up. As if someone with hot breath was blowing on her. The warm air surrounds her and strokes her. She feels it on the back of her neck. On her cheeks. On her breasts. She luxuriates in it.

"And then the voice tells her to spread her legs apart. She doesn't question his request but obeys. As she does, she hears a slow, soft moan. The sound of a wave brushing against the ocean floor. Of the wind blowing against a forest and moving thousands of limbs and leaves in unison. The sound of a man overcome when the woman he has been waiting to be with is suddenly within his grasp.

"'Now, still, stay still,' the voice commands, and so she waits, continuing to listen to the surf all mixed up with his voice. The water inches up over her ankles, up her legs, higher to her thighs, her hips, soaking her and spilling over and down between her legs, wetting her more than she is already wet. Temperate water that smells invigorating and salty.

"Suddenly the sea that is saturating her creates a whirlpool around her body, circling and circling, whipping around her, powerful caresses covering every inch of naked skin.

"There is nothing human about what is touching her,

it is nothing like being with a man except that the sensations she feels from the water are similar to what she would feel if it was a man entering her and making love to her.

"'It's me inside of you. Can you feel what you hear? That sensation is me,' he says.

"She's too overwhelmed to respond with words. But she doesn't have to. He understands what she is thinking and feeling by watching her face, by listening to the sounds she is making deep in her throat, by seeing how her fingers clench and unclench as her own waves build up inside of her. And he whispers something to her…one last phrase…the one she has been waiting for."

"What is the phrase?" he asked.

I didn't answer. It was too private. I was operating on two levels, each fighting the other.

I could see the story playing out behind my eyes, as if I had a movie projector in my head showing me scenes that already existed somewhere else. Following it as it meandered on, I narrated it, while at the same time my conscious self was horrified, surprised and incredulous that I could be speaking any of it.

There was no precedent for what I was doing—for spinning a sexual dream, for talking about a woman being seduced and aroused by her lover. It required a bravery that wasn't part of me.

Or rather, wasn't part of me anymore. It had been, but that was long ago when I was a teenager, when this kind of brazen act, this sexual showing off, came naturally to me.

Except, that was different, wasn't it?

That was about me. My own body. My own relationship.

My own feelings. This was not. This was something I was getting paid for making up. The man I was doing it for was not my lover, not anyone I was involved with. He was a client.

I heard Gideon's intake of breath as if he was getting ready to encourage me to go on again the way he had before, but I didn't want him to interrupt the man who was talking to me from inside the curve of a shell.

And so before Gideon could speak, I did.

I was hearing my voice superimposed over the ocean's song and the man whispering in my ear. I listened and then repeated what he said, as if we were both involved in reciting a responsive prayer.

"'Lie there and let me do this to you,' he says. 'I want you to feel it all.' And so she does while the whitecaps beat up into a froth that pours over me—over her—warmer than before, as warm as her own blood. It pulses against her legs and her ribs and her back and her breasts in a rhythm that she hears around her. The sounds aren't outside of her anymore. They're inside. They are in tandem. Just the way the waves inside her body advance and recede in harmony with the ebb and flow on the shore.

"'Yes…lie there,' he says. 'Keep your eyes closed. Feel the water. Feel the wind. They are my lips, my hands. The sand under you is my body.'

"What is so different about her water lover is that he doesn't want anything from her. He's not waiting for her to reciprocate or amuse him or arouse him, and his lack of a demand is a luxury she's never known before, and it overwhelms her."

I stopped. Not able to help myself this time. I could see

what was coming next and knew I wouldn't be able to describe it. Without looking, I was certain Gideon's eyes were locked on me and that he had been expecting me to stop. For a moment I was relieved. Good, if he expects it, then I can stop. This torture will be over. He's inviting me to cease my storytelling.

And then a welt of anger surged up inside me. I was furious at him. As if he'd made me come this far and now was abandoning me. He'd lost faith. I had taken this job at his insistence, I'd pushed myself to accommodate him, but none of that mattered to him. He didn't think I could do it.

And I couldn't.

No. That's not why I was angry.

It was Cole's fault.

I didn't care about Gideon having faith in me. That was pure bullshit. What was wrong was that this was about me.

It was almost as if my stepbrother had sent Gideon to me to prove to me that he, Cole, was right—I had no right to be upset with him—that what had happened when I was with him all those years ago was my fault because I was too audacious and bold, because I was too indulgent and couldn't contain my own passion. That I was the slut and Cole had not taken advantage of me—hadn't even coerced me. That everything that had happened between us had been consensual.

I was the slut then and again now.

Unable to quench my own thirst.

Except, Gideon hadn't been sent by anyone. He didn't even know Cole. Gideon was a stranger. And he had not aroused me. This story was not coming to me because I was attracted to Gideon. It wasn't about him. At all.

And it wasn't a weakness in me that had engendered it. My reactions had been honest and clean. It was what Cole had done with them that had turned them prurient.

One day I would prove that. I would even find a way to punish the man who had twisted me up in knots for so long and changed who I was, making this very moment so much more difficult than it had to be.

Chapter 16

"'I'm going to kiss you,' he says to her in her ear. The surf had slacked off but, along with his words, the water comes rushing back again, kissing her between her naked legs, creating more waves inside of her, and then rising up, over her stomach, over her rib cage, over her breasts and her neck, up to her chin and then to her mouth. The water licks at her lips and then the current pulls it back, back into the bigger body of water, and all the while he is whispering in her ear, a voice that is more ocean now than man: 'This is for you,' he says. 'This is for you.'"

I had been facing the ocean for the last few minutes that I was talking, pretending to myself that my voice was floating out to sea and that Gideon couldn't hear me anymore. I had been in a kind of daze as if the sound of the waves had put me under its trance, too. But I was going to have to turn around and face this man and worry that he might think it had been me who was talking.

"That's perfect," he said, speaking for the first time in

minutes, shocking me with the sound of his voice because of its sudden familiarity. I heard the acceptance in his words, too. As if he had been aware how difficult the recitation had been for me and wanted to acknowledge that. His words were like two strong arms coming around me, pulling me close and comforting me after a long battle that, while not won, had its first victory.

I felt the rain almost at the same time as he did. Not soft hot drops but cold pelting bullets. The sky was instantly charcoal as the wind whipped up. Out at sea, a bolt of lightning flashed.

"We'd better make a run for it," I said as I stood.

Never had I been so thankful for a storm. I wouldn't have to face him so soon after finishing up the story and speaking all of those words and images.

By the time we reached the deck we were both soaking.

"I know where the key is," I said as I fumbled around looking for the pot of geraniums that Tina had told me about. The sky flashed bright and I started counting, a childhood habit, for the crack of thunder that would follow. I got the door open a few seconds before I heard the clap and rumble so close together.

Inside, I stood in the mud room and shook off like a dog. The rain ran in rivulets down my face. My clothes were stuck to my skin and I realized how cold I was. Gideon was just as wet, his hair flat against his head, his chinos and shirt dripping.

We walked into the kitchen. The rain beat on the roof and splattered against the windows. The wind howled.

"You should take a shower," he said. "We both should. You're shivering."

There were several bathrooms, so I showed him to the one in the guest room, told him I'd get him some of Jim's clothes and leave them on the bed.

"Take your shower first, then you can bring me clothes. I don't want you to get a chill."

I didn't say anything, but was aware of his thoughtfulness.

The water was hot and I stayed under the spray for a long time, thinking only about the sensation of the heat warming me.

After I'd dried off, I borrowed a shirt and a pair of jeans for Gideon from Jim's closet and a plain white shirt and shorts from Tina's. I dressed and then took the pile of clean clothes to Gideon.

He was standing in the bathroom, towel drying his hair, with the door open. A thick white bath sheet was wrapped about his waist, and his chest was bare. I didn't stay long, just sort of threw the shirt and jeans on the bed and then walked away, saying I was going to the kitchen to make some coffee.

But even though I hadn't been looking, I'd seen him.

Despite being slender and lanky, he had well-defined muscles. His shoulders were narrow but strong. His neck was long but sturdy. His arms looked as if he lifted weights religiously. Or did manual work. His skin was olive toned and looked smooth.

I tried to wipe the image of his naked torso from my mind as I fussed with the French press and the kettle. Tried to force myself to stop seeing it. I wouldn't react.

Coffee.

Focus on making the coffee.

I set about the task I'd given myself.

Gideon came in a few minutes later, dressed in Jim's clothes. We were both standing at the kitchen counter and pouring coffee, splashing in milk, mixing in sugar, when there was another clap of thunder and the lights went out.

"Tell me how you started doing collages?" he asked when we were settled in the living room. I was on one end of the couch, he on the other. We both were looking out at the water, sipping our coffee and watching the storm.

"I painted first. It seems like I painted forever. But eventually I realized I wasn't very good at it, no matter how hard I tried."

"But you loved it?"

I nodded.

"Why?"

"The idea of capturing the colors. The streaks and swirls of lapis, vermilion, burnt umber, cerulean…even the ways the names of colors sounded made me happy. I loved the idea of taking something beautiful and, through the process of recreating it, making it last."

"It wasn't enough just to see something beautiful?"

I shook my head.

"Why not?"

"I'd see it differently if I tried to paint it. It'd be as if I'd gotten inside of the beauty or gotten it inside of me. Art was bigger than any one person. Bigger than anything else I'd ever found. Creating it…studying it…opened me up. Gave me purpose. And it mattered. Through time. Art counts. And not enough other things do."

"Do you think you gave up?"

I shrugged. "No…I moved over. It wasn't what I expected would happen, but in my senior year of college I began incorporating found images and three-dimensional objects and words into the paintings. It was Pavlovian. The more I moved away from traditional painting, the better and more praise I got from my teachers. The more they praised me, the more I moved away from the traditional."

"You sound as if you were duped."

"No, that's not what happened."

"You're upset about it."

"No. Why would you think that?"

"The expression in your eyes. You look betrayed."

I shrugged. "I just wasn't strong enough to fight for it. Besides, it's all for the best. There's too much competition in painting. I never would have gotten anywhere. Certainly never would have made a living at it."

"That's a defeatist attitude."

"That's a survivalist's attitude. How would I be able to make a living now if I hadn't become adept at collage?"

"Maybe you'd have become a fine enough painter that you wouldn't have had to do collages."

"You have no idea how hard it is to make a living as an artist. Even if you are lucky enough to get a gallery. With how long it takes to do one painting…and then you have to subtract the fifty or sixty percent that the gallery takes…"

He was making me uncomfortable, listening and watching me too intensely, even in the dark, as if he were hearing things I wasn't saying. And when he asked me the next question, his voice was too intrusive. It wasn't a breeze, but a heavy wind. Blowing open the door and tossing everything around, mixing me up.

"Do you want to go back to painting?"

Everything about Gideon was too strong, too hard to ignore. Too suggestive of a sensitivity that I knew he couldn't have but for some reason I was imagining he did.

"You don't know what it's like…art isn't a hobby or only a job. Creating, really working to find something worth saying and then struggling to make the expression worth the thought…is wrenching."

He was nodding, almost smiling. I felt—and I couldn't believe this—understood.

On the other hand I had to remind myself how susceptible I was to endowing people with qualities they didn't have, based on a few aspects I knew of them. I had taken leaps and assumed that because someone was both sensitive and intelligent then he must be understanding and fair. It was as likely that because he was strong and sure of himself then he must also be arrogant and egotistical. Seeing the way someone holds his head or says my name, I have been known to then assume he will fit other criteria that I have in my mind.

I'd been fooled. I'd been disappointed. So I had tried to break myself of the habit, to keep my imagination in check and not give people attributes they didn't have.

A man who asked questions, who seemed so interested in me, might not be at all interested. It could all very well be a well-practiced ruse, a technique, fine tuned to relax his subjects, to seduce a woman into revealing herself so that he could cull what he found and use it for his own reasons.

"What is it you are so afraid of, Marlowe?"

"I think the storm's letting up." I stood and avoided

both answering him and looking his way. "Maybe we should go while we can."

In ten minutes we were back in his Jeep and on the road. He turned the radio to a local NPR station and we listened to a news program and then classical music. Our conversation, when we had it, was as direct as the route back to the city.

It was all the things that we weren't talking about that were the loudest. And not even the most strident phrases in the symphony could drown them out.

Chapter 17

I went to work on the short story when I got home. It wasn't what I wanted to do. Anything would have been easier. Anything would have been more pleasant. Nothing would have distracted me as much.

Gideon had dropped me off at six. I didn't stop to eat anything till nine. And then all I did was heat up a bowl of soup, cut a piece of seven-grain bread from a loaf I'd bought the day before and pour myself a glass of wine. I liked to eat but not to cook, and usually kept food from one of the neighborhood gourmet stores in my freezer. But that night I didn't even want to spend the time defrosting anything.

Even though I'd taken a shower, I could still smell the salt on my skin, as if I'd been swimming in the ocean for hours, not merely walking by the shore. If I'd found seaweed in my hair, I wouldn't have questioned it. The feel of the sand on my feet wasn't gone either; I could summon up the silk grittiness as if I were still walking on it.

As I sat on the bed, propped up by pillows, working on

my laptop, my sense of the present disappeared. No longer in my loft, I was back on the beach, hearing the voice in the shell saying the things I'd told Gideon, as well as the words I'd kept from him. I was seeing the water, the clouds, the waves.

My fingers danced over the keyboard. I didn't even have to think the words. I was the conduit for the sentences and paragraphs.

In a rush, the fantasy poured out in less than three hours. At least the first draft of it. And that was all I could manage that night. Editing it would be the hard work and could wait for the next day.

I got myself another glass of wine and got back into the bed, pulling the laptop over and rereading what I'd written.

That's what I was doing when the phone rang. I might have reached for it if I hadn't been so engrossed in the story. Instead the machine answered. And a few seconds later I heard the message as it came though.

"Marlowe?"

It was my stepbrother. The aftereffects from the beach dissipated. The sensations swirling around me from the story's spell broke apart like a shattered mirror and dropped in pieces to the floor. I sucked in my breath, afraid that if I inhaled or exhaled too deeply he'd hear me. *Impossible,* I told myself. *Take a breath. It's okay. There's nothing he can do to you anymore.*

"I just left Jeff. He told me you'd been up to the office and seen the invite. I sent you one. So why did he think it was all news to you? Don't you open my mail? Marlowe, you can't hold a grudge this long. It makes me feel bad, baby. And I don't like that feeling."

I stood up, clutching the wine, gripping it too tightly in my hand. I wanted to kick the phone over. To shut off his voice. I wanted to pick up the receiver and tell Cole how selfish he was being. Ask him how he dared use that photograph on the invitation. Mostly I wanted to stop listening to him…but I was immobile. My feet stuck to the floor in the middle of my bedroom, and I heard every single word.

"I would love for you to see the exhibit, baby. Everyone's coming in for it. Dad and Isabel want us all to have dinner afterward. Can't you forgive me? You're going to love it. Everyone is saying it's going to be *the* show. Über show. What we do for art. You understand that, don't you? A little sacrifice, but what price beauty? And it is beauty. Thrilling, fucking sexy beauty. Call me, doll."

I didn't think. It wasn't about logic or sanity. It wasn't about reality or fantasy. The glass shattered against the phone as soon as it hit. Pieces scattered everywhere, appearing, in the darkened room, like stars splashing across a night sky.

Chapter 18

I worked on Gideon's story all of Saturday, revising and editing it. I was done early that night and e-mailed it to the address that Gideon had given me. I didn't check my e-mail on Sunday morning. I'd slept late and had to rush to meet Grace at a flea market on West Twenty-Sixth Street.

It was our weekly ritual. I looked for scrap and ephemera to use in my collages; she searched for vintage costume jewelry, accessories and clothes. Some days I didn't find anything. Others one or two items. She always found too much.

That morning, every time I turned around there was something else to pore over. At one booth I found two dozen old erotic postcards from France. Sepia-toned and innocent in their nakedness, the women posed and flirted with the camera, their breasts bared but with silken fabrics hiding their privates. Some of them wore stockings and garters, others wore only high heels. They entreated the viewer to come a little closer and be delighted.

I thought of Cole's nudes in relation to these. His were

erotic, too, but raw and edgy. There was no charm to the photographs he took of naked women in the throes of passion. He was a voyeur; these photographers were lotharios. He took more than his models offered; these models offered more than the photographer could capture.

I bought the postcards and tucked them into my bag. I found a long pair of silk gloves at the next booth. Cream colored and in excellent shape, I imagined them stuffed and positioned in one of my shadow boxes, the fingers beckoning.

A bolt of violet tulle sat on another booth. It sparkled with tiny diamanté flecks.

I'd come up with a new idea for the boxes I was going to do based on Gideon's sensory stories. Tease the viewer with the scenes inside. Arouse curiosity. Each would have curtains or drapes hanging over them, in different materials, but all transparent so that you had an idea of what was inside the box, but to really view the contents you would have to push apart the fabric. I wanted each box to be its own secret. Worth studying, worth spending time with. But none clear at first viewing. Layered, complicated juxtapositions of images and objects that would suggest eroticism the same way that we perceive it in other people. Under the clothes, behind the eyes, in subtle gestures and unspoken words.

I could imagine the collages, even picture how someone would inspect them—how he would push back the violet tulle to peek inside and be delighted with the gloved hand holding a tiny, naked male doll that I found at yet another table at the market.

"That fabric is amazing," Grace said, coming up next

to me. "Do you have an idea of what you are going to do with it?"

I told her about the boxes I was going to do based on Gideon's stories as we walked around and inspected all the wares, pulling dresses off racks, inspecting their old hand-stiched labels, opening ancient Vuitton bags, fingering Hermès scarves, trying on faux gem rings and Bakelite bracelets and holding extravagant pins up to our collars to see what kind of impact they'd make.

The only item Grace never looked at was shoes. In the Jewish religion you never wore the shoes of the dead, lest you follow in their footsteps, and since there was a good chance that most vintage shoes had belonged to someone now long gone, she avoided even being tempted by them.

"What do you know about the woman Gideon Brown is sending the letters to?" she asked.

"Not much, why?"

Grace looked up from investigating a box of Chanel buttons that she'd found under a cashmere sweater that someone had left on the table. "I don't know. I was wondering. That's unusual, isn't it? That you don't know anything?"

Normally I found out as much as I could about the recipient of the letters or stories. It was one way to make sure to please him. Or her. "Yes. It's unusual. But he didn't tell me much."

"Any idea why?"

I shook my head.

A woman walked up to the table, maneuvered around us and grabbed a pink sweater Grace hadn't looked twice at.

"You're usually better than that at getting information out of your clients."

"Yeah, I am…so I don't know why I couldn't do it this time. He's complicated, Grace. I'd say he makes me nervous, although that wouldn't be the right word."

"He gets to you."

"What?"

"You're interested in him. He's getting under your skin. In your head. That's why you didn't pressure him to find out more about his girlfriend."

"No, he doesn't, he—"

She put her arm though mine, the way I'd seen my grandmother walk with her friends. "Come on, let's get out of here and go get brunch. How about the Empire Diner? You're not going to want to listen to what I have to say, and if I tell you now it will be too easy for you to walk off instead of hearing me out."

"Have I ever done that in my life?"

"No, but I've never pushed you as far as I'm prepared to push you at the moment." And then she grinned. Like a medieval executioner about to behead one of Henry's wives.

Chapter 19

"You're not connected to your own feelings, Marlowe. You haven't been for a long time," Grace said over her lox, eggs and onions.

"I know you think you have a right to shrink me, but I don't understand why you think you have that right." My omelet was undercooked. I pushed it away, searched for and caught the eye of the waiter, who surprisingly came over right away. Grace waited until I'd explained what was wrong with the eggs and the waiter had taken them back before she continued.

"I think I have a right to do this because I care about you," she said.

"No. If you cared about me you wouldn't want to upset me."

"No, because I care about you I want to point out some things you're doing that are ensuring your unhappiness."

I sighed. "Okay, Grace, preach to me." I was annoyed. She knew it. But we were close and honest with each other. She needed to have this conversation with me as much as I needed to let her know it wasn't welcome.

"You look at everything so closely. Objects, colors, swatches of fabric, images—everything but your own life. And by doing that you aren't seeing what's really there. You are missing signals that might lead you forward…that might help you figure out what you really want, what might really make you happy. Or, if not happy then at least satisfied." Grace picked up her fork and took another bite of her eggs. The waiter returned my now-golden-brown, mushroom and Swiss cheese omelet.

I took a bite and expected her to continue talking. She didn't.

"That's it?" I asked finally. "No more? Short rant for you."

"That's it."

"You're not going to explain why I need to listen to you, why I need to change my way of dealing with my reality? You're not going to give me seven examples of situations that I—"

She interrupted. "No. I'm your friend, not your mother. Or your therapist."

"Or my psychic?"

She grinned. "I know better than to go there with you. You and your skepticism. This isn't about that. I'm not talking about how the stars are lined up or the *I Ching* or what I see when I read your Tarot cards."

"You don't read my Tarot cards. I've never let you do that with me."

"That doesn't mean I can't read them without you."

"Don't tell me—"

Her smile gave her away—she was teasing. "No. I can't read your cards without you being involved."

"So this is not your occult position? No witchcraft? No second sight?"

"I don't need to look that hard, sweetie. You're missing your own clues. We sense things about people we meet. We know better than we give ourselves credit for. You ignoring those intuitions doesn't make any sense. It's like turning away a life preserver when you are drowning. Those moments of insight we all have can give us the edge that helps us live more fulfilled lives. But you're doing the opposite. You're looking away from every clue and hint. You've got blinders on about your own life." She put down her fork, which she'd been using to reinforce the points she was making. "I'm finished."

"With the eggs or the lecture?"

"With both." She pushed away the plate. "No, I'm not."

"Not finished with the eggs or the lecture?"

"It's not a random conversation we're having here—"

"It's not even a conversation, Grace. It's your podium."

She looked at me askance and then continued. "There's something about this man, Gideon, that you need to pay attention to. Him coming into your life right now. It's not an accident. You're reacting to him differently. You have to figure out why. Why him? Why now?"

"I don't understand."

"No? That's okay. You don't need to understand. You just need to be aware. To be open. That's all I'm asking you to do. To take a look at the things you are feeling. To the things you aren't feeling. To look hard at the work you're doing and what's under the surface, for what's brewing."

"You're making it sound like sorcery again."

"No. You're listening to it like it's sorcery. You don't want to hear what I'm saying, do you?"

"It sounds like something a medium would tell a patient. Or a fairy godmother would whisper to her charge. You expect me to start believing in your magic because you're telling me to?"

"Well, isn't there magic to how we all relate to each other and what we can give each other?"

"That's not what I meant."

"No, but it's what I meant."

Chapter 20

Two days later, on Tuesday morning, I took a subway uptown and, because I was early for my meeting, got out on Seventy-Second Street, walking west to Fifth Avenue and then heading north.

On my left, Central Park was finally all green, and in full bloom with so many flowers and blossoming trees they perfumed the air despite the exhaust and fumes from the cars and buses that crowded the street.

Of course I knew I was going to meet Gideon, but when I saw him from a block away, standing on the top of the stone steps, immobile, his hair blowing in the May breeze, I felt a sweep of shock chill me.

It was visceral—my body reacting to the sight of him—sending messages to my nerve endings. Zinging me. Buffeting me. Pushing me to rush toward him. To breathe faster. To swallow larger gulps of air. To be aware of how my breasts felt with the soft fabric of my camisole rubbing against them. How my ankles felt cooler where the air hit them. I felt the fabric of my jeans on my hip bones: slightly rough and heavy compared to my silky underwear. I felt the back of my neck, realizing it was warm as if I'd been out in the sun. But I hadn't. The side of the street I was walking on was in heavy shade from the trees lining the avenue.

The sensations were uncomfortable and surprising enough to make me consciously shift focus off the man waiting for me and instead onto where we were going.

The Metropolitan Museum is an imposing structure. Larger and more impressive than any other museum I've ever visited except for the Louvre in Paris. But I love the Met more because it's my hometown museum. An edifice that some find cold, and a layout that many find unnavigable, is, to me, neither. Rather, I find it a comforting palace where I have always gone for inspiration, education, to be awed and to be consoled.

I never visited the Met with other people. Looking at art is something I need to be alone to do. To walk at my own pace. To rush by something that has no interest and dwell— for what might be an obscenely long time to someone else— in front of a painting, vase or sculpture that moves me.

But this was where I had told Gideon to meet me.

"It's this way," I said. I led him through the grand and formal lobby, looking as I always did at the enormous bouquets of flowers flanking the staircase. That day they were towering apple blossoms, and I silently thanked the benefactor who had left an endowment so that those two giant vases would always be filled with fresh flowers.

I was a member, so we didn't have to pay for tickets, just collect the small buttons that permitted us entry.

Ignoring the staircase ahead, I led Gideon to the left. Passing quickly through galleries of ancient Middle-Eastern jewelry, we entered the medieval church—or at least that was what I'd always called the high-ceilinged, darkened room that housed dozens of sculptures and elaborate gates acquired from a cathedral in Spain.

We walked in silence, in much the same way that one keeps reverentially silent in a library or house of worship.

Continuing on, we took another right and went through two rooms of more church artifacts. Ahead was the brightly lit Knights and Armor exhibition hall. This wasn't an area of the museum that'd I'd visited in years and I wasn't sure that what I wanted to show Gideon was still nearby. At the entrance to the gallery of gleaming silver men sitting atop their steeds, I turned left into an almost hidden hallway. Even though the museum was crowded, this corner was empty.

We were in a small anteroom. Before us was a palatial bedroom. In the center was a bed covered with ancient red silk damask. Its headboard rose up, ornate and intricate, carved by artisans hundreds of years before.

It was a luxurious bed. A bed to crawl into and stay for days. You could live in that bed, have your food brought to you there. Get drunk on sweet wine, eat figs and fresh strawberries, take naps, make love, wake up, sip hot melted chocolate out of gold demitasse cups. It was a bed that you came to dressed in peignoirs and silk robes that were handmade with rolled edges. A bed that invited you to stay as long as you wanted, that promised you there was no better place to be; a bed where you created a world away from the world of hard edges and harsh lights.

Where there was only physical pleasure or sweet slumber. Your head would lie against those pillows and there would be nothing more important than feeling someone's lips on yours.

"I always wanted to hide out in the ladies' room at closing time, so that I could sneak in here and sleep in this bed for one night," I said.

"I can see you doing that," he said, laughing.

That surprised me. It meant he'd spent time forming an impression of me. But what puzzled me even more than that was that I hadn't done the same. Since the day we'd spent at the beach, I'd avoided thinking about him. Even focusing on his project made me slightly nervous. I'd been worried that if I thought about it too much, or thought about Gideon at all, I might change my mind and pass up the job.

To the right of the bed was a window so well lit by an artificial light source that you were sure if you walked over to it, you'd be able to see beyond it to the street below. Not the New York City street, but the Italian passageway from another century.

Hanging to the left of the bed was a gilt-framed, spotted mirror, the mercury so old it had begun to flake off. The way it was positioned, I could see a reflection of not just the bed and the rest of the room, but Gideon and me.

What would anyone think if they saw us there?

I was curious. What image did we present? Did I present? Who was inside of the shell that was reflected in the ancient mirror? How much about me was revealed to anyone looking? How much of our deeper selves are expressed in the lines in our foreheads or the light in our eyes?

I've always believed we can hide who we are when we

need to. That anyone looking at my mother's photographs of me, or Cole's photos of me, would not know me any better for having seen the portraits. I would remain unknown to them because I had held back when I'd looked into their cameras.

But suddenly I wasn't sure.

And that made me concerned.

Gideon's eyes moved from the bed to the mirror to the ceiling. A small contented sigh escaped his lips.

I craned my neck, too. I had been here so long ago that it was like seeing the carving for the first time. There were dozens and dozens of fat cherubs flying around the room. The three-dimensional *putti*, celebrating the idea of both sacred and profane love, were fat and joyful.

Behind us, a mother and a child walked in, hand in hand. The mother told the child to look up, and the little girl's mouth opened. "Oh, Mommy," she said. "I never saw so many babies without any diapers before."

I smiled at the woman, who was clearly proud of her little darling's ability to be so observant. Gideon was still enthralled by the ceiling and seemed to be studying it intensely.

After another minute or two the pair left and we were alone again.

I stole a glance back at the mirror and watched the two of us, him looking up, me looking ahead. We were side by side, his dark to my light, his tall to my short.

"Can you imagine making love in this room?" he asked without turning to me, eyes still on the sculptured cherubs.

I didn't answer him. I'd noticed a placard to my right

and chose that moment to start to read it. The room, it said, had come from a sixteenth-century palazzo in Venice. Then there was a short history about the family who had owned the palazzo and the customs of the day: enough to make anyone who bothered to read it feel that they were now duly informed.

"In the mirror," I began almost without realizing that I had indeed begun talking, "she would undress and he would watch her watching herself, while the sun set beyond the window, casting both of them in a warm orange glow."

Gideon turned to me. I felt his eyes but didn't look at him. I remained where I was, staring into the mottled mirror. The idea of this second assignment—to create an erotic story about sight—was coming together in my mind in a series of disparate images. One overlapping the other.

To get through this I had to hold on to what I'd learned at the beach: that making up a fantasy for Gideon was no different from creating a collage. It took the same mental action. An ability to let go of a rational line of thinking and let the random visuals tell their own story. Not to impose structure on the piece until the internal logic revealed itself. Yes, it was a three-dimensional manifestation of the imagery that I ordinarily would have created, with papers and scissors and glue. But it was still the same process. And that gave me courage and some—well, at least a little—self-confidence.

"She wouldn't turn away from the mirror, no matter how much she wanted to…" I said a little braver, and at the same time more nervous than I'd been at the beach. I knew what to expect this time. I wanted to do this for the thrill of creating it. I just wished Gideon weren't there. That he somehow weren't so real.

"She would watch herself. Not look up or out the window or even at the bed. Her goal is to seduce him and she knows how to do that. All her energy and enthusiasm is for that. Her power will be in being powerless. He wants her to undress for him, and she obeys. Because the act will excite her, too. Knowing his eyes are on her, that he is completely riveted by her disrobing, is all the incentive she needs."

"Why are they here?" Gideon asked, almost in a whisper as if he was afraid to break the mood.

"He has brought her to show her this room, which he built and designed for her. This secret room where she can come and go from a separate entrance. A secret entrance to a secret room.

"She is his mistress, and has been for far longer than any of the others were. And he has rewarded her with this clandestine bedchamber to keep her happy. To give them a trysting place that is both comfortable, opulent and convenient for him.

"It makes him almost deliriously happy that now he can leave a dinner or a meeting in his residence, where he lives with his wife, children and many servants, and walk through a bookcase, down a short hall, then up a hidden staircase to their place. The rest of the house can carry on around them and no one can know, will know, ever, where they are.

"There is also a second exit and entrance to the room. This one can be accessed from the canal. A small door next to the servants' door, in the back. He has apologized to her for this, but she doesn't mind coming to him from near the servants' entrance. It is safer for her, because she is married, too.

"Marriages are arranged for financial and political reasons, and so it is the custom of the city, at this time, that affairs of the heart are acceptable and engaged in frequently but still conducted clandestinely.

"He's proud of the room. It's the most beautiful in Venice. He imported a sculptor from Rome, who arrived with three apprentices, to create a magical, heavenly chamber. And while she does think it's beautiful, and appreciates the effort he went to, she is most mesmerized by the mirror—the finest she has ever looked into. She can't take her eyes off it. Or off the two of them, facing each other in the reflective glass. She has never seen her own face flushed by any kind of desire before, so it comes as something of a shock to her…"

I stopped. Took a breath. Closed my eyes. I could tell Gideon was waiting for more.

"Don't—"

"What?"

"Don't stop. You're really seeing it. Seeing them. You disappeared the way you did at the ocean."

"It's getting complicated."

"You mean it's getting too erotic too quickly?"

I shrugged.

"It was even easier for you this time." He wasn't asking; he was telling. I could feel his eyes on me but I didn't turn. I kept facing the mirror. Looking at the two of us. At his fingers, flexed beside his thighs. At the dark hair falling into his eyes. He was watching, wait-

ing for me to go on or explain more about why I didn't
want to.

"Didn't I prove that I could do this with the last story?
Isn't it enough for you to see the room and know the direction I'm going in? I want to go home and write it myself in my own way."

"But I wouldn't be part of it then. I can't send the story
as something connected to me unless I'm somehow in-
trinsic to it. I need to know what you are going to write.
Besides, why do you care if it's becoming erotic? That's
what I hired you for, isn't it? Isn't that what you do for
everyone else?"

"Yes, of course…"

But I was embarrassed. There was a difference between
creating these fantasies in my own bedroom and speaking
them out loud in front of someone. Just because I'd done
it once before, that didn't mean it was any easier this time.

Like I had at the beach, I felt exposed in front of Gideon.
And I resented it.

We were at an impasse.

"You know I have three other possibilities of locales for
the sight story. Now that you know the direction this one
is going in, wouldn't you like to see the others so you can
decide?"

He shook his head.

Mixed in with my discomfort I also felt pride.

"Tell me more about them. The couple. Why they are
here. Who they are," he said, offering me a way back into
the tale.

I turned to the bed instead of the speckled mirror and
tried to imagine that no one was in the chamber with me.

"As I said, he is a Venetian prince and she is his mistress. Both are married. Each of them has had other lovers, often more than one at a time. This is the first experience they've had with being faithful—in their fashion. And because he is so in love, he's built her this room—created for her pleasure. It's full of secrets to entertain her. Magic boxes that open like puzzles, revealing jewels for her to wear. Erotic paintings on the wall that hide behind damask curtains until they are lifted. Special clothes in the closet that he has had sewn for her—gowns with pockets that are open at the other end so he can put his hand through them and stroke her under the folds of the silk. Bodices cut even lower than the current style to reveal all of her breasts, not only her décolletage.

"This is the first night that he's brought her here—slipping away during the masquerade ball going on in the main part of the residence. Over a thousand people in velvet and silk, bewigged and bejeweled, the upper part of their faces half-covered by elaborate masks, dance and eat and drink and make love in hidden alcoves, only a few hundred feet away. The two lovers have left all of them to come here. No one realized they left the party. Even if anyone saw them escape, their identities were hidden by their masks."

The present day, the museum, New York City and the man I was standing with had disappeared, and I was instead looking in on a scene to which I had not been invited. I was hiding in an alcove of the room, observing the two lovers, hearing them, smelling them, in awe of them and moved by them. I was an observer who had found a way not only to see what was going on but also viscerally experience it, feeling their emotions and the sensations in their bodies.

I knew how her heart lifted when she saw him reach out to touch her cheek. It was not the way my heart had ever soared. But I wasn't important. I was here to bear witness to their passion. I continued to talk to Gideon, no longer aware of speaking the words, the way a translator does not hear individual words consciously as she works.

"Tonight, two hours ago, she entered the villa through the front door with her husband—a nobleman twenty years older than she is. She is wearing her finest gown, blue velvet laced with silver threads in an embroidered leaf pattern. The gown is cut low in the front, as is the fashion, to show off a woman's breasts as if they are jewels.

"Her lover waited until all the guests had arrived and the eating and drinking had begun. He waited until everyone was drunk on wine and lost in the luxury of the food and the company and the mystery of the masks.

"He had sent his servant to her villa earlier in the day with a letter, written by him in private and sealed by his hand. In it he had given her instructions, a map and a key. He explained that after the party got underway, sometime around midnight, he would catch her eye. That would be her clue to make her way outside and walk west of the palazzo. The map showed her where the servants' entrance was and where the door was that she would use the key to open. She was to walk up the flight of stairs and there, he promised with all of his heart, she would find him waiting for her.

"She sees him giving her the sign shortly after midnight and has little trouble slipping away, so thick is the crowd.

She had memorized the map and finds the doorway easily. The key slips into the lock the way a man slips into a woman who is waiting for him.

"The candlelit hallway is small and intimate and there is nowhere to go except up the staircase. As she climbs, she marvels at the intricate balustrade—carved in wood, a man and a woman erotically intertwined, their forms repeating over and over in different sexual positions all the way up, so that her fingers make out the woman's waist and thighs and breasts and the man's arms and thighs and buttocks over and over as she ascends.

"At the top of the steps is a door, carved as intricately as the balustrade but with only one couple in bas-relief, embracing under a tree, heavy with fruit. The couple's limbs and the tree's limbs all intertwine, so that it appears as if they are all part of an *au naturel ménage à trois*. The man, the woman and the tree. All lovers.

"She opens the door and sees him standing by the window. In the candlelight, wearing his black silk mask and only the bottom half of the costume, he looks dangerous and delicious. His chest is bare and his skin has a slight slick to it—as if he has rushed here and is overheated. His skin draws her to him.

"She stretches out one hand. To touch him. Make sure he is real. To feel his heart beat faster under her fingertips. To know that his excitement to see her is as great as hers to see him. Her mouth is dry, the area between her legs, wet.

"She only has to glimpse him for her body to respond resoundingly.

"On the table by the window is an open bottle of wine

and two glasses already filled. He picks up both and begins to walk toward her.

"She, too, is wearing her mask—the same dark blue
shot through with silk thread as her dress—and, as always,
he is instantly aroused. Seeing her in public earlier made
him yearn for her, but now, in private, his longing has
turned into something else. A kind of fire that courses
through him and makes him hot inside his skin in a way
that no woman has done before. He wants to grab her, to
pull her to him, to kiss her and lose himself in her. But he
holds back.

"There is nothing more pleasurable than the pain of
waiting. Of knowing that she has come here for him. And
risked so much to do so. He wants to seduce her slowly.
So that she enjoys it. So that he can relish it. And he wants
to rush it and overwhelm them both all at once.

"He hands her a thick emerald-colored glass filled with
red wine. And he smiles. He whispers one word: *Welcome*. And clinks his glass against hers.

"Her eyes twinkle and she smiles at him before she
drinks. Then, to make them both wait for the taking, he
shows her around the room, slowly explaining where he'd
had everything made, where the craftspeople had come
from, why he'd wanted damask on the walls in that particular rose color. Why only a certain carpenter from
Milan could make the headboard. It would be interesting
if they weren't so anxious to take each other to bed. Instead, it is torturous. But it is a game. And they play all
games well. It is part of their mutual seduction.

"She stops in front of the mirror and stares into it. He
moves so that he stands behind her, the two of them look-

ing at each other in the glass. He lifts his left arm and wraps it around her body so that he can stroke her breast.

"With his right hand, he reaches up and pulls the elaborate jeweled comb from her hair, releasing the golden twist and with it a fresh breeze of her perfume. The finest. Imported from France.

"He breathes in deeply. She can feel his body up against her now. The broad torso. The hard stomach. The thick bulge of his erection pressing, pressing into her buttocks. She leans back. Not overtly. A discreet action he couldn't be sure was conscious, but it gave him maximum contact with her body—a pleasure for him. And it gave her the feel of the full length of him—a pleasure for her—because knowing how excited she makes him excites her. She is young and holds nothing back from him. She feels her insides tighten, getting ready. He is not her first lover since her marriage, but he is the first to show her how much pleasure can be extracted from an encounter between a man and a woman.

"He is entranced by her.

"He buries his face in her hair. And she watches this man, who is still something of a surprise to her, in the mirror, looking at his eyes heavy with want and then at his hand as it caresses her exposed skin.

"Now the wantonness she's felt all night becomes the only thing she's conscious of. The pressure and pinpricks of sensation between her legs are becoming more intense and demanding. But she waits. Like him, she's learned that the longer they can play, the more exquisite her final explosion will be. Squeezing her legs tightly together, she watches as he undoes her dress and exposes her full breasts to the mirror, and she stares at her own dark, extended nipples. It's not that they are her breasts, or that she admires them, rather it is his hands moving over them, the way his thick fingers look so masculine against her white skin, the way her nipple puckers as he flicks his fingernail over it. It's not her body, not his, it is the salaciousness of the image itself that brings her to the edge of her orgasm. It's the want and desire that can be seen—so clearly, so vividly—in the mirror. She has become a voyeur of their lovemaking.

"He has never met anyone who he cares as much about giving to as he does with her. He watches her nipple harden in the mirror and that makes him smile. It is visual proof that she isn't pretending—the way other women he has known have done. There is nothing perfunctory about the way she responds to him, and that is something he can see in the mirror.

"Her eyes are half shut, her lips are parted. Her tongue licking them, wetting them down again and again. As if she is parched from their foreplay and this is the only way that she can quench her thirst.

"Or, he thinks, she's licking her lips to make him think of her other lips, to suggest to him that they are as open to him, as slicked.

"She reaches up and puts her hand over his, covering his fingers as they linger on her breast so that she can feel him move on her.

"This desire on her part to feel his fingers move inflames him even more and he disengages her hand to pull down her bodice completely, leaving her naked from the waist up. The sight in the mirror momentarily and literally takes his breath away. In between her breasts, an emerald teardrop, hanging from a gold chain makes her appear even more naked. The contrast of the deep green stone and the soft pale skin is as artful as if Caravaggio had painted it.

"Neither of them has ever made love in front of a mirror. But that's what he tells her they are going to do. Every moment watched and felt at the same time. Eyes not looking at each other directly but into the reflective surface. It's a seduction of sight. The sight of him touching her and the sight of her watching him. She will never face him, or he her, in a way that will excite either of them more than this exchange as they face each other in the mirror.

"He pushes up her mask as he enters her, needing to see her face, to see every expression as he fills her up... Her mouth opens in a gasp as she feels him, hard and hot and so urgently moving inside her. While she watches his face, he watches her face and as the pleasure flushes her cheeks and the sensations light up his eyes, the two lovers see each other come."

Chapter 21

"Marlowe?"

Gideon's voice, like a breeze, rushed in—it was light, not quite worldly and it brought me back to the present. I was, frankly, too astonished to even be self-conscious.

And I was confused.

First because I had seemingly gone into another trance—one even deeper than the one I'd experienced at the ocean. I'd disappeared, had become unaware of where I was or that someone else was with me, or that I had been talking—creating this other world—for at least ten minutes.

Drugged? Deluded? Deranged?

I didn't know.

Where had the story I told come from? From what place had it erupted, almost as if it had already existed and I was channeling it.

How had I gone so deep into it?

And, even more than that, how had I been brazen enough to tell it?

I didn't turn around to look at Gideon but knew he was slightly behind me and to the left because I could see him in the same mirror I'd been describing. And he was looking back at me in the mirror. Exactly the way I had imagined the lovers in the story had looked at each other. Locked in each other's steady gaze.

"I don't know what happened... I..."

Gideon didn't smile, but neither did he take his eyes off me. "You got completely lost in the story."

"That's never happened before—not like that—not when everything else gets knocked out. When I'm by myself, alone, writing...it always feels like slipping over some kind of divide where the characters are real and I'm a chimera. But this...it's never been like this. Even at the beach I was still aware of being there and of you being there, but this time I wasn't even—" I broke off.

There was a long beat where neither of us said anything, but he continued to look at me in the mirror. My response started in my solar plexus. Deep and kicking, like a reminder of a hunger that you suddenly realize you are suffering from. Two seconds before, you didn't even know you felt empty and now you can't wait to get something to eat.

"It was a beautiful story," he said.

His compliment, without guile and given so willingly and easily, surprised me.

"Thanks."

"It's perfect."

"There were some other places I wanted to show you for possible story lines. I made a list of them. It never occurred to me that you would want my first choice."

"Why?"

I had turned around, and now, with our backs to the bedroom and the mirror and the ghost images of the lovers I had conjured up, the spell was broken, and we walked out of the room and back in the direction we came from.

I shrugged. "I don't know."

Gideon looked at me with a slight worry in his eyes. "Is there somewhere in the museum we can get coffee? You look a little peaked."

"Peaked?"

"Yes, it means tired, weak, overwhelmed."

"I know what it means. It's just a very old-fashioned word."

"I'm an old-fashioned kind of guy."

"Really?"

He shook his head and laughed. "No, not really. But my grandmother was a schoolteacher and she taught me one new word every single day until I turned eighteen and went off to college, where she fully expected me to keep up the habit."

"And did you?"

It was all light and silly banter, clearly a relief for me from the intensity of the story.

The Petrie Court is on the ground floor in the west wing of the museum. One of the most recent additions to the main structure, its entire back wall is made of glass and looks out onto Central Park, which was a lush green that May morning.

There were several empty tables and we took one next to the window. From where we sat, I could see Cleopatra's

Needle, flowering spring trees, people walking their dogs, nannies with their charges, mothers and children and a pair of lovers walking by more slowly than anyone else.

Gideon had coffee, black, and I had cappuccino. He'd also gotten us a plate of biscotti and had insisted I take one.

"You're embarrassed, aren't you?" he asked.

"Yes…" I blurted, sorry as soon as the words were out of my mouth. I hadn't wanted to admit that. He was a client. There was no reason to discuss my feelings with him.

"Why?" he asked.

"Really? You don't know?"

"Well, I assume because of what you were saying. But it was wonderful—both the story itself and watching you disappear into the telling like that. It's the way all artists create." He paused and then added, "Real artists."

One of his hands rested on the table, fingers splayed, veins pronounced. I saw the scars again. And again felt the urge to reach out and trace them with my fingers. I wondered what he did that he cut himself so often. And not with a straight instrument. Most of the scars curved like miniature crescent moons.

This was not a social visit. It was not for me to ask him about himself. He'd hired me, becoming my boss in a way. He hadn't offered anything personal in the car to the beach the week before and I didn't expect him to now.

"What happened to your hands?" I couldn't help myself.

"You have such a good imagination, I'm going to make you guess." There was a mischievous light in his green eyes.

"Oh, that's not fair."

He didn't offer any sympathy, but sat, still and silent, just smiling.

"Fishing?"

His burst out laughing. "Fishing? What on earth made you think of fishing?"

I shrugged.

"Do you really think I am a fisherman?"

"I don't have any idea what you do, but something about the shape of the scars on you hands made me think they might have been made by hooks."

"Hooks? Well then, you shouldn't stop at fisherman. Butchers use hooks, too, meat hooks. Maybe I'm a butcher."

I looked down at his hands again. There was a grace to the way they moved. The reverential way he had picked up the spoon to stir his coffee, his fingers curled around the cup. It was obvious to me he was very aware of the shapes he was touching. It was impossible to imagine the man sitting opposite me, with his blue shirt and black jeans and hair falling into his eyes, standing behind a counter, hacking away at a side of beef. But I knew that he worked with his hands in some way.

"No, you aren't a butcher."

"I am. And I'm mortally wounded because you have an attitude about butchers. I can tell from the way you pronounced the word and moved back in your seat away from it a little bit."

"I didn't."

He nodded. "You did."

I searched his face. Was he serious? There was no hint. He had stopped smiling and indeed seemed upset. Had I insulted him? Then he started laughing again. "No. I'm not a butcher. Don't worry. Aren't you going to take another guess?"

"I'd say a musician but the scars wouldn't make sense."

"Nope. Next?"

Around us, the room had filled up and an elderly couple walked by looking for a table. The gentleman noticed that our cups were empty and asked Gideon if we would be leaving soon.

"We're leaving right now, in fact," he said graciously, and stood, ending our guessing game.

We walked out of the café section. He still hadn't told me what he did. And I didn't want to ask again.

"I haven't been here in a long time. I'm going to wander around for a while," he said as we reached the gallery exit.

I was being dismissed, and what surprised me was that it seemed to matter to me, but before I could even focus on what I was thinking, he said, "Do you have to go back to the store? Or do you want to walk around with me?"

It pleased me too much that he'd asked, but I chose not to think about that.

We went upstairs to the European collection because Gideon wanted to see the Rodin sculptures.

The long hall was designed to resemble a nineteenth-century art gallery, with multiple paintings hanging above and below each other, and many pieces of sculpture on display. Gideon stopped in front of each one, studying it with a careful eye.

The first marble he lingered over was *The Kiss,* a full-size Carrera marble study of sensuality. Two lovers entwined in an embrace. A swirl of emotion. There was nothing urgent or unbridled about their togetherness. Rather it was a sustained moment, a frozen, emblazoned interlude of two nudes, seated, enfolded in each other.

Every point where they touched—their arms, their legs, their lips—was a loving tribute to their connection. These were not new lovers who couldn't grab fast enough, but rather a man and a woman who had been together long enough to luxuriate in themselves.

Rodin's passion was subdued. I'd read about the artist and his own boundless sexploits—but that wasn't the overriding emotion he exhibited in this work.

The marble glowed as if there were a candle inside the stone, illuminating it, making the hard surface shine like polished skin. More than anything else, I wanted to reach out and run my hand down the man's back, lay my palm there and feel his heartbeat.

Gideon didn't speak. He was engrossed in the work and absorbed by it in a way that excluded me without insulting me.

When he was done, we moved on to *The Hand of God*, another white marble of a huge masculine hand holding another embracing couple, their entire beings twisted into each other as they made love.

I'd seen this piece, how many times—two dozen? Three? In the past four years that I'd been living in the city I had come to the museum at least twice a month. And usually I walked through these galleries, stopping to focus on only one painting or one piece of sculpture. But now, standing in front of *The Hand* with Gideon by my side, I was seeing it differently. The sexuality in the piece was like an assault. A reminder of what I didn't have, hadn't had, and something I had stopped looking for—had even embraced the lack of with relief.

"What?"

I looked over at Gideon, confused again since I hadn't said anything.

"What's wrong?" he asked this time.

I shook my head.

He motioned toward the sculpture. "Something about it bothers you. Don't you like it? Some people think it's overly sentimental."

"It's not that…" There was no way I could explain what I'd been thinking. Not how the sculpture reminded me of what I didn't have. Not how he seemed to know, yet again, that something was on my mind.

"I was going to bring you to this gallery if you hadn't liked the bedroom downstairs."

"What was the story going to be here? Maybe I would like it better after all." There was teasing in his voice again. And it caught me off guard.

"No fair. You put me through my paces in the Venetian bedroom. I'm all storied out."

"How many places did you come up with? What if I hadn't liked either the bedroom or this one? Where would we have gone next? Show me."

Chapter 22

We walked to the end of the gallery, out into the hallway, where we got on an elevator and took it up to the top floor. The doors opened and we stepped out into sunshine on the roof garden of the museum.

People usually expect elaborate beds of flowers, exotic trees, artistic plantings at the museum, but the two-thousand-square-foot space is lined with very simple three-foot-high boxwood hedges and one long, geometric wooden pergola with a wisteria vine growing on it to offer shade.

This lack of adornment keeps the focus on the astonishing view. To the west, south and north, you look out at the entirety of Central Park. Tree tops, in a hundred shades of green, stretch out to the perimeter of the park, where they are bordered by skyscrapers standing like protective sentinels over the city's more fragile playground. And beyond the buildings are miles of blue sky.

It's difficult to take it all in. So much, too much, beauty and strength and creativity and delicacy all at once.

And in the immediate foreground there is the art itself.

"I've always thought," I said, "it's unfair of the museum to ask these pieces of sculpture to compete with the view."

"I don't think the sculpture minds. It's probably honored." Gideon was inspecting a large late-twentieth-century piece. Made of aluminum and echoing the shape of the buildings around us, the monolith was rubbed in such a way that the surface shone like a million suns.

"I didn't know Nelson had a piece here," Gideon said, more to himself but loud enough that I could hear. "It must be a new acquisition."

"You know him?"

He nodded. "He was my professor at school. My mentor."

Ah. So that explained the scars. He was a sculptor. I should have guessed from the way he'd examined the Rodins on the floor below. He hadn't been interested in a typical gallerygoer's way. Now I understood what I'd seen on his face: the kind of reverence that only one artist can show another.

Like the work or not, admire a style or don't, there's a respect most artists pay each other.

"A sculptor?"

He nodded, laughed. "Not a fisherman. Not a butcher. The scars are from the tools. I'm not as patient as I should be. I get caught up in what I'm doing. Move too fast."

"Do you have a studio in New York?" I asked.

"Not my own. I used to teach up at Cornell and lived in Ithaca. But I quit recently. Nelson's in Italy, and I've got his loft until I find someplace."

"Were you tenured?"

He nodded.

"And you quit?"

"It's a long story."

"Do you show?" I knew all the galleries and was suddenly very curious.

He mentioned the name of a prestigious gallery in SoHo. "I've had two solo exhibitions in the last few years. Been in a couple of group shows."

"I'd like to see your work."

"You can come to the studio sometime."

"I'd like to see it before I write any more letters for you."

"Why?"

I didn't know why I wanted to see it so badly, so suddenly, or why I'd blurted it out. I shrugged. "I need to see what you create. I can't write as if you are writing…without getting a better idea of who you are, and what you think, and especially of your art."

"But you were doing fine at the ocean and in the Venetian room."

We'd walked around the oversize Nelson sculpture and were now circling a huge Rodin bronze called *The Burghers of Calais*. We didn't speak for a few minutes as we moved to an amusing Claes Oldenburg of a giant paperclip on its side, and then taking in a reclining nude by Maillol. Finally we wound up, side by side, standing at the west wall, looking out at the park.

"What will it add to the stories, knowing more about me?"

"It will help me to include specifics that will make it perfectly clear that these visions are yours."

He shook his head. "No. Just like I didn't want to fill out the questionnaire, I don't want you to insert those things into the stories. What you do is no different than taking a mound of clay and shaping it into a form. There's a wholeness to it. I don't want to take your clay and stick my own fingers in it just because I'm giving it as a gift."

"Does that mean I can't see your sculpture?"

"You can see it, but not for the wrong reason."

"Okay. How about I'd like to see it because you've seen what I do. Because I'm curious about how talented you are. Because I am an artist and I might learn from your work. Better reasons?"

There was one more, but I wasn't offering that one up out loud. Wasn't even allowing myself to think it. Besides, I wasn't sure it was a good reason at all. Probably the worst one I'd had in a long time.

I wanted to see his sculpture because I wanted to know if it would move me. But what good would come of knowing that? I didn't want to be tempted by Gideon. I couldn't be tempted by him.

Chapter 23

We took the elevator back down to the first floor and headed for the main exit. On the way we walked through the photography gallery. I hadn't planned this route. Clearly forgetting it would naturally bring us here. While I certainly had an affinity for photography and believed it was an art as worthy as any other, it always seemed slightly out of place in the Met. An afterthought. A stepcousin. The Museum of Modern Art farther downtown, my mother and I agreed, was a much better venue.

For obvious reasons the photography gallery in the Met is always one of the most current exhibitions. They showed an eclectic mix including early examples dating back to the turn of the last century when the art form was new, but they also had a dozen or so experimental pieces from the past few decades including the present. These changed often. Photographs being—even the best ones— less expensive than original paintings or sculptures, the museum had an exhaustive collection and changed what was on view often.

As we meandered, Gideon's eyes traveled from one print to the next, and I watched, curious to see what caught his attention.

The nude in the finely developed and nuanced platinum print had her back to the photographer. There was little light in the shot. Blacks, dark grays, a dozen tones in between. Heavy like velvet. One of his trademarks. Dark interiors. Dark situations. Dark emotions. She had both hands by her sides, as if she had been standing there, watching, for a long time. Her head was turned to a partially opened door: a man was coming in. We knew that from the way his fingers were pressing on the wood. From the way the meager light poured in, illuminating the front of her—the one part of her we couldn't see.

Her nakedness was not artistic nudity. The photographer was suggesting a scenario of salaciousness. He was an interloper and voyeur. A talented, sensitive one, but still intruding.

Your eye went from the man's hand on the door to the woman's form. She evolved from the shadows and became the focus.

Her naked legs were long, drawing the viewer's eyes to where they were parted, slightly, high between her thighs. Too far apart for it to be accidental. Too far apart for it not to be suggestive.

She was not only inviting in her lover, but the viewer.

I glanced at Gideon, who was riveted to the photograph.

"What do you think of it?" I asked.

"Powerful."

Like a culprit, I stole another look, trying so hard to experience it as if it were something I'd never seen before, but aware I wasn't doing well at disassociating.

"Do you like it?" he asked.

I shrugged, not sure what I wanted to say or how much I wanted to explain to someone I didn't know that well.

I'd waited too long to respond.

"Do you think it's demeaning?" he asked, clearly trying to guess at what my issue was.

"No. I know the photographer, that's all. It's hard for me to be objective."

"Judging from your expression, you don't like him very much."

"It's complicated."

"Sorry."

"No, there's no way you could have known. I didn't even know it was here. It must be a new acquisition." And for the first time I glanced at the card beneath the photograph.

Doorway
Cole Ballinger—American, 1975–
A Gift of the Banfield Trust

For a moment I forgot about anything but the Cole I'd once known and cared for so much. He must be so pleased, I thought, to have his photograph hanging in such an important museum. And despite everything else I felt and everything I was trying not to feel, I couldn't help but think about what an honor this was. I was also thrilled for my stepfather and my mother, who I knew must be so proud.

They lived in Santa Fe now. And I didn't see them as often as I used to when they were in Vermont. But I spoke to my mother at least once a week and we exchanged e-mails on a regular basis.

We'd been through a lot together when my father died, when it was her and me and my baby sister, who lived in Los Angeles now, and was also a photographer. I grew up too fast then. I suppose I could find a therapist to complain to about that, but I never have. I'd had a rich childhood with a devoted mother who was also a fine artist. Whatever I suffered by not always having her at PTA meetings she more than made up for by including me in her life in other ways. We were close.

So why hadn't she told me about the photo in the museum? I'd never confessed how deep the rift was between Cole and me. It was easy enough to avoid since the family didn't get together en masse anymore now that everyone was living so far away from each other. She had no reason to avoid mentioning him to me unless he'd warned her not to.

"Marlowe, just because you opened yourself up once to someone—despite what happened—you can't stay shut down. It's damaging. To your soul as an artist."

"I'm not shut down—"

He interrupted. "You are. Your face is closed. You stand with your arms crossed over your breasts. You lean back when I lean forward to say something to you. You look away if—"

"I don't. I don't."

He nodded to me, indicating that I should look at my own body language. And I did. My arms were exactly as he'd described. I concentrated on my posture; I was leaning away. Any closer and I would have been uncomfortable.

His gaze was too intense and I glanced back at the photograph. Its message was even more profoundly disturbing. I was trapped. By one truth about Cole, by another about me, and by a challenge from Gideon.

"You look as if you are awaiting a terrible verdict," Gideon said.

I turned from the photo. "Not anymore."

"I'm glad," he said. But his voice was still concerned and somehow comforting I felt it around my shoulders as if he had put his arms around me. I hadn't heard a man talk to me with caring in a long time. It made me grateful and calm. I looked into his face, and our eyes caught. The connection went from being kind to kinetic. From being solicitous to penetrating.

The sexual clench deep inside me was unexpected. And unwanted. But it was real. And while I stood there, with people streaming around us, not noticing us but the artwork on the walls, Gideon stood in front of me—no longer a client. No longer a stranger, either.

He'd read the expression in my eyes and had understood it.

And I didn't know how to respond.

Chapter 24

There was a message from Vivienne Chancey on my machine when I got home, telling me that the letters I had written for her had done wonders for her blossoming relationship but that she'd hit a wall and needed me to do her a favor. "I'm going to e-mail you a photograph I took in the desert, where I'm on location. If I send it today, could you write something that has some connection to the desert and how I feel, and do it really quickly? How I feel about missing him, I mean. I know it's not fair that I'm asking you to do it so fast. But I really need it ASAP."

The message ended. The next began. At first no one spoke. There was a beat of silence. Then another. And then a third. And just when I was about to hit Erase, I heard Cole's voice.

"Marlowe, did you get my last message? I think we should work this out before your mother and my father get here and—"

Pressing the stop button, I cut him off. It didn't matter

what he was going to say. We were long past arguing or blaming each other or trying to find a middle ground where we could come to an agreement.

I was angry at Jeff all over again for telling my step-brother that I'd seen the invitation. I wanted to call him and let him know. To get in a cab and go over to his office and stand in front of him and ask him how he dared to interfere when he hadn't been asked.

But that wouldn't solve anything.

Jeff wasn't the problem. Cole was.

He hadn't even identified himself on the machine, had assumed that I would know his voice. That was so indicative of him and the way he saw himself at the center of the universe. Even more insidious was that Cole managed to manipulate people into focusing on him without them realizing it.

Almost exactly the opposite of Gideon's way of not drawing attention to himself but of shifting the attention to you.

To me.

It was hard to even admit that.

Gideon had been attentive to me; I'd felt important. As though what I had to say and offer mattered, and that in turn had encouraged me to open up to him.

Shivering, I walked away from the phone, sat down on the bed, picked up a cobalt-blue silk pillow and hugged it to my chest. I shut my eyes.

The dark curls and marble-green eyes were the first thing I saw. The olive skin, the strong cheekbones. The full bottom lip. The long fingers. The scars.

My insides ached.

After spending time with him that morning, I wasn't sure I knew Gideon any better than I had before, but I did know more about him.

He was a sculptor. He'd taught at Cornell University in Ithaca, New York, and had been tenured. Their iconoclastic artist in residence, he'd said as we'd looked at other photographs. The youngest professor there. But he'd quit.

For a reason he hadn't revealed.

I knew he liked coffee, black. And cookies. He favored blue jeans and always wore an old, beat-up Rolex watch that I bet had been his father's for all its scratches.

It was meager knowledge.

No. There was one other thing I knew.

Gideon was able to read my face. This man could tell what I was thinking by looking into my eyes and watching how I moved. And no one before him had ever been able to do that. Not even Cole. Not even with my face engraved on his pupils. Not even with the two of us living in the same house with my mother and his father, all eating at the same table night after night and morning after morning.

It kept coming back to Cole, didn't it? But that wasn't going to last. It was only because his show was opening in a couple of weeks. Only because the enfant terrible of the current photography scene, the man who was destined to inherit Helmut Newton's mantle, was about to jump to the next strata of his career.

And it kept coming back to Cole because for some reason he wanted my blessing to take that jump.

But I'm not qualified to give my blessing to anyone. I cannot absolve my stepbrother. I can't even forgive him.

If Cole needed redemption, he would have to find it

somewhere else. He'd made his choices. All centered around what was best for him. He'd never cared what I thought before. Why start now?

Certainly not for my sake.

It had to be something else.

My mother and stepfather?

No, that wasn't it. He simply didn't care about anyone else that much.

It was the photographs, wasn't it? Despite what he'd promised, he had to be using some of the photographs he'd taken of me. I knew that there was one on the invitation. Of course there must be more in the show. And he knew—somewhere deep inside of him—that what he was doing was wrong. Except Cole never felt guilt. Guilt was too selfless for him. It had to be a selfish reason.

What could that be? Was he worried that I would do something to hurt him? After all these years, what could I do?

Gideon had looked into my eyes and told me that it seemed as if I was waiting to hear a terrible verdict. And I was. I had been waiting for it for the past two years. Ever since my last conversation with Cole. The one that Kenneth had overheard.

Chapter 25

The next night I sat at my computer and looked over the museum story I'd written for Gideon. It was finally finished and, reading it, I was embarrassed all over again.

This was a new emotion, this deep blushing inside of me that no one could see. I'd been writing for the store for months, but this had never happened before.

He didn't have his computer set up yet and so had no access to e-mail; instead he'd asked me to print out the story and mail it to him. He planned on writing it out in his own handwriting and sending it as soon as he got it. But I couldn't imagine facing him again after he'd read these words and phrases.

These were not my fantasies. Nor were they his. And yet, more than anything I'd ever created, they were personal. I was certain that if I'd been on my own, without him in the museum with me, I never would have thought up the scene that took place in the Venetian bedroom.

Procrastinating, I clicked the computer keys and called

up the quick letter I'd written for Vivienne Chancey earlier that morning and reread it.

Using her photograph of an arid desert, I'd made up a scenario about a woman longing for her lover, imagining him coming to her, waiting for him. It surprised me how the two pieces I'd written for Gideon had influenced me. There was a deeper passion to this letter for Vivienne than the other's I'd written for her. There were even some similar themes in the two efforts.

At least she'd benefit from my current state of mind.

I typed out her e-mail address, attached the letter and hit Send.

Then I went back to the story I'd written for Gideon, reading it once more. After making a few corrections, I printed it out.

When the phone rang, I looked at the Caller ID before picking it up. It was my mother. I answered. After a few minutes of conversation that was clearly not what she'd called about, she told me that she'd talked to Cole and that he was worried about me.

"That's nice of him. He shouldn't bother."

I took the phone to the oversize armchair in the living room area, moved a pile of fine origami paper onto the floor and sat down.

"Marlowe, I haven't wanted to interfere. But Tyler and I are concerned. Why can't you and Cole work out your differences?"

It was so long in the past there was no reason to hurt her now. I'd never told her. Never wanted her to feel responsible nor guilty for not having noticed what was going on in front of her eyes.

"Nothing happened. We never see each other because you and Tyler moved away and we never have big family get-togethers anymore. So how is Tyler? How are you?"

"Why don't I believe you?" she asked, not answering my question.

"I don't know," I lied. "By the way, why didn't you tell me that Cole's photograph was in the Metropolitan Museum of Art? For God's sake. I was there the other day and walked by it. You know how weird that is?"

"I didn't tell you because Cole asked me not to. Back in January when he was out here and he told us about it he said he wanted to tell you himself. But tonight he told me you haven't returned any of his phone calls for *weeks*."

"Actually it's longer than weeks," I replied. "I'm surprised he said anything, though."

"Why?"

The printer had stopped and the silence presented itself as a new sound. I got up and turned on the CD player, not caring what disc was on, but needing to fill in the spaces that held all kinds of words and thoughts I didn't want to hear.

"What is the problem between you and Cole, Marlowe? Remember when you used to be joined at the hip?"

"It's nothing. We grew together, then grew apart."

"Nothing is nothing with you, Marlowe. You don't drop people. You're too sensitive for that. You get inside people's heads and understand them. You care about them. You're intensely loyal. You still have friends from grade school. Cole's your stepbrother. You don't grow apart from people you love."

"Thanks for the psychoanalysis. When did you give up photography?"

"Sarcastic now? That means I hit a little too close for comfort. What is going on, sweetie? None of this makes sense. If anything, you hold on to difficult people too long. You like their complications, their layers. You're so good at getting beneath their surfaces. And once you do, you understand and forgive."

"You're making too much of something that is probably just a bad case of sibling rivalry."

"Sibling rivalry is for toddlers."

"Okay then, professional jealousy. Mine. For him. I didn't like constantly being compared to the more successful artist in the family."

My mother didn't say anything. I knew her well enough to picture her right now. She probably was playing with the catch on her watch. The same one she'd worn since I was a little girl. It had been my father's watch before he died. And when she was thinking, or upset, she opened and closed the catch on the band. I listened hard and heard the familiar metallic snap. I didn't remember much about my father, who had been a journalist and died when I was four years old. Killed in South America while covering a story.

"You know, I almost believe you," my mother said.

"Why don't you go all the way and fully believe me?"

"Because I'm not sure you could be that jealous. A little resentful. Slightly annoyed. Angry at yourself that you haven't gotten further with your own work. But for it to all add up so that you stopped talking to Cole or taking his calls? Nope. I'm not buying it."

I sighed audibly. Not on purpose. If I'd been thinking, I would have held it in.

"Now you are getting me angry," my mother said.

"Because?"

"Because you're keeping it inside."

"My prerogative."

It was an old expression. My mother was a private person. An artist who became a mother to my sister and I and then two additional stepchildren. She believed in all of us having a right to our own privacy, and respecting hers and my stepfather's. The catch phrase in our house was "my prerogative" if we felt someone was intruding on our personal space when we needed alone time.

Now my mother laughed. It was the sound that had orchestrated the best times when I was growing up. She loved to tell jokes. To listen to us tell them. She teased us and tickled us and encouraged us to be just plain silly. Hearing the peals of her laughter, I realized how much I missed her.

Since my mother and stepfather had moved to Santa Fe, I didn't see them enough. When they were only a three-hour drive away, I went up often for weekends and always for holidays. Now it took planning and a plane trip.

"Tyler and I are coming to New York in June."

It was almost as if she'd heard my thoughts. "That's great. I can't wait to see you." I knew why they were coming, but I wanted to hear her say it. "Vacation?"

"Part of it will be, yes."

I waited. She waited. Finally I said, "The other part?"

"I thought you knew. Cole is having a one-man show at a Chelsea gallery. There's going to be a big party. We're invited. You're invited. He said he sent you—"

"That's very exciting." I knew my voice was anything but excited as I interrupted.

"He's so young to have such an honor. I was forty and Tyler was forty-five before we had solo shows."

I nodded, realized she couldn't see me, and said, "How long are you staying?"

"What the hell is going on, Marlowe? Didn't you know about the show? Why aren't you saying anything about it? No matter how annoyed you are at Cole, surely it's not that serious that you can't be happy for him about this. This is an incredible achievement."

I got up and walked over to the table in the hall where I'd thrown my bag when I walked in. Holding on to the phone with one hand, I fished around until I found my cell phone. Then, using my forefinger, I punched in my own number, waited for it to ring and for the Call Waiting click to interrupt my conversation with my mother. I let the first one go.

"Mom, listen, I don't want you to worry about this and—"

The beep of an incoming call sounded over my words.

"That's my Call Waiting. E-mail me the dates and leave some time for me. I can't wait to see you. Really."

After we got off the phone, I retrieved the four pages of white typewriter paper from the printer. Double-spaced. Helvetica, twelve-point type.

If you hold it far away from your face, so far that you can't read the words, all you see is a pattern of straight lines, curves, circles and angles. Meaningless black marks in a seeming random order. I couldn't read the searing words from that distance. It was simply an arbitrary design. But for some reason it calmed me down. My writing was not important. It was simply an escape. In the stories, men and women did things to each other that might disturb them, ignite them, illuminate them, arouse them while I remained safe and secure. Untouched and unattached. Not close to anyone who could reach into me and turn me inside out.

Chapter 26

Four days later Gideon met me in Bergdorf Goodman, one of New York City's most exclusive department stores. He was downstairs in the cosmetics department, at the Guerlain counter.

The carpet was thick under my feet, and, walking toward him, I was conscious of how little effort it was taking to get me to his side. Seeing him again, I felt a catch in my breath and I only knew I was smiling because of the way he was smiling back.

"Good morning," he said. "I got here a few minutes early. I think I'm on the verge of olfactory overdose. I never realized how serious women are when they shop. This should be more fun than most of these women make it look."

I laughed. "What you're seeing is single-minded devotion to a goal."

We stood facing the large circular counter in the center of the room. Gleaming bottles caught the lights from the chandeliers. With their soft curves and gentle angles, they cried to be held.

The liquid golds and ambers, the sea-inspired blue-greens and gray-blues, the pastels stolen from the petals of the flowers that had influenced the scents, all enticed you to open the jewel-toned or precious-metal caps and touch the perfume to your pulse points.

"Did you send the museum letter?" I asked as we strolled around the counter.

He hesitated for a few seconds. So short a time I was almost surprised I noticed it. His eyes and mine held. There was only one lost beat of time before he said, "Yes." And then he smiled. It was a secret smile, suggesting the reaction of the woman who'd received it. I wanted to know more. And at the same time, I didn't want to know at all.

Suddenly I was glad Gideon hadn't told me anything about his lover. If I could picture her, see her in my mind reading my words, it would bother me. Might even freeze me. This, too, was new for me. I'd never before been disturbed with whom my letters or stories were being sent to.

"So, do you want to hear my idea?"

"I'm breathless with anticipation."

"That's the perfume getting to you."

We laughed and then I launched into the story. "I think a man might bring his lover here to choose the perfect fragrance for her."

"How would he do that?"

We were starting to play a game, together this time as opposed to the two prior instances when I'd been on my own with an invention that sprang entirely from my imagination.

The air conditioner was strong in the store. I took my sweater from around my waist and put it on, watching Gideon pick up bottles, open them, sniff and then replace them.

"So this is what he does?" he asked.

"Yes. He wants to find exactly the right perfume."

He lifted up a bottle of Annick Goutal, in a cut-glass falcon, inhaled, frowned and returned it to the countertop.

"But it's difficult," I continued. "Each is too intense on its own. He can't tell from how the scent smells in the bottle how it will smell when he touches the liquid to her and it's warmed by her skin."

I handed him a classic, Shalimar. Gideon inhaled, then tipped the bottle, wet his fingers and pressed them to my wrist. First there was a coolness on my skin but, after it dried, the feel of his fingers lingered, the way the scent had burst forth and then lingered, filling me up, overtaking me.

I held my hand out for him and he bent over it the way he had bent over the bottles. As he breathed in, his raven hair fell in his face and brushed against my skin. The sensation made me suck in my breath.

This was wrong. I was not supposed to be reacting to him like this.

"He can't really pick out the perfume on his own, can he?"

"No. He has to ask one of the saleswomen to help him. He chooses one who he thinks looks the most like the woman he's in love with. She's happy to assist. But something starts to happen as they test out the perfumes. He smells more than the scent. He smells her. The earthiness of her beneath the synthetics and the oils and he's attracted to that smell. More attracted to it than anything he's ever smelled before. It's as if he's known her primeval essence all his life without being aware of it. He wants to be enveloped in it, in her."

Gideon's eyes were on me now, and he was nodding. Not overtly, but subtly. Just enough of a movement to let me know that he was slipping into the story with me, falling deeply into the dream.

"The saleswoman doesn't mind. She likes showing off the scents for him. And she likes the feeling of his hair, so soft against her skin when he bends over her, almost as if he is praying, to take in her smell. But they've run out of room on her wrists and so when he tries out the next scent she takes his hand and instead of pressing his fingers to her lower arm, she puts his hand up behind her ear, under her hair, in a private place on her body that is not exposed."

"Even though he knows he shouldn't, he leans toward her. Taking her shoulders in his hands, he holds on to her and puts his—" Gideon's hand was lifting up to my neck, he was moving my hair, and then he stopped. The look on his face probably mirrored the one on mine as we realized the same thing at the same time. Which one of us had warned the other off?

It didn't matter. The moment was broken as surely as if it had been one of the crystal bottles of perfume dropped on the glass counter, shattering into a hundred slivers, stinking up the air despite how fragile and gentle and sensual the scent was in the right proportion.

"Well, this won't work. I can't have you send a letter about someone seducing a poor salesgirl when his lover is pining for him."

He laughed. "Definitely projecting the wrong thing."

"I'm sorry." My own laughter sounded tight and nervous. "That's just the way the story started developing."

"Not to worry. It's amazing how you slide into telling them. Like you're putting on someone else's shadow."

I shrugged. I didn't want to tell him, didn't even want to accept it myself, but this was atypical for me. Stories didn't usually come to me this easily. And I didn't normally disappear so deeply into them.

And I didn't normally find any inspiration in my clients.

Chapter 27

We were both headed downtown and so we walked east together to take the subway.

Sitting side by side as we were whisked through tunnels under the city, we were quiet. When the train jerked to a stop at Forty-Second Street, our legs banged together. I was aware of the two inches where his jeans touched my khakis. There was a patch of heat that sizzled through the fabric. And for a few moments I couldn't figure out whether or not to move. I knew I should have. Or he should have. But neither of us did.

Everything around us disappeared. There were no other people across from me or behind me or in front of me. The sounds of the subway dissipated. All sense of the rest of my body left me. I simply was that one connection point.

There was no precedent for how I was supposed to act in this situation. I wasn't dating this man. I was working for him. Even worse, I was helping him seduce a woman he was interested in. And yet we occupied another realm when we were together. A confusing landscape that engaged my senses and my imagination in a way that was unusual.

We got out at the Spring Street station. I was going to Ephemera and Gideon was going to his studio. Both were in the same direction, and we had three blocks to walk together.

He was taller than me by at least five inches and with such long legs, he walked much faster than I did. I was hurrying to keep up with him for the first block but then he realized and slowed down.

"I'm sorry."

"Are you in a hurry? Do you have an appointment?"

"The owner of my gallery is meeting me but not for an hour. He has a buyer for a piece that I am finishing up."

"I really would like to see your work." I was surprised at myself. I'd already brought this up without getting the reaction I wanted. Now I was being pushy and overstepping my bounds. But it had simply slipped out.

If I was honest, I'd admit that I was more than curious. The night before I'd wanted to look him up on the Internet and see if any of his work was online, but I'd held back. I didn't want to give in to the urge to scope him out. It was too much like being a high school girl with a crush, waiting outside a boy's house and pretending to bump into him.

"I hope you won't be upset but I've told Tyler Fisk—he's the owner of the gallery, the man I'm meeting—about your collages."

"You did?"

"Do you mind?"

I shook my head.

Cole had promised me years ago that he was going to help me find a gallery. He'd had such an easy time of it—with his father's and my mother's connections to the photographic community all kinds of doors had opened for him. At twenty he had already been shooting for *Vogue* and *Bazaar*. At twenty-five, he'd seen one of his photographs sold at an auction at Sotheby's for $25,000. Now, at thirty-one, he was having a solo show. Meanwhile, I'd gone nowhere with my work. It didn't fit into an established area. It couldn't be categorized. The dealers my mother knew handled only photography and said my pieces belonged in a gallery that specialized in the fine arts. Fine art galleries said my work was too photographic.

It had turned into a matter of pride. I needed to prove that my work was of interest to people because of the art itself and not because of who my mother or my stepfather or my stepbrother were.

Now Gideon was offering me help, and I felt different about it. Why? "That's extremely nice of you."

"I know what it's like to be where you are and how demoralizing it can be. Making art that no one sees. Yes, I know creating what you believe in and doing it for yourself is what matters. But after a while you need someone to respond, to watch someone looking at your work and know you're communicating."

"All that's important is doing the work. Success isn't my goal," I said.

"It's not success that I'm talking about. It's interaction. When we paint or sculpt or assemble a collage, we're using our senses and our souls to make something out of thin air. We're saying something. And the act of saying it, and the process we go through in presenting it, doesn't teach us everything we need to know until we can discuss it and argue about it and listen to other people talking about it. It's like making love versus masturbating."

I had been nodding vigorously. He was expressing everything I was feeling, had been feeling for the last few years. But when he used the sexual analogy, I stopped. Suddenly he was taking me to a place I didn't want to go.

I no longer understood the act of making love the way I thought Gideon meant it. Had no idea what it would be like to communicate with someone through the act of fucking. I thought I'd known once, but when I'd found out that man had used me, had tricked me into opening up to him before I realized he was going to take advantage of me, I began to second-guess myself. He'd taken a lot from me. Too much. I hadn't known that you could give that much of yourself away during sex. Hadn't known it until it was gone. Until he was gone.

After that I became cautious and held back. Kept my own fantasies in check. I watched. I tried to learn. I listened. I didn't stay with anyone long because I never could figure out what it was anyone really wanted. Even when it seemed simple and uncomplicated, I questioned it. And they sensed that.

I couldn't figure out what I wanted, either.

So it became easier to want nothing.

With Kenneth, my reticence had worked. He'd found it attractive, he said—that I didn't open up easily meant, to him, that I had not shared how I felt with many men.

It was refreshing, he told me. But he'd been too invested in my lack of any commitment to anyone before him. It prevented him from noticing that there was something missing from my emotional commitment to him.

And then we'd had the fight about my past the night before he'd left for Venice.

It was only in the past six months, since I'd been writing letters and stories for Grace's store that, despite myself, I'd begun to think about my own sexuality. As I wrote about other people and their sexual releases and comminglings, I acknowledged how much I hadn't allowed myself to experience.

"Where'd you just go?" Gideon asked.

"What?"

"You disappeared on me. Looked like you were far away."

"I was thinking about what you said. About how much I agreed with it."

We'd arrived at my destination.

"Am I going to see you in the morning?" he asked. "We have to nail down this smell story."

I nodded.

For a moment I was overwhelmed with sadness. I didn't want him to walk away. It made no sense.

"Where?" he asked.

"I'll call you later. I need to figure out what we should try next," I said, hearing the harshness in my own voice. I'd retreated already. Reacting to him leaving as if I'd been rejected.

"And I'll let you know what my dealer says about setting up a meeting to see your work."

I shrugged. "Oh, right."

"Don't sound too excited." His voice was colder than it had been ten seconds ago.

I didn't know what to say or how to explain why I wasn't more thankful or enthusiastic.

He'd shown me a wall and where the loose bricks were. He'd even offered to help me pull them out and I hadn't responded. I didn't want his help—a man's help. Not with my personal life, not with my art. Because I knew, I'd learned, that even a man who has your best interests at heart, will, if it comes down to his work, do the selfish thing.

Chapter 28

I hadn't been sure what else to suggest for smell until I was walking home later that afternoon and passed a man carrying a large bouquet of flowers.

What about focusing not on one smell but an abundance of fragrance?

What would it be like to overwhelm someone with a bouquet of smells and drench them in scent?

That's what I suggested to Gideon's answering machine that night. I gave him the address of where to meet me the next day and told him to call me if he had a problem with that.

Lying in bed a few hours later, I thought about the woman I was writing these stories for. I tried to imagine her again but I had nothing to go on except the person she was attracted to, perhaps even in love with: Gideon.

I'd been in love. In very different ways, with two men. There were others I'd had crushes on, but only those two had aroused a serious depth of emotion in me. Not only were *they* opposites, but the kind of emotion I'd felt for them was completely opposite, too.

The first was a hurricane. I was in its thrall. Incapable of fighting it. It undressed me and stripped me bare. It made me feel every inch of my naked skin and every nerve ending in my body. It took away my want of food, of sleep, of entertainment, of social situations. There was nothing mild or calming about the storm of sensations that swirled in me when I was with Cole. And there was nothing I couldn't imagine doing for him or with him. And so I did it all. Brazen and shameless, I split open for him, like a tree struck by lightning, shearing down the middle and immodestly showing its core.

He took from me what I offered, never considering if it was for my good or not. Cole wanted what I wanted, I thought. Certainly what he gave back was precisely that: his blatant desire.

I basked in knowing that there was nothing that I could say or do that would disturb him or frighten him away. The deeper I went inside myself to shock him, the more I delighted him. I spun on him. I rained for him. I lit up the sky, giving him everything I had to offer.

Ten years later nothing was the same. Falling in love with Kenneth was like skimming a pond in a small but well-tended teak rowboat, bright with brass fittings. Each of us rowing, the oars dipping only lightly into the water. It was feeling sunshine on your face. Looking up and closing your eyes and looking only out, never in. My reflection in the surface of the water was serene. Clear. And the water itself was not dark or murky but a sparkling sky-blue. All of my features were distinct in the mirror image that looked up at me.

As time went on, I offered Kenneth no more and waited to see how much he would demand, only to find he demanded nothing. It was easy giving. No wrenching pulls, no dragging. If I wondered what I was losing by loving him simply, without the old craving and longing and hunger, I don't remember it.

Kenneth was a relief. I could forget about the girl who had stripped off her clothes and spread her legs and opened her mouth and couldn't get enough of the lanky, long-haired boy who couldn't get enough of her.

She faded more and more into a past I didn't think about. I forgot about her the way you forget about a cut that leaves a scar so thin and so pale it all but disappears. I cherished Kenneth for who I was able to be with him—someone who did not suffer passion.

At the time I didn't think I was pretending.

After all, we change. We morph. We evolve into who we are based not only on the experiences we have but the ones we realize we are not strong enough to have again. And I was not brave enough to go back to being even a grown-up version of that teenager who didn't understand the concept of shame or the idea of betrayal.

I turned over on my side and moved the pillows so that a fresh, cooler one was under my cheek. I tried to think of something that wouldn't keep me awake but would soothe me to sleep. Instead, my mind went back to Gideon.

What was he like with the woman who was getting my stories? Did she lay herself bare before him and wait to see what he wanted, or did she reach out and take his hand and put it on her breast and show him how desperate she was to have him inside her?

What did she write to him in her letters that had made him decide to embark on this campaign of his own? How long had he known her? How well did he know her? Did he know the inside of her? Were the taste and smell of her in his memory? Or was he one step removed? Was he simply responding to her wanting him?

Which one of them had opened their mouth first during that kiss that is the first marker of how things will progress? When a simple movement turns into an invitation.

I could see him, facing someone, his hair falling into his face, his green-black eyes focused on her, putting his hands on either side of her face, holding back a moment so he could study her even more closely, set her features in his mind, catch her eye and tease her with what was going to happen.

I knew—how did I know?—that for him the anticipation was as important as the act. That his wanting was as pleasurable as his release.

It made me feel something I hadn't remembered for a long time.

Not what *want* is. But what *craving* is.

How much I had savored every second of it and played with it and shared it and used it with my first lover. And how it flavored all of our time together.

We were bitter and sweet, dark rich chocolate perfumed with oranges. The kind of chocolate that you don't eat quickly, but hold on your tongue, almost like a communion wafer, and let dissolve, your mouth alive with subtle bursting flavors too complicated to identify.

Who was she?

What did she write to Gideon?

What would he add to the end of the stories I wrote for him to make the letters more personal, more wicked, more promising, more salacious, sweeter, more loving?

And then, as I was finally falling asleep, I realized none of those questions mattered. There was only one I needed to understand before morning:

Why did any of this matter to me?

Chapter 29

The flower district opens early, before other businesses do. Midtown Manhattan, on the west side, is where hordes of small florists, restaurant owners and retailers come to pore over the day's offerings and choose from among the hundreds of thousands of flowers that are delivered fresh each morning.

By the time I got there, at 9:00 a.m., the foot traffic was slowing down. To be standing on a street corner, with traffic whizzing by and bus fumes filling the air and yet have the overwhelming scent of flowers waft over you, is incongruous.

The late-May day was unusually warm, and I'd taken off my black sweater and tied it around my waist. My crisp white shirt and khakis were already starting to stick to me.

I saw Gideon before he saw me, and I watched him cross the street: his long strides, his observant eye taking in everything around him. It was an artist's trick. My mother and Cole and my stepdad did it, but through the lens of a camera. My mentor and teacher, Kim Cassidy, did it by making tiny drawings in a sketchbook that she always kept with her. No matter what other kind of art she created, it was those minute observations she drew in a flurry of movement in less than sixty seconds that were her best work. I had a notebook, too. But my drawings were mediocre. I wondered how Gideon stored his impressions.

"This place is amazing," he said as he handed me a cardboard cup. "Cappuccino, right?" he asked.

I took the coffee. "That was really nice of you."

He shook his head. "That's me, courteous to the core."

"What about that bothers you?"

Now it was his turn to be surprised by something I'd said. "In everything but my work, I can be far too accommodating."

"Do you know why?"

"Yes, I do. But it doesn't help that I know."

"So why?"

"I just feel so damn grateful that I get to do what I do with my life. I almost lost my hand once. In an auto accident." He pushed up his shirt cuff and showed me the old scars on his wrist and arm. "I was in the hospital for a long time. Worrying about whether or not I'd still be able to sculpt…it changed me."

I nodded. "What did you mean about not being accommodating when it comes to your work?"

"I'm too stubborn for my own good. I won't bend. That's why I left Cornell. Me and my damn principles."

I sipped the coffee. It was good and strong. "What happened?"

He laughed sardonically. "The dean of the art school relaxed the requirement of figure drawing for students majoring in fine arts. I went crazy. How can you break the rules if you don't know what they are? I refused to teach unless the figure drawing requirements were reinstated. They weren't. So, I'm here." Then he shrugged as if the conversation were irrelevant. "Now, where are all these flowers?"

The first small stall was filled with tulips. Long-stemmed French tulips, tight in the bud, in soft colors that looked like faded curtains in a chateau. The flowers were elegant and lush, in bunches so big that their opulence was almost an embarrassment.

But tulips don't have a strong scent, and so we moved on.

Have you ever spent an hour walking among cut flowers? Touching them and smelling them? Letting their perfumes mix and mingle and impregnate your pores?

We began with lilacs, buying two large bunches of pale lavender blooms that emitted fragrance without you having to bury your nose in them. Their smell was sweet without being cloying, and fresh the way no perfume can be.

Next we found precious bundles of hyacinths with a scent more exotic and deeper than the lilacs. It opened my heart to sniff them. I had to close my eyes and hold my breath once the smell was inside me.

In a corner of the next stall we found rubrum lilies rife with their aroma of ritual and passion. These are Easter flowers, the only ones worthy of the story of Christ rising from the dead. But when I breathe them in, I don't think of resurrection. I think of Mary, finding solace in this fragrance. Of a man's mother weeping and of her tears turning into this scent.

We bought roses, too.

Alone, they can be too sweet and too familiar. But not mixed in with all the others. These were white and fat, and their edges were tinged with a blush of pink. They perfumed the rest of the bouquet with an edge of nostalgia and old-fashioned seduction.

"What kind of flowers does she like?" I asked him as we walked to the next stall, our arms laden with flowers.

He looked at me but was picturing her. But something in his expression wasn't what I expected. No smile. No softening of his features. And then he refocused so that he was seeing me again.

"I don't know her that well yet. Didn't I tell you that?"

"No."

I wanted more explanation. How had he gotten to be so obsessed with her without knowing her? I didn't want him to be shallow. To have fallen for an image without soul or substance. Except why the fuck did that matter? Why did I care what kind of man he was?

"I don't want to talk about her. Tell me what kind of flowers you like best," he said. "Show me."

We went in search of them.

The next few stalls said they were out but finally, after six more tries, we found them.

Pure white peonies.

Each flower was more than eight inches wide. Overwhelming, lush and provocative. I wanted to take them and pull them apart, and dig deeper to find the odd center of the flower where a few blood-tinged petals and saffron-colored stamens were hiding.

I pointed them out to Gideon.

He reached down, scooping up two dozen, and took them over to the owner, who quoted a price. Gideon paid.

"What else do we need?" he asked.

If he noticed my surprised smile, he didn't comment on it.

We spent another fifteen minutes walking through the flower market, buying more and more until, finally, we couldn't carry anything else, and then we hailed a taxi.

As soon as the door closed the driver said, "I hope you're not going far. I have allergies."

"Where *are* we going?" Gideon asked me.

I realized I had no idea. My loft? His? I hadn't thought it through. Where should we take the flowers? And then I knew, absolutely.

"The Seventy-Ninth Street entrance to Central Park," I told the driver. And with a grunt of something I didn't understand, he took off.

Twenty minutes later Gideon followed me as I led him north past a playground, down a path until it forked, then left onto another path. To one side was a deep green lawn, to the other, wooden park benches where young mothers with baby carriages and elderly retirees sat enjoying the morning.

We reached the toy sailboat pond and walked halfway around it. Exactly where the oversize sculpture of Hans Christian Andersen sat, I stepped off the path and started climbing up the hill to a grove of cherry trees, thick with blossoms.

There was a very slight breeze. As we reached the trees, the wind blew and petals fell like a pink rain. There was grass beneath the trees but it was almost invisible under the thick carpet of foliage.

This was my destination.

I laid down my share of flowers, as did he.

Once they were out of our arms, I could survey them, and was surprised to see how many we'd bought. There must have been two hundred stems.

The only flowers he didn't put down on the ground under the tree were the peonies. Instead, he handed them to me. "These are for you. Not for the story."

I bent my head into the fat open blossoms. Surprised by the gesture. Seduced by the man or the flowers? I wasn't sure which. They were so obscenely lush, it was as if he was handing me a bouquet of erotic suggestions.

I remembered the first peonies I had ever noticed. At our house in Vermont. Those had been pink and Cole had picked them for me from my mother's garden and brought them to me in the dead of night, into my bedroom, stealing in silently when everyone else was asleep. He had undressed me first, slipping my thin nightgown off my shoulders and down my hips so that I was lying in bed, naked, the only light coming from the half-moon shining through the window. Then, one by one, he had laid the flowers on top of me. Covering me with them. Dressing me with them. Until I was blanketed by flowers. Finally, when there was no bare skin showing, he smiled at me and said, "As pretty as a picture."

That was when it began.

When we made love that first night, our bodies crushed the flowers. In the morning when I tried to gather them up and make them into a bouquet, I found that our twisting and turning had ruined them. But I'd kept the petals in an envelope. For years.

It wouldn't matter if I borrowed that story for Gideon. Its emotion had disintegrated for me along with the foliage years ago. I could at least make some use of it now. Maybe by recreating it for him, I could even salvage some of what had made the flowers so beautiful that night and redeem them, turning them into something other than another memory that I kept at the bottom of a drawer along with the rest of the detritus of that old affair.

"You keep leaving," he said.

"I was thinking of how to start."

We sat down, surrounded by the flowers. He was leaning against the trunk of the tree, watching me.

I wanted to look away, but I didn't.

"The woman is sleeping. She thinks you are away. That it will be weeks until she will see you again. She goes to bed every night trying to think only of you so that while she sleeps she'll dream about you, because sometimes in a dream you can make something real. You can taste and touch and feel it and, for a while, be lulled into thinking that you aren't dreaming at all but awake. And that's what she wishes. That while she sleeps she can make you come to her in that way, so that she might miss you less. Because the missing is turning her pale and making her cheeks hollow and her eyes dull. And it's leaving an ache inside that she is aware of all day long.

"Women can't feel their wombs—we can't feel our cavities—except we can feel their emptiness. The lustful pangs it causes in her interrupt her while she is doing other things.

"That night she thinks she is dreaming of a garden. Even in her sleep she smells the scent of flowers. Jasmine. Lilac. Gardenia. Rose. Hyacinth. In her dream these scents all combine until she is floating on them and they are holding her aloft in their stem-and-leaf arms.

"She knows she is naked. Can touch her own skin. And then she feels something softer and lighter than fingers can be. She shivers in her sleep. Tingles. Her nipples harden. And she's wet between her legs, too.

"As if the smell has aroused her.

"The perfume is intensifying. At first it was one layer deep, like a single fine cotton sheet had been laid over her body. And then it thickened, as if an almost weightless blanket had been placed on top of the sheet. The scents are commingling and becoming more complicated.

"She moans. Feeling for a moment as if she is being kissed by the perfume of the lilacs and roses. And then yet another layer is added. Still the combined weight of them is featherlight. But the fragrances themselves grow heavier. Making her drowsy even in her sleep but stirring her at the same time. She wants to hold on to the aromas. To stay in their thrall for as long as she can.

"She wants to breathe in the perfume, and press it into her skin, and have it fuck her pores. She wants to soak it up the way you soak up a lover's kisses. Swallow it so that the scent becomes part of her and makes her skin and her hair fragrant."

I didn't realize I had shut my eyes until I opened them. And then the first thing—the only thing—I saw was Gideon's face. His marble-green eyes staring at me.

"Don't stop." His voice was husky and sounded a warning. But for a perverse reason I couldn't name, that only made me want to go further. Nothing mattered anymore. It was as if I was trampling on something that had once been important but wasn't any longer and it was all right for me to ruin it. I needed to keep going. To defile it.

I knew that I wouldn't understand what I was doing or how I was finding the guts to do it without being ashamed until much later. There was time for all that. For now, it felt too good to see these things in my mind and to say them out loud.

"You have been watching her sleep. Seeing the expression change on her face, and it goes from peaceful to wanton. And the longer you watch, the more you want to touch her. Not only with the flowers, the way you have been doing, but with your fingers and your tongue and your cock."

A chill went down my spine. I had crossed a line. It felt like I was shouting the words now. As if I'd thrown off some heavy winter coat and was finally able to breathe.

"You've been covering her with the flowers. Making a blanket of them that hides her body from you. And still she sleeps. You want her to wake up so you can go to her and hold her. So that she will open to you and swallow you whole with her body. But at the same time you don't want to lose the expression on her face. Because you've never seen a woman like this before. Unaware. Not acting. Not conscious of being watched. Showing a desire that is most like the way desire feels inside you. Not some shy kind of wanting. Or brazen greed that is almost angry in its insistence. This is neither feminine nor masculine, pushy nor restrained. It is simply a true feeling. It's longing.

"You have put the last of the lilacs around her shoulders. And now you cover her chest with the roses. A necklace of rubies that open as they touch her skin.

"What you have left are the peonies. The pure, white, full, open flowers. But she is covered. There is nowhere for them. Except, you think, between her legs.

"One of the peonies is open wider than the others, this is the one you choose. Slowly, you kneel down between her thighs and brush it against her vagina. You stroke her with it in one direction and then go the opposite way. You feather her with it. And then tease her with it. You crush it against her.

"Your own body is responding and you want to sweep all the flowers off her skin and get on top of her, but you don't because there's one thing you want more.

"She opens her eyes. But you don't see her do that. You are looking between her legs at the flower you are pressing into her, mashing into her. Then you bring it up to your face. You bend over it and lower your face to it.

"And then you breathe. Deeply. Now the aroma that the flower gives off is not its own, but a mixture of a floral scent and her musky scent. Now the flower smells like the deep earth center of a woman—this woman. And this is what sends you over the edge, what pushes you finally past wanting her, past thinking, into sensation. The scent is a more potent perfume than the roses and the lilacs, heliotrope and lilies, all together. It is more powerful than the hyacinths and jasmine.

"She sees that in your face. And that is when she gives herself to you."

Chapter 30

A kiss is something that you take for granted when you have been in a relationship for a long time. It's given easily. As a thank-you, a goodbye, a hello, a punctuation mark, a prelude to lovemaking, a show of comfort or support.

But a first kiss is none of those things. It is an invitation to a sensate world that is yet unknown. It is dark in the light and light in the dark. It is foreign in its tastes and smells. It may begin with your lips but it moves along your body in a way that brings your blood to the surface. It turns you inside out so that you become your feelings, and your thoughts retreat, bowing to the physicality of the kiss's moment. The rest of you withdraws to allow the coming together of a mere two inches of flesh that fly you to an unknown place—the way you can travel to a new city or town and recognize that you are in its center without knowing the particular buildings, foliage, storefronts.

There is one kind of first kiss that is like a meal. It begins with a taste. Sweet like honey and fresh like mint. It feeds you, giving you immediate nutrients. It is delicious in the way that only something you have never eaten can be.

It has a beginning that is soft and patient. And sometimes stays in that place. Which is all right.

Or else it slips into a more potent activity.

While it is only one kiss, two pairs of lips coming together, it has sensors that seek out the empty crevices in your psyche where you have forgotten feelings that are waiting, dormant, ready to bloom and burst and then explode. Firecrackers of blossoms.

This one kiss, if it lasts, turns into a kind of cut. Slicing open those places where want rises and surges, up, up, up though your blood vessels and nerve endings. And mixed in with the spirit of that kiss can be a palatable sadness if you can't find what you need from it because it is so new you don't know where to look.

It teases. It suggests a road unfurling in front of you and you think that if you follow where it leads, you will find the end of the kiss, which will be a beginning of more kisses that will lead to other tastes and touches and sensations.

Except, deep inside of you there is another reality you don't want to accept. It nudges you, reminds you that you have had first kisses before and you know, as miraculous as they are, you cannot count on them. As much as it seems as if worlds are opening up, they might not stay open. One of you will walk in a straight line and the other will zigzag. And even if it appears that you both want to take that road, and keep up the same pace, the road itself will reach a hill only one of you will climb or a valley only one of you will be willing to descend into.

Our first kiss was a promise.

And it was more.

It was both gentle and passionate. As light as the fragrance of the lilacs and as deep as the color of the roses. It was as much about discovery as it was about destination.

It was those things for both of us. I could tell that. And that alone made it astonishing. We were exchanging the same kiss.

Under the trees that rained petals on us, our lips pressed to each other's and our mouths opened at the same time and, as much as I knew better, the kiss seemed to answer questions that I had never before been willing to ask, much less hear the answers.

When we broke apart, both breathless and overwhelmed, neither of us said anything. We sat, surrounded by the hundreds of flowers we'd bought at the market, many of them now crushed and bruised, and we simply looked at each other.

Then Gideon smiled.

The business that had brought us there was, for the moment, beyond recollection. Who we had been before was changed. What had happened to us with other people didn't matter.

I forgot, and he forgot, that we were there to compose a story for the woman he was having a relationship with. And in those few minutes before we remembered, neither of us said anything. We reveled in what it had been like to come together.

He took my hand and turned it over and brought my palm to his mouth and kissed me again in a very different way. Giving. Not taking anything back this time. Not asking for any knowledge of me, but bestowing information to another part of my body which accepted it, willingly. It was more intimate because I watched it, saw his head bowed over my hand, felt his fingers holding me, saw his shoulders strain over me.

"We can't do this," I said finally.

"Why?"

"You're with someone," I said with chagrin. Shocked that he could forget. Elated that he could.

"Are you?"

I shook my head.

"I'm sorry," he said.

I wasn't even sure what he meant by that—was he sorry I wasn't with someone, or that he was sorry he was? Or was he just sorry that he had kissed me?

It didn't matter. I couldn't ask. Instead, I said, "Don't be."

"Are you frightened?"

I nodded. "How did you know? No. Don't tell me—something in my face."

"In your eyes. But it doesn't have anything to do with me being involved with someone, does it? Something else made you frightened."

I nodded.

"What?"

"I don't know."

"Really?"

"I wasn't. Frightened. Not when you were kissing me."

"No. I could tell that. If you had been I would have stopped. What happened since then?"

I didn't know. I wanted to turn away. Away from him.

I couldn't stand looking into his eyes anymore because every time I did he figured out more about me.

That was what frightened me, I suddenly realized.

"You know what it is, don't you?" he said.

I took my hand back from him, surprised that he was still holding it, that he had been gripping me the whole time we'd been talking.

"Do you want to stop?" I asked him, not answering his last question.

"Stop what?"

"The stories. Should I stop writing them for you? I won't hold you to the deal. It's all right. I don't even want to get paid for what I've done."

I could read *his* eyes now and saw worry fill them. A frown creased his forehead. "No. I don't want to stop." He was talking about the stories, wasn't he? Why did I think he might be talking about the kiss? About another kiss? About more than a kiss?

"Why not?"

"Because I'm frightened, too, Marlowe. And when I get that feeling, I want to throw myself into the center of what's scaring me."

"That makes you perverse."

"Because your way of dealing with fear is to walk away from it?"

"I know how to protect myself."

"Or you think you know."

I felt sad then. Sensing the edges of a thought forming but not wanting to focus on it, I looked down at all of the crushed flowers under us and around us. Couldn't we go backward to where we had been before the kiss? Before the silent promises that, I told myself, over and over, were in my imagination.

I stood up. "What should we do with the flowers?"

"Leave them here," he said. "Think how it will be for people who walk by this spot today. What they will imagine."

We began to walk away and were halfway down the hill when he stopped.

"Wait. Wait for me here." He left me and ran back up to the trees and bent down. I couldn't see what he was doing until he turned around. He was holding out a bouquet of pure white peonies with red-tipped centers, offering them to me.

He watched as I started to reach, but then I hesitated. It seemed that if I took them I would be agreeing to something. And I wasn't sure I should. I wasn't certain that it was the best thing for me.

Before, a long time ago, I'd been this scared. But that was a fearless alarm. The way only someone who is younger can know they are doing something wrong and be frightened but also be brave and daring at the same time. To know there is danger but not to care. In fact, to crave the risks.

Then I wanted to feel everything being offered to me.

Now I wanted to reject the offer itself and feel nothing.

I meant to drop my hand and not take the peonies. I think Gideon expected it, too. But that was not what happened.

Part Three

"Come!
Come!!
Come!!!"

—Sarah Bernhardt in a letter to
Charles Haas in 1869

Chapter 31

At home that night, I wandered around my own loft, dazed and slightly bewildered by what had happened earlier. Finally at seven o'clock, I made myself scrambled eggs and a toasted English muffin, which I pretended to eat. I wasn't hungry. I kept replaying the kiss, actually feeling the sensations all over again and being stunned by them.

I finally gave up on the eggs, poured a glass of wine and climbed onto my bed to watch *Sabrina* with Audrey Hepburn, which I'd seen at least a dozen times. With the movie playing in the background, I turned on my laptop and wrote out the fantasy I'd talked out in front of Gideon that morning.

I hoped that the movie would distract me, that I wouldn't connect to what I was writing in a personal way.

I couldn't have done it by hand. It would have been too painful to form all those words with my fingers, to see the shapes swirl and curve and climb in my own handwriting. I needed to separate from the story. It wasn't me lying in the bower of flowers. I wasn't smelling them and feeling their fragrance overwhelm me. It was a nameless, faceless woman. Narrower than I was. Blonder. She was sweet looking without the cruel set to her mouth that I see on my own when I look in the mirror. In her eyes there was nothing of the sense of cynicism that hardly ever leaves mine. She could believe in the fantasy because Gideon was falling in love with her. And what had happened in the park with me was only a momentary confusion that she didn't know about.

I finished up at about nine-thirty. Unable to reread it, I printed it out, folded the sheets in thirds, put them in an envelope and set that on the little table by the front door. I'd mail it in the morning.

It was like having a small fire burning, unprotected in the grate, building up to a frenzied heat that might at any moment blaze brighter and reach out to do even more damage.

I got up, grabbed my keys and the envelope and left my loft. I wanted the story out of there.

Even though it was ten o'clock, my neighborhood was busy. SoHo, which had once been an isolated part of New York, was now simply another gentrified section of the city. There were people coming home, going out to walk the dog or meet friends for drinks, or simply strolling on a warm May night. There was nothing to fear from the well-lit streets and pedestrians. The thing I was afraid of had been inside of me. Hopefully, I'd exorcised it with the writing, but had I?

The kiss had been a momentary aberration.

I knew better than to be fooled by a man's passion. Or

my own. Lust is so fickle, motivated by so many of the wrong impulses. Fooling us into thinking it has some significance when it has none.

Gideon's studio was close by, and it didn't take me long to walk the two blocks downtown and three blocks west to 35 Broome Street. The red stone building was a mid-nineteenth-century structure. Five stories high, renovated and refurbished, it had an elegance that I marveled at—these buildings had been factories and yet they were artfully designed.

The glass-and-iron front door was locked. Of course it was. And of course the mailboxes were inside the vestibule. I should have known that. It was the same in my building.

Suddenly feeling foolish, I turned and walked down the two front stone steps. At the corner, while I stood waiting for traffic to pass, I glimpsed Gideon on the other side of the street. Clearly, he was coming home.

How could I disappear so he couldn't see me?

It was too late. He'd already noticed me and waved, motioning to me that I should stay where I was and he would cross the street. There was no escape.

"Hi." His smile was too intimate. His eyes too focused on mine. "You on your way home?"

"Yes." I lied because I didn't want to explain why I'd needed to drop off the story and get it out of my apartment, out of my sight.

"You live nearby, don't you?"

"Just a few blocks away, not far from the store."

"I think you told me that."

"Maybe. I think I did. I might have."

"This is stupid, Marlowe. For us to stand here and make small talk. Do you have to go home right now? Can you come upstairs?"

"I don't think I should."

"That's not what I asked you. No. You probably shouldn't. But I want you to. And you want to. So you will, won't you? I'll make you a drink. I'll even show you some of my work."

Maybe if he hadn't mentioned showing me his work I might have been able to walk away. But by then I was desperate to see it because I was so badly hoping that it was going to be terrible. And, if it was, then I'd feel different about him. No matter how attracted I was to him, if I hated his sculpture, if he had no talent, if his work was as pointless and vapid as most of the artwork I saw at the majority of the shows I went to, I'd be immune to him. I could go back to doing my job for him and not be tempted anymore.

And his work *would* be awful. I was sure of that. Because there were so few people who really studied their craft anymore, so few artists who stretched and tried to create anything using a moral compass as well as they used a blowtorch or a brush or chisel or shining silver camera.

We climbed three flights of old marble stairs. On the fourth floor we walked down the hallway to a metal door with three locks on it. One by one Gideon opened them and then held the door open for me.

"The locks came with the place," he explained.

"They're not a bad idea."

"Three? They're overkill."

The first thing I saw before Gideon turned on the

light was a roomful of people in shadow. They conveyed an immediate sense of power and purpose and their stances and size immediately communicated heroism.

Once he flicked the switch for the overheads, the six full-size people were revealed as bronze sculptures. Three women. Three men. Nudes.

They were all of a piece—so you didn't feel as if you were looking at separate people but a planned grouping. The surface of each shone with a rich patina on the metal that called out to me to come closer.

I stepped forward and saw them all for the first time, not in profile but from the front: each of the six people was split in half, lengthwise, and between each half was a foot of space, large enough to walk through. Gideon didn't have to tell me what to do. The work insisted I take a journey though them. And when I did, I was surprised yet again, to find that the insides were mirrored.

I stood in between the two halves of a young man and looked to my right and then my left, seeing my own face and body reflected back at me.

It took about ten minutes for me to walk through the group, stopping often to examine each and to notice how I fit into each of them.

It was an unearthly feeling. To find myself inside each of them, part of all six of them—a woman my age, a boy much younger than me, a pregnant woman, an older man.

There was a theme and a meaning to this work, an investigation into how we interact. Questions raised about separateness, isolation and connections.

This was not what I'd expected. It was, though, what I

had feared: a powerful statement by an accomplished artist. Careful, creative, wildly thought provoking.

I found Gideon in the kitchen where he was opening a bottle of wine.

"Do you want some of this? Or would you rather have coffee?"

"Wine, please."

I watched him take glasses out of the cabinet and pour us each deep red burgundy. And then I followed him back into the living area, which consisted of two deep-cushioned dark brown leather sofas and a slab of glass sitting atop rocks that had been shaved clean to make a base.

"What are they called?" I gestured back to the sculpture.

"The show is called Mirroring. Each of the people is numbered but not named."

I was still looking at them across the room, not sure of what I wanted to say, or even knowing if I'd be able to express it. "I'm surprised," I finally offered, and then realized how vapid I sounded. "I didn't expect anything that strong."

"Because?" He was smiling.

"This is silly. You know how good you are, don't you? It's redundant for me to say anything."

"I know that my work says what I want it to say. And I know that certain people get it. I knew you would. But I try not to worry about whether I'm good or not. That's a judgment call I'm satisfied to let other people make."

"Why? How can you be?" I was thinking, damn it, I was thinking of Cole who was so preoccupied with how other people viewed his work, obsessed actually over what they said about it and how they perceived him.

"How can what other people say matter to me? The minute you create something you have a choice—you can be satisfied you've been true to your own ethics and aesthetics and judge yourself only on how well you succeeded at creating what you wanted to this time. Or you can give it to the world and let them tell you what to think about yourself and your efforts. I think the latter would be setting yourself up for misery."

"But what they think makes a difference in how you will be received. On your success or failure."

"Not in my own eyes. If someone judges my work poorly, I have the right to reject or accept their opinion. I also get to judge them back. If I find them wanting, or uneducated, or incapable of making the kinds of distinctions that are necessary in making an informed opinion, then what they say simply can't matter."

"You're that strong? That sure of yourself?"

"If you want to call it that. I think I'm clear about what I need to do in order to survive as an artist."

"I'm not sure I understand the difference."

"Marlowe, I need to create. This—" he gestured toward the sculpture "—is what feeds me and makes me feel alive. So I have to be protective about the place in me where the creativity lives. If I started to take other people's opinions into account it would pollute me. I know that. I've seen it happen with other artists. There are people whose work I admire, who I trust and whose opinions matter. But the random critic or stranger who comes to my work with their own subjective likes and dislikes and prejudices? Nope, I can't give in to that kind of self-flagellation."

"Well, I'm envious of you. And actually a little bit in awe of you. After what I—"

I had been about to tell him about Cole. About his work and his need for strangers' admiration. About his willingness to break faith with me in order to be provocative and ensure attention. I wanted badly to tell someone about the position Cole was putting me in. About how worried I was about my family finding out about us. But I couldn't. No one knew. I'd kept it secret so long.

What bothered me the most, I realized as I twisted around on Gideon's couch to look at his work again, was that Cole had tricked me into being someone I wasn't. He had seduced me into playing a role that I wasn't right for. For the wrong reasons, I had gone along with it, and now I was going to have to pay the price, in public.

"You have secrets, don't you?" he asked.

I nodded. Wondering how he knew, guessing from other instances that he'd read something in my face.

"Ever since I was a kid I wanted to have friends who had secrets," he added.

"Why?"

"What a funny response. *Why?*"

"I didn't know what else to say."

"You didn't? Or is it that you didn't know if you should say what you wanted to?"

"Don't you ever have meaningless conversations?" I asked.

"I try not to. Do you like being bored?"

"It's better than being in pain."

"No it's not. And you know it."

I sipped my wine. It was rich and heady with a deep taste and a fruity smell. Delicious.

"What kind of secrets did you want your friends to have?"

"The kind that come from taking chances. From trying to do more, to push limits."

"Did you get what you wanted? Do you have friends who have secrets?"

"Not till you."

I felt myself blush as heat suffused my cheeks.

He laughed. It was a strong sound. Impenetrable. As if, no matter what happened to him, he would be able to withstand what was thrown at him.

"Listen, Marlowe, I'm not good at duplicity. What happened in the park is something I'm glad I did. I wanted to kiss you. I want to do more than that. The rest of my life isn't what you think. I need you to trust me about that."

My skin started to tingle and I felt pressure building up behind my eyes.

"You're in the middle of another relationship. Of sending my stories to her."

"I know you think that I don't know what I'm doing. But I do. I need you to give me some time."

I nodded. Stupidly. But said nothing.

"I'd like to continue working with you if you feel comfortable with that."

"You want me to write more stories?" I didn't understand.

"Yes. Two more. As we planned. It will be all right in the end. I promise."

"Sure. We can write off what happened as intoxication from the scent of all those flowers."

"Even if neither of us thinks for a minute that that's what happened?"

The pressure increased.

"I don't understand."

He nodded, then got up and came over and sat down next to me.

"Just give me today. Tonight. Tomorrow we go back to writing the stories."

I knew before he did it, what he was going to do.

I didn't fight him. This was an interlude. Something that I wanted even though I knew it wouldn't lead anywhere. Even though I knew it had a time limit on it.

Or maybe I wanted it exactly because of the time limit.

This kiss was more complicated than the one in the park. It was not lighthearted or easy. It was not simple. There was no sun warming our skin and no overwhelming perfume. It was dark in the loft; the air was cool; there was the taste of wine in his mouth and the feeling that this was hurting him, that he was fighting himself and me at the same time. This kiss was a bruise.

It battered me, too. Buffeted me. I was lost. Not at his mercy, but at my own. Because I knew this feeling from a long time ago. I knew how helpless I was to fight it. How addictive it was to experience passion this deep. How this kind of pleasure had once turned me into someone who was a stranger to me now—a stranger who had embarrassed me. I had abandoned her years earlier because of Cole's duplicity. Now, I was afraid. Not of Gideon, but of myself and my lack of control. Mostly I was afraid that she was back, and I was not going to know how to banish her again if she got too great a taste of this night's pleasure.

I was the one who pulled back. Who stood up. Who walked away from him. And facing the window, I was the one who laid the ground rules. Holding on to my own arms, wrapped up in myself, afraid of what I was saying, I spoke in a monotone. "We have two stories left to write. I think that's what we should do, not this. Not now. Is that all right with you?"

"Of course," he said. But he didn't apologize for what had happened.

And I was glad. If he had, I don't know whether I could have gone on.

I picked up my bag to leave.

"When we're finished working on the stories, at some point in the future, I'd like to ask you to pose for me. I'd like to sculpt your secrets."

"You think that you'll be able to find them?"

"Yes."

"I don't think you will. And I don't think I want to pose for you. I'm not a very good model. I've had some bad luck with doing that."

"Maybe it would be different with me."

I knew we weren't only talking about my posing. But it didn't matter. I didn't want to explain the past or even think about it, but I did want to get away from his deep green-and-black cat eyes and his swollen lips and his voice that, like the wind, had blown me off course.

Chapter 32

I stood at the door and reached out for the knob.

"I don't think you should leave yet," he said.

"Why?" I turned around.

"Because you're upset."

I didn't say anything but I didn't open the door, either.

"And it's not only about me. It's something that being with me is making you think about." It wasn't a question. He didn't ask if he was right. He knew he was.

He came over to me and took my hand and led me back to the couch where I sat down. I was suddenly very tired.

"Let me get you some more wine. You can tell me."

"I can't."

He went into the kitchen and came out with the bottle that we'd started. He poured more in my glass and handed it to me. I drank from it as if it were water and I was very thirsty.

"Who did you model for?" he asked.

"Of all the things you could have picked up on from our conversation, how and why did you zero in on that one?"

He came and knelt at my feet. Reaching up, he caressed my cheek with his fingers, tracing the line a tear would take if I had let it fall. This more than the kiss, more than anything that had happened so far with us, touched me in a place that I had forgotten existed inside of me.

"When you told me, your eyes filled up. I saw you blink the tears back. You succeeded. But you couldn't stop the initial reaction. It has to be very powerful to do that to you. So far you've proven that you have very good control over your emotions."

I felt defeated. And elated. And brazen. It didn't matter anymore. "My stepbrother asked me to model for him."

I'd never said it before, and it came out so much more easily than I'd imagined it would and much more violently. It filled the room with a dark fog that had a putrid sulfur smell, and I had to put my hand up to my mouth to stop from gagging.

"When?"

"When I was sixteen, seventeen. Eighteen. Nineteen."

The expression on his face was a mix of horror and an effort to hide that horror. "Your brother?"

"No. My stepbrother. My mother remarried when I was fifteen. Her husband had two children. A son who was two years older than me and a daughter four years older. Cole and I were never siblings. We never lived together in our parents' house for longer than a few months at a time."

"Is he a painter?"

"A photographer. You actually saw his work. In the museum last week. Cole Ballinger."

He thought about it and then nodded. "Did he photograph you?"

"Yes."

"Was the photograph in the museum you?"

I shook my head.

"But there are photographs of you."

"That's an understatement."

He was looking at me, but I turned away. It was all too complicated. I got up and walked over to the desk where I'd left my bag and saw the corner of an envelope under a stack of papers. I noticed the stamp and stared, the way you do when you are unfocused. There was something about it, but I was too distracted to focus.

"What happened?"

I turned on him.

"It was a long time ago. It doesn't matter anymore."

"Except it does. You're still angry about it."

"What will you do if I tell you? Say how sorry you are and I didn't deserve it? That won't make it go away. I won't get myself back. The photographs are still out there. His first show will open in a week. And there I'll be. At least in black and white. Everything he stole from me. Up on the wall."

He came up to me and took me by the arm and brought me back to the couch and then he pushed my head so that it was resting on his shoulder.

Neither of us said anything for a while. I was smelling his cologne and still tasting the wine, and listening to him breathing and thinking that if things were different it would be so easy to be there with him.

"I don't understand," he finally said. "What is it about the photographs that make them so awful?"

Chapter 33

"My mother is a photographer," I told him. "Mostly landscape work. Lush, evocative work. When I was four my father died." I thought I was repeating myself but I wasn't sure. I could only tell the story in sequence. Like a litany.

"When I was fifteen she remarried Tyler Ballinger, a Pulitzer Prize–winning photojournalist. He had two children and was divorced. We never lived with his children, who were both older than my sister and me. But his son, Cole, spent a lot of time with us. Vacations, summers. We lived in Vermont on a large, old farm. I had a crush on Cole from the minute I saw him. He was a bad boy, the kind that is irresistible to teenage girls. Irreverent, arrogant, sure of himself, and he was a photographer like his father. But he wasn't going to work in journalism. He was enamored of the artistry and cutting-edge imagery of Helmut Newton and Chris Von Wagenheim. He wanted to push boundaries. His photography was all about sex. My mother used to say he'd grow out of it. That it was merely hormones. His father fought with him and urged Cole to get a job with a newspaper and get some news experience. But Cole was rebellious. And the summer I was sixteen and he was eighteen, I was part of his rebellion."

I was sitting in Gideon's living room, but I was seeing the farm.

The air was redolent of the smell of cut grass. The strawberries were fat and shiny and, as I picked them, I couldn't resist eating some. A fresh strawberry, warm from the sun and just plucked, is not like anything you can buy in a store. My fingers were stained red and I'm sure my lips were, too. I was wearing shorts and an old shirt—open—with a tank top underneath and I'd smeared the juice from the fruit on my chest while trying to chase away mosquitoes.

It was like being at the beach or in the museum: Gideon, the room we were in, his work, the night; it was all disappearing, and I was seeing a story play out behind my eyes....

Cole walked up from the direction of the house. It had been seven months since I'd seen him last, when he'd come home for Christmas. He was a sophomore at Cooper Union in Manhattan, living with a group of other art students in Greenwich Village, and he looked older than he had in December. More sophisticated.

Cole always seemed as if he was from another world than mine. But it was more exaggerated now. His clothes were all black, even though it was summer, and his hair was more styled than anyone I knew. He looked like a movie star.

"Hi, Picasso," he joked, using his pet name for me. I was always drawing, painting, working on some sort of art project, and he teased me about my seriousness. I was already obsessed with becoming a painter. Actually, my artistic passion was a bond between us since he was obsessed with making a name for himself as a photographer.

"Hi, Cole." I had a private nickname for him but never had the nerve to use it. Instead, when he was around, I became quieter than usual, self-conscious and aware.

"Can I have some of those?" he asked after he'd already reached down into my basket and eaten three of the berries.

I laughed.

He had his Nikon around his neck. He wore it constantly. At meals he took it off but hung it on his chair where he could feel its strap against his back.

Cole was looking at me as if he hadn't noticed me before that afternoon, and I grew uncomfortable under his gaze.

"If you're going to stand there, grab the basket and start picking," I said, channeling my mother, knowing that's what she would have said if she were there with us. "There are too many ripe berries. The sudden heat and everything."

"You are putting me to work? You're the midget." Another nickname. Cole used nicknames all the time. I hated midget. Almost as much as I loved Picasso.

I threw a berry at him and it landed splat on his face. He laughed and brushed the wet spot, and then sucked on his fingers. "I can't believe I forgot how good these were." He picked up the basket and followed me up and down the aisles of plantings.

"How have you been?" he asked.

"Good. I got the art prize at school this year."

"I wouldn't have expected anything less from my Picasso."

Something thrilled in me—the use of the possessive—the intimate tone. I'd had three boyfriends that year, but none of them lasted for long. Eventually I started to compare them to Cole in my mind and none of them measured up. They weren't as charming, as good looking, as worldly, as talented. My mother teased me about being picky, but she also let me know she liked that I wasn't getting serious with anyone. She didn't know, no one knew, that I wasn't taking my time. I'd chosen who I wanted to be with. He just didn't know it yet.

And there was no way I was ever going to tell him.

My crush on Cole fit in with my overly romantic imaginings. He was the cruel and handsome hero of the books I read when I wasn't painting. Max DeWinter in *Rebecca*. Mr. Rochester in *Jane Eyre*. Heathcliffe in *Wuthering Heights*. Jane Austen's Mr. Darcy and D. H. Lawrence's Mellors.

"You seem different," he said after we'd picked a few dozen more berries.

I turned around. He was standing behind me. Camera up to his eyes, its lens trained on me.

Looking at someone who was looking at me with a camera was nothing new to me. My mother had been shooting me since I was an infant. My stepfather took pictures of us all. And when Cole was home, he did, too. The three of them versus the two of us—my sister and me. She was going to be a writer. Nothing visual for her. I was going to paint. Create images the old-fashioned way.

The sun was reflecting off a side button on the camera case; like a diamond, it gleamed.

Click. Click.

It was nothing. No big deal. A snapshot. He took a few more.

And then I sensed something.

I've wondered about this for a long time. What was it? Something in Cole's stance? Or was it his energy reaching out to me at a time when I was receptive to even the slightest shift in his mood from studying him too much.

I became self-conscious and brave at the same time. Shifting my hip, throwing out my chin, I posed for him for the first time. It wasn't the same as standing still for my mother. Nor was it the same as the previous three or four shots had been.

Frozen, there in the sunshine, listening to hot summer sounds of the buzzing of the bees and the low thrum of the katydids, I watched him approach, retreat, circle, taking picture after picture. The shutter the only mechanical sound in the noisy field.

He'd take a shot, step forward, take a shot, step back, take a shot, step forward, all the while murmuring small sounds of encouragement, not so much words as nonverbal clues. A seductive music that I'd never heard before but responded to viscerally. I was in his eye. He was watching me. I could see myself reflected in the lens and I didn't look like anyone I knew. I could tell that I looked sexy. I tried to look sexier. Not that I really knew what that meant…except that Cole was responding to it and I liked that. I wasn't the midget anymore. I wasn't Picasso the painter, either. I was the woman who was the object of his attention.

He got so close that the camera was right up to my face. And finally, teasing and slightly insane in the way teenagers can be, not thinking, not caring, not worrying about what it meant or why I was doing it, I put a strawberry in my mouth the way a pin-up girl would.

His fingers flew out as fast as one of the summer mosquitoes and knocked it out.

My lips hurt as if I'd been stung. He dropped the camera around his neck and glared at me. "What are you doing?" he yelled.

"I…I…was only kidding around."

"Don't ever do that. Don't ever ever do that!"

His eyes were bright and brilliant and his lips were almost white with anger. I was frightened but something else, too. Excited that I'd elicited that kind of emotion in him.

"Do what?"

"Cheapen yourself like that. You looked like some little slut."

I laughed. In his face.

He didn't say anything but reached out and grabbed me and pulled me to him and then kissed me. Hard. In a way none of the boys I'd been with had even come close to. My imagination kicked in. It wasn't just Cole kissing me. It was Heathcliffe. It was Rhett Butler. It was all my fantasies coming to life. And with his lips on top of mine, I opened my mouth.

After the kiss, he brought the camera back up and he shot me. He kissed me again. Then he took another photograph. He made my lips swollen and then documented them.

I took strawberries and smeared them on my mouth.

He licked them off and then photographed the bits that were left.

He pulled off my shirt and touched my breasts, streaking strawberry juice on them. He licked that off, too. Then photographed what was left of the stain.

I don't know what excited him more: the shots he was getting or what we were doing.

Well, I do know. Now I know. But I didn't then.

Chapter 34

I stopped talking. This was very different from the stories I'd invented in the process of doing my job. I'd told Gideon more than I'd planned to. It wasn't enough of an excuse that talking to him was unlike talking to most of the people I'd met.

Why?

The way he listened was like an embrace, as if what I had to say was important to him. The eye contact, which, once made, he never broke.

He had no agenda. He simply was there to listen to what I wanted to tell him.

Despite my silence, he continued to sit still, his head slightly cocked to one side, and somehow his energy reached across the room, accepting me, cajoling me into telling him more of the things I'd never told anyone. Yes, it happened each time we'd worked on one of the erotic stories, but the way it happened again that night was different.

"How long did it go on?"

"Three, almost four, years."

"Were you in love with him?"

"Yes. Too much. So much so that I didn't see what was going on. I missed all the clues."

"What was going on?"

"I… I thought…" I couldn't tell him. It was too personal. Sure, what I'd already told him was personal, but what had happened afterward was also humiliating.

"I'm not going to judge you, Marlowe."

"When you sculpt, when you have people pose for you…" I gestured toward the silent giants that filled the rest of the large space. "How much of the real people do you capture?"

"Capture? You make it sound as if I'm raping them." He thought for a moment and then continued. "I try to glean something from them that I can add to my work to make it more about humanity and less about artifact."

He had been watching my face when he spoke. "Why did that make you grimace?"

I didn't know what to say. Any answer I gave would be too revealing.

Gideon didn't move. He wasn't in a hurry. He didn't pressure me. And it was that lack of determination that worked on me. I kept thinking it would be a relief to finally tell someone who might actually understand what I was talking about. I'd never met anyone before who'd have any insight into the odd relationship that a model has with an artist, that an artist has with a muse. But he might.

"Did you ever use any of your lovers as your models?" I asked.

He hesitated. There was a serious look in his eyes as if he knew that the crux of my problem was tied up in this question and he wanted to give me an answer that would help.

The CD he had put on when we'd gotten to the loft had stopped playing. From the *swish, swish* of cars driving by in the street, I suddenly realized it was raining outside.

"I have asked two of the women I've been with to pose for me. One was self-conscious and couldn't. The other did but I still haven't finished that piece. It was complicated to know someone that well and not use what I knew about her—by way of our private relationship—in the sculpture. That would have been unfair to her. To us. To what we'd meant to each other. I only use the outer shell of people who pose for me. I don't go traipsing through their souls. And that's what finishing that sculpture would have been. I use models to give me the muscle and bones. The heart, the themes, the meaning—" he put his free hand on his chest "—that comes from me."

"Cole did the opposite of what you do. He only wanted to get to the private part of me. The sexual part. He needed to have a relationship with me so that I'd open up to him and he could take the kind of pictures he wanted. He was like Rasputin. Lulling, mesmerizing, so he could steal what he needed from me. And then as soon as I wanted it to stop—it was over."

"You mean as soon as you wanted to stop the relationship he—"

I was talking too fast and too loudly when I interrupted him, but I didn't care. Maybe if I told the story it would stop mattering so much. Maybe then Cole's upcoming show wouldn't scare me so much.

"No. As soon as I asked him to stop taking the pictures—when I finally had had enough of them, when I finally started to worry about what he was going to do with them—he broke off the relationship with me. He ended it. What he loved wasn't ever me. Or us. God, how I wished it was. He was in love with having his very own private poser. His very own model who would let him explore his art on her body."

"Damn him."

That was all he said, but he'd said it with so much disgust and vehemence it was enough.

I nodded.

"And you were sixteen when it started?"

"Yes, and nineteen when it ended."

"What a prick."

"It gets worse."

"What?"

"Two years ago I met someone and started seeing him seriously, and the fact of the photos being out there bothered me. I went and asked Cole to give me the negatives. Or to destroy them. He refused. We fought. I didn't let up. He didn't give in. We stopped talking. I've been dreading seeing any of those shots show up in print.

"And now, in ten days, he's having his first one-man show. I saw the invitation. I have it here—"

I grabbed for my bag, opened it and pulled out the worn, torn postcard I'd thrown out and then, for some perverse reason retrieved and handed it to him.

Gideon looked down at the black-and-white photograph of the woman's open mouth. The lips moist and swollen. The unmistakable expression of passion. And the mark on her cheek. It was a smear of strawberry juice—recognizable only if you knew that's what to look for.

Gideon knew.

"This is you." He didn't ask, but I nodded anyway.

"He's showing the photographs. He's showing me. To anyone who wants to see. And there's nothing I can do about it. Everything about me that's private will be public. On display. Sexually. Out there."

I was certain that no one could do anything to stop him. Certainly, I couldn't. I knew Cole. Knew how much his career meant to him, knew nothing else mattered.

Except, the expression on Gideon's face suggested something else.

Chapter 35

We sat in the darkened living room for a few minutes without speaking. I was depleted. Putting the story into words had left me with a deeper sense of anger than I'd felt before. And at the same time, a deeper sense of sadness.

"Do you want to take a walk? Get out of here?"

I nodded.

When we reached the street he took my arm and practically led me the three blocks to a French bistro called Lucky Strike. I'd been to the dark-paneled, crowded restaurant before, and its noisy familiarity was welcome.

He ordered a bottle of Cabernet and we talked about inconsequential things that I don't remember now. But what I can remember was the way he never took his eyes off me and the way he leaned in whenever I spoke. The sense of intimacy I felt. Sharing my history with him was so novel, and so shocking, that I wasn't sure of myself.

I'd been with several men since Cole, even had fallen in love with Kenneth, and yet I'd never told anyone about my stepbrother. My mother and sister didn't know. My closest girlfriends didn't know. And Grace, who was closer to me than my own sister, had no idea.

I realized I was hungry, that I hadn't eaten those eggs I'd made myself hours before, and when the waiter came I ordered mussels and *pomme frites* and Gideon ordered the same thing. After we'd started into our second glasses of the smooth, velvet wine, the waiter came out carrying big white stoneware bowls full of glistening black shells with steam rising from them and a huge plate of thin, golden, salty and crunchy French fries. The scent of the broth the mussels were simmering in wafted up. Garlic and wine and butter and the briny smell of the shellfish themselves. Using my fingers I spread apart the shell, felt the ligament break, put the half that held the meat up to my mouth and sucked the mussel in. It was hot, wet, sweet and full of the sea all at once with only a tiny bite of the onions that had been used to flavor the dish.

The contrast of the French fries, which were light and crunchy to the chewiness of the mussels, was perfect, and for a few minutes we gorged on the food without bothering to talk.

Halfway through the meal, Gideon leaned over with his finger and wiped the corner of my mouth.

I stopped eating. Didn't take anything to drink. The action had been so natural and at the same time so provocative that I was stunned with the sudden knowledge of how much I wanted him.

It didn't matter that he was with someone else, that he was a client, that I might never see him again, or that if I gave in to how I felt he might not want to go forward and finish the last two stories with me.

I just wanted him.

It wasn't something I can articulate. It was an urgency that was far down and high up inside me. I wanted Gideon there. His arms around me. My face buried in his neck. My legs around him. I wanted the whole world to fall off and leave us alone, wrapped up in each other. For as long as it could last.

What is it that happens to our bodies when desire stings us awake like that? Where is it in us? What feels it first? The brain? The womb? The nerve endings? And how do you manage to translate it so quickly and share it so seamlessly with the person you are with? What happens to your eyes, the lay of your lips, the muscles in your face that tells the other what you are feeling? I don't know. It happens too fast to notice. It happened too fast that night. I knew that Cole had pictures of a face—my face—being transformed by passion. But it had been ten years since I'd seen them, and when I had, I hadn't really recognized the transformation.

It didn't matter. Cole didn't matter. Not anymore. I didn't have to say anything, Gideon knew and paid the check and we walked out into the street. He turned me to him, there on the sidewalk, and slid his hands around my back and pulled me to him hard. He kissed me even harder.

I could feel the entire length of his body against me and hear the traffic and knew that people were walking by us, but I didn't care. It was the first time in years that I didn't care who was watching.

It had been ten years since I had been unselfconscious about being with a man.

That night I could have made love standing on the sidewalk. And we almost did. We kissed until our lips burned and then we walked back to his loft, alternately taking steps and then stopping to kiss each other again.

He put his hand up my shirt and brushed my breasts with his fingertips, my nipples hardening under their light touch. I felt weak-kneed and couldn't walk forward. He took the opportunity to push me up against a wall and kiss me again, this time his hand snaking into the waistband of my jeans and down, down to where it was dark and damp. His fingers played there long enough for me to feel my insides tightening. A moan escaped from my mouth.

He pulled his hand out, his fingers glistening in the streetlamps and when he was sure my eyes were on him, he sucked off the slick. Smiling at me. I wasn't sure I could keep standing. Or that I could walk. Or that I could wait.

"You have no idea how damn fucking hard it has been to listen to you spinning those fantasies and keep my hands to myself," he said.

He took my arm and smiled. Despite the heavy sexuality that I could read in his eyes, there was a sweetness to the expression on his face that was so kind I wanted to stand there and cry.

But not as much as I wanted something else.

We walked up the steps, and he opened the door to his loft and turned on the light and started to make love to me there in the entranceway.

And even though the light was on I didn't shy away.

Cole had always needed the lights on when we had sex

because he needed to shoot me in the light. Not even our fucking had been a camera-free zone. The camera came to bed with us. The lights. The clicking. His fingers. His tongue. His cock. The lens. It was all part of the same haze.

And so it had been ten years since I had not asked a man to turn off the lights. And ten years since I had stood in front of someone who watched me as I took off my clothes. Piece by piece. Slowly. Openly. Facing him. Not caring that he wasn't doing anything but watching.

No. That's not true. It wasn't that I didn't care that he was watching. It was that I wanted him to watch.

And then when all my clothes were on the floor and I was naked, I didn't go to him. The sculpture was behind me. And that was where I went. I wasn't thinking, it was not planned. But as soon as all my clothes were off I knew that I wanted to walk among his work.

I walked up to the first man and stepped forward. I took the path between his two halves, watching myself in his mirrored interior.

Gideon walked over to where I was and watched my strange dance through his people.

Inside the first man, I faced one side and then the other, looking at myself reflecting back at me in the man's silhouette. My breasts, my thighs, my feet strangely superimposed on the man's mirrored insides.

Next, I walked around to the youngest woman and into her, this time putting my hands up to the mirror. Touching the reflection of my face. My shoulders, my hips. Making sure that it was me I was looking at and not the woman Gideon had sculpted.

It was as if I was showing him that I was different from his static people. Making sure he understood that I was flesh and they were metal and that I moved of my own accord, that I could not be posed or frozen.

I needed to walk naked in his work and show him that I wasn't afraid.

Gideon stood and watched me walk through the second man. And then while he held me with his eyes and stripped off his shirt and his pants. Once he was naked he walked to me and I waited for him, there in the protection of the tall bronze man.

I looked at Gideon's reflection in the mirror. I watched as his arms went around me. As his erection nestled between my legs. I watched my legs move to accommodate him. Watched my hands go around to his ass and grab hold of him.

I was two people—one performing for an audience and the other watching the performance. A participant and a player at the same time. He buried his head on my chest and I watched his mouth open to suck the nipple of my right breast and I watched myself push him away because that wasn't what I wanted, even if he did. I pulled him down with me so that we were on the floor, and I climbed up on him, straddling him, lowering myself onto him. It didn't matter what he wanted. Not right then. It didn't matter if he wanted to go slower or taste me more or feel more of my body or have me do something to him that I wasn't doing. I had to have him up inside of me the way I wanted it. I had to have him watch himself go in and have him watch my face as he did and for me to watch my own face as I did.

And that was what happened.

We watched ourselves in his mirrors and I made love to him and he responded. I watched my face get thick with the wanting and my eyes half close and my mouth open of its own accord. And I never stopped looking.

Chapter 36

"Will you stay tonight and sleep here with me?" Gideon asked.

At first I didn't think I should, but he wrapped me up in his robe and ran a bath and then sat beside the tub and rubbed soap into my back and between my legs and under my arms and then he pulled me up out of the warm water and surrounded me in towels and carried me to his bed.

I stayed. And I slept. Wrapped in his arms, in the empty loft, not dreaming at all. When I woke up, he was lying next to me, his almond-shaped eyes focused on me. The green even more vibrant in the morning sun that flooded the room.

His smile came slowly, but it made me happy that I was there. That I had stayed. Until I suddenly remembered about the woman whose name I didn't know but who I was helping him seduce.

"What?" he asked.

"How do you do that?"

"Do what?"

"Read me so well. I think it scares me."

"No, it doesn't. It awes you and amazes you," he teased.

I laughed. What might be arrogant in someone else was sweet and certain in Gideon. And the truth was that the connection between us did in fact awe me. I didn't understand telepathy. I'd never experienced it before.

"You have some trick way of doing this."

"How could I? I told you. It's in your eyes. I can see what you're thinking."

"Have you ever done it before with anyone else?"

"Yes," he said, and paused.

My breath stuck in my throat while I waited to hear the name, finally of the woman I'd been helping him woo. Or, worse. The name of a woman who'd broken his heart and who he'd never gotten over. Or—

"I can do it with Dana." Another pause. "My sister."

"Really?" I think I said it too fast and with too much delight. But he didn't react.

"We can tell so much about each other. But it's never happened with anyone else. So this is as odd to me as it is to you."

The way he was looking at me made me suddenly realize I was naked under the sheets and that my breasts were exposed. Before I could cover myself, Gideon reached out and pulled the sheet down lower.

This time I knew what the look in *his* eyes meant.

"You want me to pose for you now?" I said it half shocked and half as if it was the most natural thought in the world.

"I do. But I know this isn't the time. You have things to

work out, and I want to help you do that. It's much too important to you, too tainted. I never would have brought it up, but since you guessed, yes, one day I want to sculpt you like this, lying in my bed."

"One day? You talk as if we have a future."

There was no reaction on his face. He simply looked thoughtful. I waited. He said nothing.

"It's okay." I pulled the sheet up to cover myself. "I knew you were involved. Hell, I'm helping you be involved. I'm still happy that this happened. It makes it easier in a way that this has an end point."

"Easier? How?"

"There's an honesty that is hard to find when every action has another possible meaning and subtext."

Something about the way his eyes narrowed made me think he was going to argue, but then he changed his mind.

"I'm going to take a shower. Why don't you get dressed? I'm going to take you out to breakfast and then we're going to see your stepbrother."

Chapter 37

Cole's studio overlooked Union Square, in a turn-of-the-century building that housed over a half-dozen photographers' studios. I'd been there only once before in the last few years.

There was a shoot going on, the receptionist told us when we asked to see Cole. "Would you like to leave your number and—"

"It's urgent. We'll wait until Mr. Ballinger takes a break," Gideon said.

She left us in the front room, which was high-tech and filled with expensive chairs and end tables, exotic orchids and a state-of-the-art computer and phone system on a marble slab that functioned—though not too well—as her desk.

"I don't know if interrupting him is the best way to get him to listen to us," I suggested once we'd sat down in side-by-side leather chairs.

As attractive as they were, they weren't at all comfortable, and I felt as if I'd slid backward onto a contraption that was going to be difficult to extricate myself from.

"I do."

"Why?"

"I know enough about him from what you've told me to understand what kind of man he is. Or at least what kind of artist he is. And the only place to talk to him is on his home turf and at an inopportune time."

I shook my head. "I don't know. He's likely to be aloof and angry. I've seen him like that. *Entitled* would be the perfect word."

"I know the type," Gideon said in a voice tinged with sadness.

I struggled to name what I heard. What I'd heard before. There seemed to be words that lived underneath the ones he said aloud. Whole thoughts and ideas that he wanted to talk about but was hesitant to even bring up. But why? And what were they?

"How?"

"Do I know the type?"

I nodded.

"I knew a writer once…he felt totally comfortable taking what he wanted from someone's life and using it in his books. It never mattered to him what the repercussions were. Only that it furthered his career."

"Someone did that to you?"

"No. To my father."

"Who?"

"His own father. He used him. Damaged him. He died when I was fifteen. But I have the books. And my father's letters. And his suicide note."

Before I got a chance to respond, just as I was reaching for Gideon to put my hand on his to say something sympathetic, I heard a familiar voice. Cold, etched with superficial delight.

"I won't say anything as clichéd as 'long time no see,' sis, but it has been forever, hasn't it?" Cole was striding across the room, arms out, looking as handsome and sophisticated as ever with his short buzz-cut hair, open-neck shirt, tanned skin and sparkling black eyes that were impossible to read.

He was expecting me to stand up so he could embrace me, but I didn't. The idea of feeling his arms around me, of smelling him, especially so soon after being with Gideon and being wrapped in such sheltering, giving arms, was an anathema to me.

Beside me, Gideon stood and extended his hand.

"Gideon Brown."

Cole shook his hand. "Cole Ballinger," he said, his eyes examining Gideon with a haughty expression, as if he'd already summed him up and wasn't impressed.

"I know you're in the middle of a shoot. And we don't want to keep you any longer than we have to, so we'll get right to the point…" Gideon turned to me slightly. Cole was already looking at me. I'd stood up by that point but hadn't stepped forward. Cole and I had not touched.

"Is something the matter, Marlowe? Do you need help? Is there trouble at home?"

"I…" I took a breath and started again. Gideon and I had worked out exactly what I needed to say on the walk over. I just needed to stop being afraid long enough to say it. And I was afraid. Because I hadn't seen Cole in six years, hadn't looked into his eyes. Hadn't confronted him or his betrayal ever. It was like looking at a piece of me, broken and shattered. To be caught in Cole's glance was to be faced with how unimportant I'd been to him. How easy it had been for him to use me. Facing Cole was like facing all of my weaknesses at once.

"I know you are about to have a show, and since the shot on the invitation is one of me...of my mouth...I need to know...you have to tell me...are you using other shots of me?"

Cole had found a thread on the cuff of his fine-cotton shirt and was slowly twisting it around and around the button. "Marlowe, I would never do anything to embarrass you."

His voice poured like a viscous liquid. Too heavy. Too studied. His voice wasn't like that when I'd first met him. As a teenager he hadn't yet been frozen into the persona that he'd created of himself.

"Cole, I didn't ask you if you were going to embarrass me. I want to know if there are other shots of me in the show?"

"You signed a release, Marlowe. The photos are mine to do with as I please."

I felt Gideon's eyes on me. He'd asked me about a release, and I told him that I hadn't signed anything.

"There was never a release," Gideon said.

Cole turned, gave him a dismissive glance. "I think I know best on that score." He turned back to me. "I have a letter from you telling me that I could use the photographs."

"A letter?"

He laughed. "Yes, dear. One of your love letters. All sweet and sexy. Back when you were like that. I'd written and told you I was doing a class presentation and asked if you minded. And you wrote back and told me that you'd never mind. That you'd loved my taking pictures of you when you were—"

"That was before—" I interrupted.

"I have the letter, sis. Have them all." His eyes glittered, like cold hard stones.

I hadn't thought about my letters to him in a long time. There were dozens of them. Written from me to Cole when he was in college and I was still in high school—before I knew better, before I understood that Cole was anything but my fictional hero.

"She was underage," Gideon said.

Cole laughed. "This is all an exercise in futility. Marlowe, you posed for me from the time you were sixteen to nineteen. You were not underage in all the photos. And you gave me that release when you were eighteen."

"So there are pictures of me in the show."

"I didn't say that, did I?"

My head was pounding. He was so slick. I searched his eyes for the boy that I'd fallen in love with and caught a glint of recognition. I latched on to it. Saw his face muscles relax a little and some of the masklike quality dissipate.

"Marlowe, I promise. There is nothing in the show that will upset you at all. I've taken hundreds of photographs since then, thousands. Please, don't worry. Do you think I'd invite our parents to a show of naked photographs of you?"

Our eyes held again. It sent shivers through me. There never had been anything like having Cole look at me. He could see right through to the other side of me, even as we stood there in his studio with Gideon next to me. The old pull. The old attraction.

But I knew better. I hadn't always known better, but I did now. "Do you still have all those photographs?"

"Of course. But I'd like to remind you that there's a difference between keeping them and having them all to myself, and showing them."

This was the more recent Cole. The look in his eye that I'd connected to had disappeared. He turned and glanced at the studio. He'd left the door open and inside his clients were milling around. "I wish I could stay and reassure you further, but I've got to get back. Will I see you at the opening?" He didn't pause long enough for me to answer. He was looking at my mouth now. "Isn't the invitation wonderful? That's one of the best shots of you I ever took." He reached out with one finger and drew a line in the air that followed the outline of my lips. It might have been seductive if it weren't so crass and if it weren't Cole who'd done it. "Only a piece of your beautiful mouth. Unrecognizable. You always think the worst of me."

"I don't…but—"

His expression was rueful as he interrupted me. "Give me a little credit. And please come to the show." He leaned past me and picked up a glossy invitation off of the end table and held one out for Gideon, who didn't take it. "Please, Mr. Brown. You should come, too. Now, I'm sorry, but I really have to get back in there."

Cole tilted his head forward to kiss me but I stepped back, managing to bump into Gideon, who reached out and grabbed my arm to steady me. But Cole had gotten close enough so that I could smell him—his cologne was the same as it had been when we'd been together. Bile rose in my throat. It tasted of sweet memories gone rancid.

No matter how many years had passed, the girl I'd been was still in me, lurking, sleeping, hiding, but she was there. The young woman he'd encouraged to come out and play with him.

She humiliated me, and it was Cole's fault that I was forced into facing her again over the wide divide of years that had passed between then and now.

Chapter 38

"Thank you for trying," I said when we got back down-stairs and were out on the street. My voice was flat. See-ing Cole had pulled all the energy out of me. Around us people passed. Some noticed us; some walked by. One of these people might wander by the gallery in Chelsea in two weeks. If the photographs attracted him to go inside, what would he see? If it was a seventeen-year-old girl posing for an invisible photographer, how lurid would it seem? What would anyone think of that girl?

Of me?

"Do you believe him?" Gideon asked. "You know him. You're in a better position to judge whether or not he was telling you the truth."

"I don't know."

"You're not okay, are you?"

I shook my head, the tears were hovering right behind my eyes. All I wanted to do was go home and let them flow. Bury my head in the pillows and give in to the anger and frustration.

But Gideon didn't let me go. He took my arm and walked me to the corner where there was a coffeehouse.

We both ordered espresso, and Gideon added a package of chocolate-dipped graham crackers, and we sat down at a table by the window. Gideon had put his attaché case on the floor. The type that has a middle section with a zipper and two side pockets, which were open and filled with papers. The leather was old and worn.

We drank our coffee. Gideon tried, but failed, to get me to share his cookies. We didn't do very much talking.

He told me he had a meeting at noon and was going to drop me off at the store and then head uptown to Cooper Union, but before we were ready to leave, he went to use the men's room.

As he got up, he kicked over his briefcase but didn't notice.

I bent over to pick up the sheaf of papers and envelopes that had spilled out.

Dazed, I wasn't paying much attention as I shuffled the papers back into a pile. I don't remember the actual moment when I noticed the envelope. It was the stamp, though, that caught my attention first. I'd seen it the night before on Gideon's desk, and something about it had attracted my attention then but I didn't know why.

Now, in the coffee shop, I knew exactly why it looked familiar. I'd received a letter with the same Spanish stamp last week.

My eyes traveled to the return address and I read her

name on the envelope. Without thinking it through, I pulled out the letter that was inside.

It wasn't my upright printing with the fat Os and rounded letters and the extra tall ascenders. It was slim and cursive and in a dark blue ink that I didn't like.

How could the letter be in that color ink? Why was it in that handwriting? The words were mine. I knew every one of them. I could tell what sentence was going to follow the one preceding it without even looking.

"Dear Gideon,"

It began—but I had never written to Gideon.

"The light here is naked light. The heat is naked heat…"

My eyes jumped to the end of the letter, and the full force of what I was holding hit me. No, it wasn't my handwriting. It wasn't my signature. But they were my words.

I had been hired to write that letter for Vivienne Chancey. One of four I'd written for her in the past two months.

What was it doing addressed to Gideon? What was it doing among Gideon's papers?

It wasn't possible. It didn't make sense. It couldn't be what I thought it was.

Yet it couldn't be anything else.

Chapter 39

I was still squatting on the floor of the coffeehouse, next to his briefcase.

If I didn't get up, Gideon was going to come out of the men's room any minute and find me there, and he would certainly ask me what was wrong. And even if I didn't tell him, he'd know. Because he always knew with that crazy sixth sense of his.

He'd know that something was bothering me. Even if I wouldn't tell him.

And then it hit me again. The way a second wave comes up and slams you just when you've finally gotten up after the blow of the first. There was no time to recover. Shock on top of shock.

Gideon was involved with Vivienne. She had been sending him letters I had written for her. He, in response to my letters, was sending her back erotic stories I'd written.

I wasn't just in between these two people, I was helping them connect to each other, helping them seduce each other. It was ludicrous. Impossible.

Except that it wasn't.

Gideon must have seen the photographs Vivienne shot of my letters, or the actual article in the magazine. Certainly she wouldn't have told him she'd hired me—she'd pass the letters off as her own. The way Gideon was passing off the stories as his own. The way all of my clients did.

The night Gideon and I had spent together was too fresh for it to be anything but an insult now.

I got up and left.

As soon as I was out in the street, I turned right, ran down the block and found a cab. I was due at the store, but I could call Grace once I got home and tell her I was sick. I gave the driver my address.

I needed to figure out what had happened. How it had happened. And what I should do about it.

Inside, I already knew there was nothing I could do about it. The sick feeling in my stomach told me. The pain starting behind my eyes told me.

I couldn't see Gideon anymore.

I couldn't write his stories for him. He and Vivienne were involved with each other and I might have facilitated that. I certainly would not stay in the middle of it.

Running away from him, not explaining, not confronting him might have seemed a cowardly way to handle what I'd found out. But I didn't have any choice.

If I told Gideon that I was the one who'd been writing Vivienne's letters I would be destroying his idea of her. I'd be exposing her. He wouldn't be able to see her the same way ever again.

I'd hurt him.

Possibly ruin a relationship that meant a lot to him. Or that was headed that way.

And I couldn't do that to him.

The whole ride home, and then once I got upstairs, I kept thinking of Gideon's bronze sculptures and the one I had been standing inside when he'd come over to me and made love to me. When I'd watched the two of us, naked and hungry, acting out our passion in the mirror.

I had stood in the middle of his sculpture and looked at myself. Now I was in the middle of his relationship with another woman and looking at myself again.

Chapter 40

Sleep eluded me for the next two nights and the days dragged slowly. I cried. And then admonished myself for doing it. I took food out of the refrigerator and then let it sit on the counter without touching it. I forced myself to take showers and get dressed and work. But nothing I tried to do was any good.

It rained steadily for those two days, too. In late May, it's usually mild and lovely in Manhattan. But we were having a heat wave and the humidity was extreme. Thunderstorms clapped with a sound that was angry, and the rain fell in a steady downpour that flooded the streets and tore petals off the flowering trees.

I had letters to write. Clients who wanted to meet with me. There were assignments I'd taken in the last month that were due. And I spent those two days trying to focus on them, trying to use them to push away all my thoughts about Gideon.

I didn't succeed.

He was inside me.

It was not that we had made love. It was how we had made love. How we had explored the idea of touching and kissing and examining our erotic selves through my stories. How he had looked at me when I was spinning each story. How his eyes had locked on mine and not let go. What I had opened and given him. How he had taken it. It was how he reached out and, with one finger, touched my cheek and knew everything about me. It was how he had watched me undress. How he had kissed me in the light.

I spent hours looking at my body in the mirror during those two days. Searching for where I had changed. How I had changed. I touched myself—the soft place inside my wrist, the hollows under my collarbone, my thighs.

No. Nothing had changed, I told myself.

Except it had.

He'd embraced my body with his fingers and his tongue and his lips and his cock and his eyes and it had woken up someone who I'd let go to sleep. Someone I'd forgotten existed.

I shuddered every time I thought about his body, naked, above me, skimming my skin. I'd made his veins throb. I'd kissed the heartbeat that I saw beat harder because of what we were doing to each other that night.

And now it was over. Almost as immediately as it had started. What made it worse was that it was my fault. I'd opened for him. I'd taken him inside me—not just his body, his flesh—but his passionate desire to connect, to explore, to see where we could go and if we could get there together, and we had.

I was a fool.

Gideon called me several times over those two days, but I didn't answer the phone. I finally turned the sound down so when he left messages I couldn't hear what he was saying.

On the third day I dragged myself to the store, knowing that I looked exhausted and drawn and that Grace would certainly believe that I had been sick.

She was working with a client when I got there, but a half hour later she came into my office with a cup of hot tea laced with honey.

"Sweetie, you look like you should still be home in bed."

"I know. But I have too much to do."

"Drink this. You need someone to take care of you. You should have called. I would have come over."

"I'm really getting better."

She sat across the desk from me and made sure I drank the tea, which did make me feel slightly less shaky. It wasn't really a lie when I told her I'd had a stomach virus. I was, by then, sick over what had happened. What I'd let happen. What I'd found out.

"I hate to tell you about this when you are feeling bad…but you need to know about it," she said.

She put a letter addressed to her on the desk and pushed it toward me. For a second I froze, afraid it was from Gideon, that he'd gotten in touch with her and that he was complaining about me for not finishing the work we started. Afraid that Grace would ask me what had happened and that I'd have to explain.

I took the letter, opened it and read it.

It was from a woman named Clara Loomis. She explained that she had met a man named Philip Drawson on a vacation. They'd only gone out to dinner twice and then both had gone back to their homes—three hundred miles apart. In the ensuing weeks, Philip had written her several erotic love letters.

I knew Philip Drawson. I had written those letters for him, three months earlier.

Clara wrote that, based on those letters, she had gotten more and more involved with Philip and fell in love with him. Ultimately she flew out to see him and spent the weekend with him.

The first night she was there, he had become physically violent with her and she'd wound up in the hospital.

She was blaming Lady Chatterley's Letters, because I had written the letters that her lover had sent her.

I put the sheet of ordinary typewriter paper down on my desk. The letters I'd written for Philip had been artfully designed in red ink on heavy vellum. "I'm having a hard time understanding the reason for her sending this. Is there a threat in here? A lawsuit? What does she want?"

"I wasn't sure, either. I spoke to a lawyer today, and he said it's either a prelude to a lawsuit or someone who is angry and venting her frustration. You aren't responsible if it does turn out to be a lawsuit. I own Lady Chatterley's Letters, but we are living in a litigious society and he suggested we amend our contract with clients to include a release, in case anything like this happens again."

I nodded. I knew I should be focusing on what she was saying but it was the word *release* that had stopped me. I was thinking about my old love letter that Cole had insisted to Gideon was as good as a release.

Could my letter to Cole, written when I was eighteen years old, agreeing that he could show the photos he took of me to his college professor, hold up in court if I were to sue him?

"Marlowe, you really aren't better yet, are you? You don't have any color. I want you to get out of here. I'll handle your clients. Go home."

"No. I've been out for two days. I can handle it." I picked up the letter and stared down at it. "The poor woman…"

"I hate to sound like a cynic, but we don't know anything in this letter is true."

"I never thought there was anything wrong with what I was doing. Facilitating romance never seemed like a serious offense. But suddenly it seems false and dangerous."

"Something else is going on, isn't it?"

I didn't have the energy to explain to her about Gideon and Vivienne Chancey and how, in my attempt to help them express their feelings for each other, I'd played with their emotions and allowed them to pursue a relationship that was partially based on lies.

"I don't feel well." Now it was the truth.

"Go home, please. The releases can wait till next week, okay?"

I nodded.

I'd send them, though. Send them to everyone but Gideon. I couldn't write to him. Couldn't contact him. He'd already called me at home again that morning. This last message had started out less concerned and more terse, asking again why I'd run out of the coffeehouse. And then he'd said, "If this is about Cole and those photographs, you can't let them bother you anymore. You were a kid. You were in love. You didn't do anything to be ashamed of."

Even if the photographs had been the reason I was avoiding Gideon, it wasn't because I was embarrassed by them.

I had loved posing for Cole. Loved being sexy and provocative and having him take my photograph. I was in love with him, and it seemed to me that everything we did was fine. I didn't know any better. In my naiveté, I'd thought that posing was part of showing him how I felt, and that he was reciprocating by taking the pictures. It had never occurred to me that when I'd finally had enough of the photographs, he would have had enough of me.

I'd been so hungry for Cole that I'd fed his addiction and wound up starved.

And even now, years later, the part of me that had been ripped apart had not completely healed. The exuberance I'd felt with him when we made love turned sour, and until I'd met Gideon I hadn't ever imagined I could feel it again.

I'd shown Cole everything about me that he'd wanted to see, and rather than enjoy it and take pleasure in it, he'd turned it around, regardless of what it would do to me. And now it was possible he was going to reopen the cut he'd made in my psyche.

How stupid I'd been not to see that all I'd been to him was another body to use for his precious art.

His art.

"Maybe what I'm doing here is wrong?" I blurted out to Grace who was about to walk out of my office. She turned.

"What you do is an art form, Marlowe."

"If that's true, if even a little bit of that is true, then it's even worse."

"Why?"

I wanted to explain it but I didn't know how. It was all complicated in my head. What part was Cole, what part Gideon, and what part Vivienne?

If Grace didn't know what had happened, if I didn't tell her, then to her I was still who I'd always been. So as long as I could keep it from her, I could remain myself, and maybe I'd be okay.

I couldn't answer her question. She came back and sat down again at my desk.

"What you're doing isn't wrong. But how your clients use the letters can be dangerous."

"But how can I know that when someone comes to me?"

"You can't."

I sighed.

Grace put her hand on mine. She was wearing a huge amethyst ring, surrounded by light green peridots, that sparkled on her finger.

"It's not only that you are sick, is it?"

"I'm fine."

"You're lying."

"You're wrong."

"Something is bothering you. Tell me."

"Did you get an invitation to the opening for my stepbrother's show?" I was sure she had; she and Jeff were good friends and I was certain he'd put her on the guest list.

"Yes, I got it."

"Are you going?"

"Jeff asked me to go with him. He suggested we bring you. I was going to ask you about that. Why?"

"Do you have to go?"

"No. Would you prefer if I didn't go?"

I nodded.

"Can you tell me why?"

But I couldn't. To talk about it, to draw attention to it, would only make it worse. "Cole and I don't get along. You know that. I don't know what kind of lies he tells. About me. It bothers me that he'll tell them to you."

"I can tell the difference between the truth and a lie. Why don't I walk you home? We can stop and pick up some soup. I'll heat it up for you. Get you into bed."

"I don't need you to do all that."

"Yes, you do. Come on. The girls can spare me for a while."

She took my umbrella and we walked out.

First she ushered me across the street to Dean & Deluca to pick up some ready-made food. We passed the long marble table in the window and in my mind's eye, I saw the ghostlike image of me and Gideon sitting there that day, when he found me seemingly by accident.

The store wasn't too busy yet, it was only three-thirty, and we made our way down the aisles, getting a seven-grain bread, some corn and crab chowder, a bottle of Stewart's lime soda, a box of glistening strawberries and a package of chocolate dipped butter cookies. Comfort food.

Back out on the street, Grace carried the bag. I held the umbrella over us. We didn't talk until we were back in my apartment, both a little wet from the overwhelming rain.

"You get undressed and get into bed. I'll heat this up."

"You don't have to do that. It's early. I'm not ready to eat. You don't have to hang around here."

"No. I don't have to. But I want to. If you're really not hungry, how about some more tea?"

I nodded.

She came back a few minutes later with steaming mugs of strong green tea. "Don't you think it would help if you told me, finally, what Cole did to you and what's wrong?"

"It won't help."

"Do your parents know what happened?"

"No."

"Did you tell Kenneth?"

"No. But we fought about it. It was the only thing we fought about. And I never got the chance to explain it to him."

"You can't blame Cole for that."

"That's not what I blame him for."

"Okay. Don't tell me. But you need to tell someone. You can't hold on to whatever it is. It's destructive."

"What I'm doing is deceptive. Writing these letters for other people."

"You changed the subject."

"I'm sorry. I didn't realize it." I laughed sardonically. "I guess I don't know what's bothering me more—Cole and his show, or that I'm doing something wrong with the letters. That I'm setting people up for disappointment."

"People are disappointed all the time. What you're doing is the opposite. It gives people a chance to express themselves in a way that they can't."

What would be easier—to tread into unknown waters

and tell her about Gideon, examining parts of myself that I wasn't interested in exploring? Or explain about the past and Cole?

At least I knew the terrain.

Chapter 41

The next morning I didn't go into the store again because Grace called first thing and told me to take one more day at home.

"Work if you want, but I want you to rest, too."

I worked through the day, beginning early in the morning, without taking a break, on a collage that I had started before I'd met Gideon or found out about Cole's show. I didn't shower or get dressed but threw on a big shirt, pushed up my sleeves, pulled my hair back, turned on the stereo and filled the CD changer with classical music, and focused on the collage.

It consisted of words, ripped up and arranged in the shape of a flower that was placed inside the silhouette of a woman standing in a park with leaves raining down on her.

It was awful—one of the worst things I'd ever done. After slaving on it for the whole day, I took a pair of stainless steel scissors, cut it into pieces and threw it all in my wastepaper basket.

At 6:00 p.m. I splashed some vodka over four ice cubes and sat down on the bed, clicking through three dozen channels before settling on an old black-and-white movie—*The Ghost and Mrs. Muir.* I had seen it before. At least three times. I wanted something that was familiar and sad and that would keep me from thinking.

The buzzer rang at seven and I got up, pressed on the intercom button and said hello, fully expecting it to be some delivery—of pizza or Chinese food—for a different apartment.

"Marlowe? It's Gideon."

I didn't say anything, but I felt his voice in my stomach and behind my knees.

"Marlowe?"

"Yes."

"Can I come up?"

"No."

There was a silence on his end but I knew he was still there. I could hear the traffic.

"If you won't let me up, I'm leaving something for you down here. Please call me," he said, and then I heard the click of the intercom shutting off.

I went to the window and watched the street below. I wasn't going to go down there if he was waiting for me. I really didn't want to see him again. So I waited until, twenty or thirty seconds later, I saw him emerge from the building. He stood there for a few more seconds. The wind blowing in his hair. His hands by his side. Still and not moving.

Should I go down?

No.

There was nothing I could do. No way to explain. As

much as I wanted to, I knew the right thing was to let him go back to his loft and his bronze figures and his relationship with Vivienne. I had to remember that. Despite our night together and his kindness to me and his odd way of knowing what I was thinking from reading my face, he was already involved with a woman. He cared enough about her to hire me to further his seduction of her. Despite his iron will and adherence to principles, he'd been willing to lie to her to make her happy. Pretending to write the stories, paying for them, because he knew how much they would please her.

Then I realized I was mimicking his stance. Standing exactly the way he stood, six floors below me. My hands clenched by my sides. My feet rooted to the floor.

I had forbidden myself to move for fear I would go down there after all.

Finally he turned and walked off.

Still, I watched. He had reached the corner. The light was red.

If I hurried, if I ran downstairs and out into the street I might be able to get to him before he disappeared into the night.

What was I thinking?

I wasn't even dressed.

My oversize white shirt had splotches of paint on it, there was newsprint glued to the righthand sleeve and sparkle on the left corner. I was barefoot.

The light changed. I leaned against the window and rested my forehead on the glass. He was getting smaller. In a few seconds I'd lose sight of him and then I'd never see him again.

Would he and Vivienne ever figure out that they'd both hired me? Would it even matter, or would they love each other all the more for having gone to so much trouble to seduce the other with fantasies? Would they sit up in bed at night and drink wine and laugh over the utter silliness of what they'd done? And of how stupid I'd been not to have realized what was happening?

The scene was clear—the bed, the tangled sheets, the sound of the music on the stereo, the empty wineglasses on the nightstands, the smells of their lovemaking—I could even see Vivienne lying back on pale green pillows, leaning on him—I could see it all, except I couldn't see him. Couldn't imagine Gideon laughing over what had happened. Couldn't picture him kissing her, holding her, couldn't see his hands on her bare breasts, his long legs intertwined in hers.

The street below was empty now. The night glowed silver. But it wasn't lunar light. It was a false brightness from the streetlamps. My stories had been equally as misleading. They were imitations of lust. They implied passion. But they were fakes.

I pulled on a pair of black leggings, stepped into black ballet slippers. My hair was coming out of its ponytail and I had glitter and leaves on my face, hands and shirt, but it didn't matter. I wouldn't see anyone downstairs in the vestibule.

I didn't look inside the shopping bag until I brought it back to my apartment.

On top was a sheet of paper torn out of a notebook. In the middle were three lines, scrawled in pencil. The kind of soft lead that artists use to sketch with. The letters had smeared a little where the side of his hand must have moved over them.

Marlowe—
It would be a shame to let all this go to waste.
Gideon

I reached out and touched his handwriting with my forefinger. My only letter from Gideon. The only words he'd ever written me, after all the words I'd written for him.

The tears started then and I stood in the living room, holding on to the bag, hugging it to my chest as if it were a living person. I wasn't crying for what I'd lost, but because I finally understood that I'd been writing those stories to Gideon. They were how *I* felt. Not how I imagined someone else felt. I was telling him what *I* wanted us to do, how I wanted us to be together.

Hugging the bag, I slipped down to the floor. Holding on as if I were afraid to let go of it. For a few more minutes I cried, hard, choking sobs that only made me feel worse. And then I looked inside and my crying turned hard and silent.

I'd written three stories out of the five that Gideon had commissioned—Sound, Sight and Smell. Taste was supposed to be next. We had planned on going on a food shopping spree, we'd even made a list of all the foods we'd buy and then talked about how we'd bring them back to his studio and find a story in the flavors and textures.

He'd remembered everything.

In the bag was a mix of exotic fruits: lychee nuts in their hard, prickly, outer shells, a cellophane bag of fat, dried apricots, two pomegranates and a box of pale yellow raspberries.

There were two cheeses, both soft to my touch: a small wheel of Brillat Savarin and a wedge of St. André.

The two loaves of bread beneath them emanated a rich, yeasty smell; the walnut raisin was as heavy as the French baguette was light.

The writing on the small jar of honey was in French and proclaimed it was from Provence and contained lavender. I opened it, bent over and breathed in.

You could smell the sunshine and fields of flowers.

There was a container of olives glistening in rich oil. Another of pistachio nuts, out of their shell, bright green and inviting—sprinkled with cayenne pepper.

Inside a pastry box was a chocolate mousse tart covered with whipped cream and chocolate shavings.

A bottle of champagne.

And when I thought I'd emptied the bag of everything, I found, wrapped in shiny gold foil, like a last present almost forgotten, a thin bar of expensive dark chocolate.

Sad and miserable, I sat down on the floor with all the food. Touching it. Leaning over, sniffing at it like a feral cat, starved and lost, coming upon a treasure trove of possibilities. Suddenly I was hungry, desperately hungry.

I ripped off pieces of the walnut bread and dipped it into the honey, not caring that the sticky sweetness got all over my fingers. I didn't bother to get a knife but used a crust of the baguette to break into the St. André, scooping up too much of the rich, creamy cheese to fit in my mouth all at once. It didn't matter. I licked it off the bread, like the cat would, lapping it, feeling its silky texture on my tongue, scooping up more, not eating the bread at all now, only using it as a utensil. Then, I picked out the soft inner middle of the baguette and dipped it in the oil the olives came in. More of the walnut bread with more of the honey. Now more of the soft bread with the St. André. Was anything richer?

Honey spilled on my leggings, I pulled them off, then, still not satiated, I tore at the rough outsides of a lychee nut with my fingers and popped the juicy fruit into my mouth, working the flesh off it with my teeth, my salivary glands exploding. The texture of the opalescent fruit was smooth and wet and lush until I had eaten it all and was left with a smooth polished pit that was hard as wood.

I smashed the raspberries on my tongue. One after another. After another.

Still hungry, I tore the paper off the chocolate and broke off too big a piece. After the fruit, the chocolate was bitter. I tasted coffee and burnt beans. I sucked on slivers of it, letting it dissolve in my mouth, thick and rich. As dense as fog. As black as the middle of the night. As overwhelming as being caught in a storm.

I was still hungry. Still unfilled. I ate more of the bread and honey and then I peeled away the papery cover of the pomegranate.

The juice stained my fingers as I picked out the small seeds covered with the clear jewellike scarlet sweetness. But there was a dryness to the taste of the fruit, too. And if I worked each cluster too much, my mouth puckered from the ugly taste of the seeds.

I pulled apart more of the pomegranate, peeling away the inner membrane that kept the sections separate. I stuffed another handful of seeds into my mouth. The juice dripped. By now my chin was stained the color of the fruit. So were my fingers.

How would this food have led to an erotic story? How would I turn all the tastes and textures into a seduction?

I couldn't see anything beyond my gluttonous orgy. A woman alone devouring food, salty and sweet and thick and rich and dark and fruity. Trying to satiate herself with flavors because she couldn't have what she wanted: the man she'd met. She wanted his mouth, not raspberries. His fingers, not bread. His lips, not cheese. And his cock, not champagne.

It was nothing I would ever be able to sell.

I looked down and saw my shirt was stained with ruby splatters. It looked like I was bleeding.

I stood and tore it off.

What would we have done with all this food? Even though it didn't matter anymore, even though I'd never write this story for Gideon, my imagination refused to obey my logic, and I searched for the key to how to turn the experience from gluttony to seduction.

I looked down at my bare chest to see the juice had not only gotten on my shirt but seeped through and left streaks on my chest. An accidental and violent design.

I picked up a few of the pomegranate seeds, but instead of putting them in my mouth and sucking off their flesh, I used them like a paintbrush, drawing long swaying lines down my neck and my chest adding to the pattern already there.

More fruit.

More vermilion lines around and around my breasts.

More fruit.

I continued painting.

Colorful swirling lines, down across my stomach, over my thighs, all the lines leading to and ending at my sex disappearing into my thatch of hair. But I wasn't done. There were more seeds left, full of blood.

I drew with those on my inner thighs. Big Xs. One over the other until they became a crosshatch of angry lines. My skin was covered. At least the skin outside of my body. But inside was untouched. I rubbed the seeds up and down the lips of my sex. Teasing and tickling, cruelly confusing my nerve endings into thinking someone was touching me when it was no one at all.

My stupid body didn't know the difference.

I was wet in seconds. Primed. My cunt was waiting. For who? Gideon? That fast?

I'd been with him once and my skin and my bones were already craving him. Longing for him.

And all I gave it was fruit.

The loft was dark, the mess was all around me on the floor. Crusts of bread. An almost empty champagne bottle. Cheese rinds. Spat-out and gnawed-bare olive pits in a pile along with the pomegranate pits. Foil and paper ripped off the chocolate bar.

I wasn't focusing on the garbage. My head was full of images of Gideon. I could see his green-black marble eyes and smell his cologne between my thighs. I twitched for more. Using my hand, I thought about his scarred hands and stroked faster and then slower, working out a rhythm that would have matched the rhythm of his breathing. If he were here.

I imagined his breath on my neck.

My hand did more. Rapid then slow, hard then soft. Rapid then slow, hard then soft.

My body, stupidly, responded, stumbling over itself to get to the end of the effort, wanting the release, thinking maybe the explosion would satiate the hunger that the food had not.

I fell deep into the fantasy that Gideon was with me, that one of his hands was gripping my buttocks, pulling me closer and closer to him, that his other hand was touching my clit while his erection thrust into and out of me in slow and easy pulls and pushes and all the while he was whispering in my ear—words that I was whispering out loud, fooling my poor ears into thinking they were listening to him.

"Marlowe, let me inside. Let me go deeper. Tell me how it feels. How it pleases you…"

And I did what he asked and told him how it felt and that his sixth sense about me was informing him well. How the way he was biting my shoulder was sending perfect shivers down my side. How the pain of his fingers, digging deep into my muscles, was making me quake. How this fucking was closer to something divine than I had ever felt.

I heard him respond then, clearly as if he really were with me at that moment. "Yes. It is. We are."

It was hearing his voice say that—or thinking I'd heard it—that sent me crashing over the rising swell, and as I came I started to cry, realizing as my orgasm beat at my bones and boiled my blood that I was alone, that Gideon was gone. That he had never even been a possibility. And wondering, at the same time, how even the idea of him pushed me into a passion that I'd never even guessed I was capable of.

Chapter 42

The next week moved slowly. I watched the clock, not knowing why or what I expected. I didn't connect to anything I was doing. As requested by Grace, I'd sent out the letters to all of my clients asking them to sign the release form, wondering as I wrote out each envelope if perhaps it was time to move on. If writing other people's letters or telling stories for them wasn't that good an idea.

I called Jeff and asked him how many covers he thought he might be able to give me a year, told him that I wanted to get more involved. He gave me a number that would more than make up for the letters and stories. I thought about how I would tell Grace.

And then, after we'd finished talking, as I was about to say goodbye, Jeff asked if I was going to Cole's show that night.

"No."

"I think you should. Cole's pretty shook up over what happened between the two of you at his studio."

"He told you?"

"We had dinner. Marlowe, let me take you. Grace and I are going. Come with us. It's the right thing to do. Cole wants you there. And you have to get past this."

"I can't."

Jeff didn't argue; his silence was a worse indictment than if he had.

He was right, though, I thought, after we got off the phone. And Gideon also had been right. I couldn't run away from this, too. I had to deal with Cole, finally.

The gallery was in Chelsea, about twenty blocks from my loft, so I walked. Slowly. It was the first week of June and the sun had started to drop, bathing the streets in its glow. People were going home from work or going out for the night and, as I passed through their groups, I wished I could walk up to them and ask if I could join and go where they were going, become part of their lives for this one night so that I didn't have to be part of mine.

Desperately slowly, I walked the last two blocks. Wishing something would happen so that I'd have a good excuse for turning back.

Step after excruciating step, I got closer, until I was standing in front of the gallery.

With great trepidation I peered in through the large plate glass windows, wanting to see the photographs on the wall before I went inside, to reassure myself that Cole had been telling me the truth, that there were no shots of me.

But there were too many people milling around, and I couldn't see the walls.

I noticed my mother in a peach-colored jacket, white shirt and black pants. She was standing with my step-father. If I could catch her eye maybe she'd come out, so that I wouldn't have to walk in alone.

While I watched, I saw Cole walk up to them, smiling and gesturing with his hands. He was in his element, with all the attention on him.

Two people passed me on their way to the door. It must have looked strange. I was, like the poor little match seller, standing outside looking in.

How long could I wait? Until the crowd thinned out? Until the party ended? Until tomorrow?

And then, like an answered prayer, my mother did notice me. Smiling her broad grin, waving, gesturing to me to come inside. But I couldn't move. She frowned then, gestured again. And finally seeing that I wasn't making any progress, excused herself from the people around her and came outside.

"Marlowe," she cried as she hurried over and enclosed me in a big hug. Oh, how I wanted to stay there, safe in her arms, pretending to be six or seven years old, having her take care of me.

"What are you doing outside? This is so exciting. Come in. Come in. We've been waiting for you. It's so wonderful. Everyone's here." And then she rattled off a list of names: dealers, collectors, critics, old friends of hers and my stepfather's. The who's who of the photography world. It was a proud night for her and for Cole's father, who both had stood on this same precipice years before.

My mother was usually more sensitive to my emotions, but she was too excited to notice that something was wrong with me, that I was petrified. Taking me by the hand, she pulled me inside.

The air smelled of all the different colognes and perfumes and fresh flowers arranged in large vases around the wide-open space. The crowd was thick, and I almost lost her as she led me toward my stepfather.

Tyler took me in his arms and kissed my cheek. And it was when he finally let go of me that the people in front of us moved, revealing, at last, the wall beyond.

That's when I got my first glimpse of Cole's photographs.

Breaking away, I walked closer, toward a black-and-white shot of a woman's naked torso, twisted in obvious passion, sweat glistening on her skin.

Her skin.

Not mine.

I took a breath that felt like my first in a while. And then, more quickly I began to make my way around the room, almost racing as I looked at each photograph just long enough to check.

Not me.

Not me.

Not me.

I'd done two walls of the front room and started on the third.

Not me.

Not me.

And then, there I was.

Me: half of my naked torso thrust out in a blatantly sexual pose.

Heat rose to my face. My cheeks burned. I was afraid to take the next step, to look at the next photograph.

But I did.

My mouth. Open. Waiting. Ready. The lips pouting. The tip of my tongue the center of the shot. Damn. I moved on.

In the next photo, a woman—from midhip level—naked, standing in a thicket of daylilies. The flowers all open and full. My legs were partially covered by the leaves. My thatch of pubic hair was half-hidden by blossoms. So suggestive.

I spun around and found my mother in the opposite corner of the room. Had she seen these, looked at them, studied them? Of course she had. And yet she hadn't guessed?

How was that possible? I was her daughter.

But she didn't know what my eighteen-year-old body, my nineteen-year-old legs, my seventeen-year-old mouth, looked like out of context and in such lascivious poses.

A mother doesn't know her children naked as adults, or their features suffused with desire.

Three walls done. One left.

Damn you, Cole.

The next wall was all me. Eight separate shots of my bare breasts. A sequence of a headless female taking off her bra, then touching herself, exploring, arousing, brazenly showing off for someone beyond the frame.

I went up to the first in the sequence. Eighteen by twenty-four inches. Simple, two-inch, flat, black wooden frame. A single sheet of glass.

I only had to reach a little to pull the first one off the wall. It was in my hands, I was holding on to it. I never thought about being strong or weak until then. Lifting it as high over my head as I could, I took a deep breath and threw it down hard on the floor at my feet.

I watched it fall, saw my own breasts flying through the air and then landing, and saw the glass shatter. With my foot, I kicked at it, and then took three steps and stood on the photograph. Feeling the heels of my shoes breaking through the paper, hearing it tear.

I don't know how many people turned and looked, I didn't care. I was pulling the second photograph off the wall. Now smarter, not bothering with throwing it on the floor, but instead, taking it with both hands and smashing it against the wall. I reached for a shard of glass and ripped at the photograph with it, slashing my torso into thin irregular strips, turning my breasts into meaningless pulp.

If anyone was speaking, I couldn't hear them.

I pulled off a third photograph. Like all the others, it was black-and-white, but there was red on the glass. I didn't stop to wonder where it had come from; it didn't matter. I had to destroy this one, too. This one most of all. My hands holding my breasts, offering them to him as if they were food. I dropped it. Stomped on it. Heard cruel music, like ice breaking, felt my feet sinking into the paper.

"You're hurt."

I didn't stop.

"Marlowe. You've cut your hands. Stop. You are bleeding." The voice was like wind in a storm.

I looked up.

Gideon was standing in front of me, pulling the frame out of my hands, letting it drop to the floor, gently taking my hands and inspecting them. Then quickly, no longer gentle, he grabbed my sweater off my shoulders and wrapped it tightly around my right hand, making a tourniquet. He worked fast and was done in seconds.

I heard the screaming now: a deep lion's roar. So loud I wondered how I had not heard it before.

"You crazy, lunatic bitch…" Cole's voice was coming from somewhere in the background.

Gideon wrapped the sleeve around my hand once more.

"How dare you? Who do you think you are to come in here and do this to me?" Cole was only inches away, screaming.

"You think you ruined my show? You think I don't have the negatives?" His words were like a crazy rain coming down on me but not bothering me at all. I was protected from him now. But still he yelled. "This will make everyone want to see them more."

Gideon finished making the knot. There was blood seeping through the fabric already. He had me by the other arm, walking me quickly toward the door. I saw faces, astonished, frightened, fascinated. None I knew. Then I saw my mother. Gideon was on a cell phone, talking about an ambulance, saying yes, yes, we're on Twenty-Sixth Street. My mother was by my side, telling me I was going to be fine, holding me.

"We are close enough to get there in a cab. They said it would be faster," he told me and my mother.

We approached the door. Behind me Cole was still screaming. I turned. Looked at him. Fought off Gideon's pull. I had something to say. "If you don't take the photographs of me out of the show, if you put one of them back up, I'll tell everyone how old I was. I'll tell everyone the truth." I was hissing. A voice I didn't recognize. Not mine. But a fearless voice. The voice of someone very brave who didn't care who knew about her. Who knew that it didn't really matter anymore.

I'd taken back whatever Cole had taken from me. It was all mine again. He hadn't really ever touched me, had he? Hadn't taken anything that was precious or real. It was all my perception. I'd allowed myself to be shamed by what I'd done.

He had stopped speaking and stood there staring at me. Finally he looked afraid.

I laughed. My mother and Gideon, his hand still on my arm, ushered me out and into the street. We all got into a taxi and rushed the eight blocks to the hospital.

Chapter 43

The cut on the fleshy part of my forefinger was deep enough to require dozens of stitches, but I hadn't done any nerve damage.

While the doctor worked on me, Gideon stood beside me on one side, my mother stood on the other with her hand on my shoulder. I could hear her rapid breath.

When the doctor was done, he gave my mother instructions on how to take care of the wound. "I'd like your daughter to stay here for another half hour. I'll let the nurse know. And then you can take her home." He focused on me. "I'm going to give you a scrip for painkillers. There's an all-night drugstore about three blocks from here. You're going to need them." He wrote out a prescription and held it out toward me. Gideon took it.

After the doctor left, my mother turned to me.

They'd given me something and I felt light-headed and sleepy. I tried to concentrate and connect to her emotional words but couldn't.

"I don't understand." Her eyes were filled with tears. "Why didn't you tell me?"

Gideon stood up. He looked from her to me. "I'm going. You two need to talk."

"I…Mom, I can't…not now…" There was too much for me to figure out. Gideon was getting ready to leave. I didn't want him to go until I found out why he had been there. That he had been at the gallery was astounding to me. I hadn't seen him there until he was standing next to me taking the photograph out of my hands. Why had he been there?

My mother was watching me, waiting for me to answer her. I didn't. Instead I asked Gideon, "I don't understand, why were you there?"

"I'll explain that to you when you're feeling better. Call me, tomorrow, when you wake up. I'd like you to. Please?" He put his hand on my shoulder, bent down and brushed the top of my head with his lips.

"I will."

"Does it hurt much?" he asked.

I shook my head.

"It will. It will throb later. Don't suffer with it. Take the meds."

I nodded.

"The other pain, it's gone now, isn't it?"

I couldn't answer but there was no question what he was talking about. The release I'd felt while I was smashing the photographs. I didn't have to ask him how he knew. I was used to him knowing by now. But what was I supposed to do about him? The man who'd gotten under my skin and opened me up wasn't free. Where did that leave me?

Chapter 44

My mother took me home, tucked me into bed and let me sleep.

I woke up at eleven and she was still there. Working at cleaning the piles of papers and magazines, and trying to bring some order to the mess. I watched her before I said anything. It was just so comforting to be there, my head resting on the pillow, the covers pulled around me, with her there, taking care of me.

"You don't need to do that," I finally said.

"No. But it was something to do. Are you hungry?"

"Thirsty."

She came back with a glass of ginger ale for me and a glass of wine for herself, and then she climbed onto the bed and sat beside me and we finally talked about what had happened all those years ago that she hadn't noticed.

"Don't blame yourself. We were very good at sneaking off by ourselves," I told her.

"But it never occurred to me to even worry about the

two of you. He was such a wonderful older brother to you. Showing you how to do so many things you didn't know how to do—" She broke off realizing what she'd said.

I laughed. She looked horrified. "Mom, it was so long ago."

"But he took advantage of you. Terrible advantage of you. And I didn't even know what you were going through."

"I wasn't going through anything until we broke up. For three years I thought I was in love with him."

"He hurt you," she said, her voice cracking now. My mother didn't often cry. She was strong and always the reasonable, logical one. "Your father was the first person I was in love with. Did you know that? I was seventeen. I wish you could have had a first experience like that. One you'd look back on without regret."

"I don't regret it. Even now, knowing I wasn't…that it wasn't him at all…but who I was with him…I'm not sorry about it. Not anymore." I looked down at the bandage on my hand. The novocaine was starting to wear off, and the throbbing was beginning.

My mother noticed the expression on my face. "Do you want some of your pills?"

I nodded and she got up, reached into her purse, pulled out the painkillers.

"When did you get those?" I asked. I didn't remember us stopping at a drugstore.

"Gideon picked them up for me and dropped them off on his way home. You were already asleep by then."

I took the pills from her and then lay there quietly, waiting for them to start working. I didn't want to talk about Cole anymore. But I also knew that my mother was still upset, she needed more.

"I snuck around, Mom. There was no way you could have found out. There were so many places to go on the farm. Out past the orchards. Down by the lake. You couldn't be in all those places at once."

"I should have sensed something."

"You couldn't have. I lied, Mom. I was so good at lying. There's no way you ever could have guessed."

"Are you still?"

"Good at lying?"

She nodded.

"I think I have been. But I might be ready to try the truth for a while. The lies haven't done me much good."

Chapter 45

In the morning there was a note for me from my mother, in the kitchen, propped up against the coffeemaker.

Dear Marlowe,

You were sleeping so deeply, I didn't want to wake you. I've gone back to the hotel to shower and change and can come back in a minute if you need me. Just call. Well, call either way when you wake up. I want to know that you're all right.

I spent some time with all your collages last night after you went back to sleep. And you've really found your art, haven't you? I can see you in each one. Clear and strong and so sure of your voice. I'm very proud of you! Your stepfather and I would love to take you out to dinner tonight—call.

Love,

Mom

P.S. Gideon called. He wanted to know how you were.

And asked me to tell you that he'd like you to call him, too, when you get up. We had a nice conversation. He seemed very concerned about you. Why haven't you mentioned him???

I smiled at the three question marks. My mother was a photographer, not a writer. She always overused punctuation.

My hand hurt, but it was a dull ache. Not bad enough for the painkillers that I knew would make me groggy. Instead, I took two extrastrength ibuprofen while the coffee machine worked its magic. And then I poured myself a mug and sat down in the living room, with the sun pouring in through the windows, bathing the room in lemon light, and let my mind go over and over what had happened the night before.

I don't know what was harder to believe.

That I had gone on such a violent rampage—so suddenly a victim of my own emotions, or that Gideon had been there to stop me, to take me to the hospital, to make sure I wasn't alone?

I understood what had happened. How seeing those photographs up on the wall, on display, had triggered my fury. Like my mother's overused question marks and exclamation points, the explosion had been my own punctuation to a long, unresolved conflict.

What, I wondered, had happened at the gallery after I'd left?

I turned on my computer and clicked on the *New York Times* Web site and then went to the art section. It was there. A full-column review of Cole's show.

If I had worried about ruining his night, I could put that to rest. The exhibition had gotten raves and the "incident" as the reviewer had referred to it, would go far, she said, "to explain how incendiary Ballinger's nakedly erotic photographs are."

The day before, I might have gotten angry at the idea that Cole's star had risen another notch. But I didn't care that much anymore. His fragmented images of me were only paper reflections of a young girl who'd been in love, in her way, with him. They were nothing but a record of the past.

Yes, I had lost that part of myself. But not because he'd stolen them. Because I'd given them up. I'd deaccessioned them. Divorced myself from that ripe and willing young woman who was more in love with the idea of love and more aroused by arousal itself than she'd realized.

I'd tried to be with other men since Cole. To find some depth of emotional connection with them. Of course it hadn't worked. Not even with Kenneth. How could it have?

I'd kept part of myself on ice. Removed. Remote. Hidden. I'd disowned my sexual self.

I hadn't wanted the passionate woman who Cole had known to show up with any of the men I dated afterward. I didn't want her to get me in any more trouble.

But it hadn't worked. She'd scrunched down deep inside me and hidden inside my heart, like a poisoned seed. As long as I was unwilling to accept her, I wouldn't be able to feel.

I even started to understand why I'd almost been able to come alive with Gideon. He had never been real to me.

He was attached to another woman from the first moment I met him. I didn't have to worry that ultimately he'd reject me if my succubus reared her wanton head.

I poured myself a second cup of coffee.

Gideon wanted me to call but I couldn't because I was afraid that he'd hear what I was feeling in my voice. That he'd use that damn sixth sense of his and guess. And then I'd be chagrined. Because I didn't want to be a soulful woman with longing in her voice, lusting after a man who was with someone else.

Chapter 46

I had dinner with my mother and Tyler.

It was awkward at first. Tyler didn't know what to say or how to act, until I told him that I didn't expect him to apologize for his son. We worked at it through the meal and by the time dessert came we were okay. I knew it would take more time to heal, but we were clearly going to be all right.

I was tired when I got home and didn't even turn on the lights. I undressed in the semidarkness and, as I got into bed, saw the blinking light of the answering machine.

There were three messages.

"Marlowe, it's Gideon. I'd like you to call me. I need to come clean. I wasn't fair to you and now I'm paying the price. I think that by trying to give you—give us a chance—oh, this is so ridiculous. Talking to your machine instead of you…"

There was a pause and the machine, which operated on a system that cut off after a certain amount of dead time, disconnected him.

The machine's beep sounded again and the second message started.

"Marlowe, its me again. Listen, I hired you to write stories for a woman who was writing me—letters that were making me fall in love with her. And then I started working with you, I listened to you at the beach, spinning that story…" He had stopped talking again.

The machine shut off again and I couldn't help myself, I laughed, thinking of how frustrated he must have been.

The third message started.

"I got it now. I can't take any long pauses on this machine. Okay. Let me get this out—short and sweet—and fast. So I realized that you were writing the letters Vivienne was sending me. It wasn't that much of a coincidence. I'd seen her photos of your work in that magazine. So I called her after that day at the beach and broke it off with her. I was going to tell you at the museum. I didn't. I don't know why. I think because I wanted to spend time with you, the letter writer, the woman behind those words. I wanted to tell you a dozen times to stop the charade. But I sensed that you wouldn't let me in if you knew the truth. I thought that the way I was doing it would give us a chance to get to know each other without the false expectations that relationships create."

There was another pause. The machine cut off again.

Even though I was angry, no, furious at the lie he'd told and the game he'd played, I smiled in the dark, at how the machine had hung up on him a third time while he was trying so hard to explain what had happened.

I thought about the deeper meaning of what I'd just heard.

Gideon hadn't been unfaithful. He hadn't cheated on anyone with me. And all the things I'd felt, he'd been feeling, too.

Continuing to lie about there being a woman might have been dishonest. But…I remembered something I'd tried to explain to Kenneth two years before. "There is no glory in honesty if it is destructive. And no shame in dishonesty if its goal is to offer grace."

There was another beep on the machine and then Gideon's voice returned.

"I'm clearly not having any luck with your damn machine. So I'm not going to try and explain the rest of it. Except to ask you to call me when you get in. Or come over to the loft. Either. Please. And, oh, one other thing. I don't know if this will make any more sense to you than anything else or any difference—but I know what the shells were saying on the beach—'I can love the darkness in you.'"

There was a click as Gideon hung up his phone.

I was lying in bed, thinking through what I'd heard. Not understanding it all.

I hadn't told him what it had sounded like the shells were saying when we'd stood by the ocean. In the story I'd made up something else.

But he'd known.

I had to make a decision. To trust him—to trust someone who seemed to know me better than anyone else ever had, who didn't seem to be afraid to know me and all the darkness that was part of me.

Or to stay away and protect myself from being hurt again.

I put my hand on the phone. I left it there for a minute. But I didn't call.

I couldn't.

Instead I got up and walked over to my desk.

I looked down at the array of pens. The antique glass stylus from Venice that Kenneth had sent me so long ago. The curved black lacquer Waterman. The thick and sleek Mont Blanc pen.

I chose a simple fountain pen I'd had before I'd started to write for clients.

Then I began to riffle through the papers.

None of the vellum or rice paper or rare marbleized sheets was right.

I wanted white paper. Clean and pure and plain. This wasn't for a client. Not for a husband or wife or lover. This wasn't a story I was creating for someone else, trying to keep myself out of it.

This was a letter *I* was writing.

For myself and for the man I was writing it to.

This was my heart, in words, on paper.

An invitation to a man who I'd met and who had gotten inside of my head and helped me get inside my soul.

And for that, I didn't want artifice or artfulness or fancy colors.

I'd never written a love letter in my life. I'd never answered Kenneth's apology. I'd never written for my own pleasure or to satisfy my creativity. Every word I'd inscribed with ink on paper until that night had been for someone else.

I'd disappeared into an eroticism that didn't belong to me while I'd tried to pretend that my own eroticism didn't matter. That my own feelings were immaterial.

But I'd been lying. To myself.

And so I started to write my own letter.
From me.
To him.
"Dear Gideon,"
I began, and then the rest flowed.

To Loretta Barrett, Nick Mullendore,
Margaret Marbury, Dianne Moggy, Donna Hayes and
everyone at MIRA Books, with great appreciation for
all your efforts. As always, to my wonderful friends
and loving family for their support.

International bestselling author **M. J. Rose** graduated from the School of Visual Arts at Syracuse University and spent the next ten years in advertising. She is the author of five previous novels, including *Lip Service,* which was published in 1999 and was excerpted in Susie Bright's *Best American Erotica.* Her psychological suspense series, which includes *The Halo Effect* and *The Delilah Complex* features a New York City sex therapist. Rose is also the co-author of two non-fiction books on marketing and is on the board of directors of International Thriller Writers.

Visit M. J. Rose's Web site at www.mjrose.com.

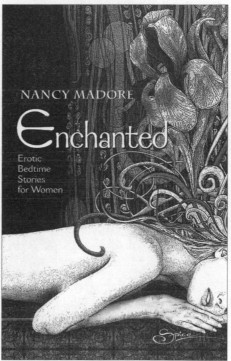

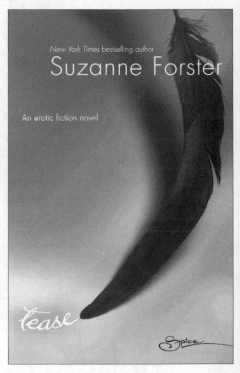

SPICE & BootyParlor.com
live your fantasy CONTEST

For the launch of our Spice line of books, we've teamed up with our friends at BootyParlor.com™ to offer you a chance to win an irresistibly sexy contest. Why not enter today?

Live Your Fantasy Romantic Island Getaway Contest

You could win a trip for two to the beautiful Jalousie Plantation Hotel™ on the gorgeous island of St. Lucia! Nothing is sexier than spending a full week at this tropical all-inclusive resort. All accommodations, airfares and meals are included! Even spa treatments— nothing's more sensuous.

Simply tell us about your most romantic fantasy—in 100 words or less— and you could win!